ANNA SPARROWS

Josh's Jackpot
Littles & Lace Book 6

Cover Design by: Ky at Blue Brolli Graphics

First edition

This book was professionally typeset on Reedsy.
Find out more at reedsy.com

For anyone still looking for their HEA, whatever* that might be.

(*Mine involves winning the lotto. They say money can't buy happiness, but it can buy me a lot more time spent alone with my laptop. I mean my family. Yep. That's what I meant.
Damn typos...)

Contents

Preface

This is Book 6 of the *Littles & Lace* series, however it can be read as a standalone.

While this is a low-angst, sweet & cute, instant-attraction romance, this book contains mentions of **gun violence, kidnapping/abduction, guilt complexes, middle-child inadequacy, insecurity, anxiety, nightmares, bed-wetting, and panic attacks**.

Similarly, this book is an MMM Age Play/Age Regression romance between consenting adults and **does** include significant age gaps, mentions of impact play, size differences, 2 Daddies and 1 boy, orgasm denial, cock warming, use of a chastity cage, intimate scenes with a plush toy, ABDL and wetting. This book contains elements that are suitable for ages 18 and over.

I am still a firm believer in not yucking someone else's yum, so if these kinks aren't for you, don't read them.

Life's too short to read something you don't enjoy.

Acknowledgement

Firstly, I want to thank my wonderful alpha readers, Megan and Ky, for reading the rough, unedited first draft of this book and not running for the hills. Let's be even more honest: thank you for responding to my hundreds of messages asking for advice as I wrote and rewrote the draft.

Megan, your feedback added integral moments that helped give the story a complete feeling. Ky, your commentary wasn't just entertaining, but it also highlighted things I had missed in my rush to get to the finish line. I wouldn't be as happy with this story without either of you or the guidance you gave me along the way, so thank you.

Similarly, I want to thank my beautiful beta readers, Amur and Cindy, for reading the not-quite-ready-for-publication version of this book and for helping me polish it into the version you're now reading.

Cindy, you made sure Max's needs were addressed properly when I couldn't quite get the balance right. I know MMM is not your thing, but you made me feel so good about this one. Amur, you pointed out continuity errors that sneaked through past editing, and you also helped me put a big bow around the relationships in this series as a whole.

Honestly, I don't think I could have published this without any of you. You're not only amazing alpha & beta readers, you are also wonderful friends I am so glad to have found.

And on that note, I also want to thank you, the person holding this story in your hands right now, regardless of whether this is the first of my books you've picked up, or whether you've followed the whole series through. Even if you DNF this one for whatever reason (and any reason is valid - if you're not feeling a book, don't force yourself to finish it), thank you for giving it a go. It means a lot to me. I know there are literally hundreds of thousands of books to choose from, so it's a big deal that you've got your eyes on mine at this very moment. Thank you. I hope it's everything you wanted when you read the blurb, or saw the cover, or for whatever reason caught your attention.

Prologue – Roughly 6 Years Ago – Josh

I am an absolute wreck right now.

I am standing under fluorescent hospital lights and wondering whether my big brother is going to pull through from surgery after being shot on the job. He's a cop just like me. I followed him into the force. Everything Charlie ever did, I wanted to do, too.

I've always idolized him.

When I first heard the reports of an officer down from my precinct, I'd been concerned, but I'd never imagined that it would be Charlie. He was on an easy day shift, for fuck's sake. He wasn't even working the 'rough' parts of town.

I was wrong.

Our Captain let me leave work early, knowing I'd be too worried to be of any use anyway. And, instead of driving straight here, I went directly to Charlie's best friend's offices, where I knew I'd find both him (Ted) and Charlie's boyfriend,

Ash.

I like Ash, don't get me wrong. I'm the one who introduced him to Charlie, albeit without the foresight that they might actually hook up. But he's a Little, and Charlie's his Daddy, and I was wholly unprepared for his irrational reaction when I broke the news about the shooting.

So sue me for snapping at him, okay? Ted made it very clear that *my* reaction was unjustified. Never mind that my big brother is currently on a table getting bullets pulled out of him, or that *I* don't have a Daddy to cuddle and reassure me right now, either. And having Ted scold me while he was simultaneously comforting Ash was a little hard to swallow given the circumstances.

Not that any of the guys know that I want a Daddy.

Oh, don't get me wrong: they know I'm a Little. But I've always maintained that I'm just a scene Little. They think that I'm just down for some kinky fun with a bratty twist, and that it's easy for me to step away from the headspace and live 'normally' outside of that.

'Normally'.

Ugh.

I don't like that word. What is 'normal' anyway?

Whatever it is, it's not me.

I'm just as kinky as the rest of my social group, but I've been pigeonholed and, to be honest, it's easier for me if they think I'm not a lifestyle Little. Could you imagine what might happen if they knew? Not to mention what they might say about me being a cop and all the stress the job brings, and the control I need to have over my Little side in order to make it work. All those protective Daddy types would become unbearable, especially if I ever found a Daddy of my own. They'd probably chase the guy away, or tell him how unbearably bratty I am, or *both*.

I can't have that. Especially when I haven't actually found anyone I've sparked with.

But I'm still young. There's time.

Charlie might not have time.

Fuck. So much for being able to distract myself.

The clock on the wall of this waiting room is ticking the seconds away, but to me it sounds like it's in slow motion.

Tick...tick...tick...tick.

Further into the room, Mom and my big sister, Maisy, are doting on Ash, with Ted hovering worriedly as well. My little brother, Axel, is sitting in one of the uncomfortable plastic chairs, looking stoic next to Dad. I feel like an outsider in this group right now, even though they're my family.

Thankfully, I don't have too much time to think about that before a knock on the waiting room door has my head swiveling in that direction.

A series of complicated feelings wash over me as I take in Max Dalton, Charlie's partner. He's maybe an inch or two shorter than me, and, even though he's muscular, he's nowhere as buff, either. I'm not sure exactly how much older than Charlie he is, but I know he's getting close to forty, even though his blonde hair and bright blue eyes make him seem much younger than that. But today he looks tired and stressed. His uniform is unkempt and stained, and I don't want to concentrate too hard about where those stains came from.

Without thinking, I make my way over to the doorway and embrace him, knowing that if it hadn't been for his quick thinking during the shooting, Charlie might have bled out before he could even make it into surgery.

"I'm so sorry, Josh," he murmurs into my ear. I shiver, but I don't know whether it's because of the situation or the proximity of his lips to my skin. I hope it's the former. Right now is a very shitty time to think about my crush on the man. Especially when he's clearly rattled. "I didn't see it coming. Neither of us did. It happened so fast."

"Nobody blames you, Max," I tell him, keeping my voice equally low. "If anything, they said that you compressed the wound and called it in in record time – fast enough to keep him alive so the bus could get there."

Max squeezes me, then thumps my back: a gesture that I return. "He's gonna be okay," he says, but I don't know if he's trying to reassure me or convince himself. Either way, of all the people in this room, he's the one I relate to most right now.

Obviously, I can't know what it's like to watch your partner get shot —*twice*— in front of you, but I know what the job itself is like. I know how much we care about our partners and our whole unit. Max's guilt is palpable, as is his worry. I'm right there with him.

Remembering our audience, I pull away from the hug and lead Max over to my family and Ted. I've barely introduced him before Ash's knees buckle and he drops to the ground, looking pale and horrified at Max's uniform.

Ash stammers out an explanation about the blood —*Charlie's blood*— and it's all I can do to not feel woozy as well.

"Shit," Max says, as if he's finally realizing that he's still wearing his uniform. He's immediately apologetic. "I didn't think. The paramedics let me go, I had to give my statement, and then I came straight here." As if he can sense how close I am to my own panic attack, he looks at me, his gaze piercing and fortifying all at once. "Any update?"

4

Unfortunately, all that does is make me antsy. That's better than close to hyperventilating or bursting into tears, I suppose. I shake my head. "Not yet. I only just got here."

Nodding, he chooses a seat near the door and lowers himself into it, waiting in tense silence while my mom peppers Ash with ridiculous questions partly to get to know him, and partly to distract herself (and him) from the situation at hand.

It's a relief when a doctor finally walks through the door in clean scrubs and tells us that Charlie made it through surgery and is awake, though heavily medicated. They're only going to let two people in to see him tonight and, knowing it's not likely to be me anyway, I voice my thoughts that Ash should be one of them. Charlie's gonna be asking for him, I just know it.

Dad agrees because he's a nice guy and, before I can blink, Mom and Ash are following the doctor out of the room, leaving the rest of us standing around awkwardly.

With the adrenaline rush over, I feel bone tired and shaky.

"Come on," Max says, giving me a gentle nudge towards the door. I find the weight and warmth of his hand on the back of my shoulder a comfort. Grounding. "Let's get you home. Did you drive here?"

I shake my head. My partner, Sam, dropped me at Ted's office building, and then Ted drove himself, Ash, and me here. I know I'll need to check in with Sam at some point, but right now I don't have the energy, and she's not expecting me back at work until Charlie's officially out of the woods anyway.

"You still living with your folks?" Max's question gets me to refocus, and I sigh.

"Unfortunately."

I'm almost twenty-five but, to save money while I attended

5

the academy, I remained living at home. It's not like I spent all of my time there: my last relationship was kind of serious, so I'd spent most nights at Declan's place. Until he dumped me almost a year ago, anyway. Since then, I've had the odd one-night stand, but I haven't gone out of my way to find a new relationship or a place of my own. I've been stagnant.

"Unfortunately?" Max questions, steering me down the rabbit warren of hospital hallways which all look the same to me, not that I'm really paying any attention to where we're going. I trust that Max knows the way out of here.

It's not that I don't love my family, because I do. But they're kind of a lot to deal with. Mom is a drama queen, Dad's an enabler, Axel is…well, he's a high school kid coming up on closing out his senior year. Maisy lives with her husband but is usually having some sort of feud with Mom, and Charlie's probably the only one I can put up with for extended periods of time. Right now, with Charlie just out of life saving surgery, I just want a quiet space without all the drama.

I must be closer to breaking point than I thought because those words tumble out of my mouth without a filter, and I end on a confession that I would *never* make if I was in my right mind. "I need to be Little for a while."

Max's footsteps beside me falter for only a second as the blush creeps over my cheeks, but then he's walking just a little bit faster, the press of his hand between my shoulder blades just a tiny bit firmer, and I have no idea what he's thinking. I'm too embarrassed and exhausted to ask.

It's only as we finally approach his car in the multi-story car park attached to the hospital that he speaks. "Would you be comfortable at my place? I don't have any stuffies or anything, but we can make a stop on the way." I'm surprised by the question and the confidence with which he asks it. He meets my gaze head on, his expression open and non-judgmental. When I don't answer, he says, "I'll be honest, Josh. I'm a Dom, not a Daddy. But I'm here for you. Whatever you need."

I'm surprised by his confession. I have never seen him at The Grove, but I know it's not the only BDSM club in town. The Grove is the best, though. It is high end, with exclusive memberships, NDAs, and intense vetting procedures. A part of me wants to ask why he's not a member there instead of wherever it is he goes instead, but I know that's just my squirrel brain focusing on the wrong details because I'm stressed and on the verge of unintentionally regressing.

"Does Charlie know?" I find myself asking instead of answering his question, still standing beside his car, my hand hovering over the door handle. He drives a dark blue sedan of some kind. I wasn't really paying that much attention to the make or model as we approached. It's definitely a good thing that I'm not at work if I'm not picking up those kinds of details right now.

He arches a light blonde eyebrow as he rounds the car and stands on the driver's side. "Does Charlie know what?"

"That you're a Dom."

He sighs and looks away. That's not a great sign. Then again, Sam doesn't know my secrets, either, though I wouldn't be surprised if she suspected them. She's a pretty switched-on cop.

"He knows I'm familiar with various BDSM lifestyles," Max eventually tells me, then he bends to open his door. I do the same on my side and we both slide into our seats.

"So that's a no, then?"

I watch him nod. "But he knows that I know about him

and Ash. About their kink." He winces. "I told him earlier today. Before we got the call out..." he trails off and shakes his head, then pops the key into the ignition but doesn't turn it. "I should have done a lot of things differently today."

I frown, realizing that he's as close to losing it as I am, and I make my decision without any further thought, rationalizing that he mightn't be a Daddy, but a Dom's needs are to take care of their subs. It's close enough for me. "If the offer's still on the table, I'd like to stay at your place tonight."

* * *

An hour and a half later, Max opens the door to his apartment and nudges me inside. We swung by my parents' place so I could grab my overnight bag with clean clothes and some comfort items, and then by his local Chinese restaurant for some takeout. It's still only early evening, but it feels like I've been awake forever. The need to just let go and be Little and let someone else take care of me is growing stronger with every passing minute.

Unfortunately, that usually makes me whiny and bratty: not the kind of attitude I want to have around a Dom. And not just any Dom, but my brother's hot older work partner who I have been crushing on since the day we were introduced.

"I'm just going to get changed," Max tells me, dropping his keys in a bowl on a little stand just inside the entryway of his apartment. He waves a hand around the space as he places the plastic bag of our takeout on the table. "Make yourself at home."

I nod, clutching my duffel bag closer to my chest as I step into the main living area. It's a small apartment, clearly only designed for one person or a very close couple. It's basically just a studio, though the bedroom and bathroom are separate to the rest of the living/dining/kitchen open-plan space.

Max has a big-screen TV mounted on the wall, with a soft looking three-seater couch upholstered in a light cream color. There's a worn timber coffee table in between both items. Behind the couch is a little square dining table, also timber and scuffed, with two matching chairs. That leads into the U-shaped kitchen, with its windows looking out over the scrawl of suburbia with the city proper in the distance.

It's all neat and tidy, beige, and plain. A basic bachelor pad if ever I saw one. There's no evidence here that Max is a Dom, so anything of that nature must be in the bedroom.

I sit on the couch and nibble my lip when I realize that it's not a fold out or a futon. I'm 6'1", so I could sleep on it as it is, but it'll be a tight fit, especially with how broad I am. Still, I'd rather this than home right now.

"Josh?" his voice startles me, and I swivel around to where he's leaning against the jamb of the door which I assume leads to his bedroom. He's changed into loose gray sweats and a tight white t-shirt. He mightn't be as broad as me, but the man is toned and fit, and I try not to visibly salivate. His expression softens and he points towards the table. "Dinner?"

"Oh. Right. Yeah." I get up and walk over to the table while he grabs cutlery and a couple of cans of soda from the fridge.

As we dig into our boxes of noodles, I can't help but wish that I didn't have to do this for myself; that he would step in as the Daddy I need right now and feed me forkfuls like the overgrown toddler I want to be in the moment. I don't say anything, though. I just play with my food sullenly.

"Hey," I look up to see concern etched across his handsome

face. He gestures down to my box of barely touched food. "Not hungry?"

I am. I'm starving. But how do I explain that I'm so exhausted and stressed that I'm regressing beyond my ability to control it? That I want to eat, but I don't have the motivation or coordination to feed myself.

I just shrug.

That gets a reaction.

"*Joshua*," he says firmly, and fuck it if my dick doesn't take interest at the same time as my brain lights up like a Christmas tree, because Dom voice sounds a *lot* like Daddy voice. "Use words, please. I am not a mind reader."

With my cheeks burning, I blurt, "Can you feed me?"

Max's eyes widen, first in surprise and then with understanding. "*Oh*. Oh, yeah. Of course."

He pushes his own meal aside and then brings his chair around from opposite me to the space to my left, reaching for my box of noodles and fork. There's a gentle smile playing around the edges of his lips as he swirls the fork in the delicious umami mix then brings it to my mouth. "Open up," the instruction is quiet, but firm, and I comply without any of the brattiness that I'm otherwise known for.

For Max, I want to be good. At least for tonight. I want to be praised, cuddled, and cared for.

We repeat the process over and over, and it's not long before the comforting fog of being Little sets in properly. Later, I'll think back on how irresponsible it was to do this without negotiating first. To not discuss safe words or limits. Even though we're not doing this for sexual reasons (no matter how badly I wish he'd see me that way), leaping in without having that talk was a stupid idea. But right now, I don't think about such things. I just think about how Da—*Max* is being so kind and caring, and about how much I trust him to take care of me.

And take care of me he does. He finishes feeding me, then gets a washcloth to wipe my face clean. Then he ushers me into the bathroom and helps free me from my constrictive uniform while I whine and squirm and complain that "I gotta go real bad". We both breathe a sigh of relief when I make it in time. While I'm taking care of business, he throws my uniform in his hamper. Afterwards, he makes sure I wash my hands and brush my teeth, then he leads me back into the living room to grab my duffel bag.

Da—*Max* takes one look at the couch, then shakes his head, taking me by the hand and leading me into the bedroom where he gets me to lie on the bed as he pulls out the outfit he'd watched me pack earlier.

He also pulls out my diaper. If I were big, I'd question his limits. Ask him his traffic light color. Almost anything to make sure that he's really okay with this. But I'm not. I'm Little, and he's doing *exactly* what I need right now, so I let him pull my underwear down and awkwardly diaper me. I suck my thumb while he does, watching him from underneath my lashes, daydreaming that he could be my Daddy every day. Those thoughts don't go away. In fact, they get worse as he helps me into my pajamas —the *Paw Patrol* ones that feature Chase the police pup— and then hands me my matching Chase stuffie.

"Into bed, Josh," he says, gesturing towards the headboard. "I'll go sleep on the couch."

"No!" I cry out angrily. "No! Want Max here." 'Here' comes out as a whine, the 'r' sounding more like a 'w'. I'm a lost cause now.

Max hesitates.

I bring out the big guns, widening my eyes, not needing to force the tears that well up at the thought of being left alone in this strange room after the day I've had. *"Pwease* Da—*Maxxie?"*

"Okay, shh, it's okay," Max agrees when the tears actually do fall. He drops onto the mattress and reaches for me, pulling me against his side for a cuddle. I clutch my stuffie under my arm, sucking on my thumb as I press my face against his warm, solid chest.

He rubs my back and continues to murmur sweet, soothing words until sleep finally claims me.

I wake suddenly in the morning after a nightmare. My heart is pounding, my diaper is wet, and the bed is cold and empty beside me. But I'm big again and I smother the desire to seek Max out, slipping into the bathroom next door and taking care of my needs myself.

My biggest mistake comes later when we're back at the hospital, having just seen Charlie. Max and I leave the room after Charlie and I both try to assure him that he's not at fault, and we walk silently back down the hallways towards the multi-level car park. Halfway there, I stop and grab his arm, tugging him into an empty room.

I don't like the resigned expression on his face, but I have to say my piece. "I just wanted to thank you for last night. For taking care of me like you did. It meant a lot."

Those blue eyes of his gentle again. "Don't mention it, Josh." Even though the words are kind, there's warning in them. I don't like that. Neither grown up nor little Josh likes being told no.

I don't know why I push it. Not really. But I lose all sense of reason, stepping into Max's personal space, even as he backs up against the wall.

"Josh…"

I ignore the more obvious warning there, too, pressing my lips to his.

I keep it chaste, but it's still sweet and affectionate. I probably give far too much away about my hidden feelings. But he kisses me back, if only for a moment, and it is *everything*.

Until it's not.

Hands as large as my own find my shoulders and gently push me back. "We can't do this, Josh," he tells me, and I swear I can feel my heart squeezing so hard it might stop. Last night was so good, so perfect, and my crush turned into something stronger. He was my Daddy, if only for a moment, and it's destroying me to know that the same man from last night is rejecting me now. "Not now, not ever. I'm sorry."

Then he walks away, and I'm right back to standing under the fluorescent lights of a hospital feeling absolutely wrecked.

Chapter One – Josh

Number one on my list of things that suck? Not being able to find an available Daddy at The Grove on short notice.

Ever since I made Detective, the stress of being a police officer has increased. Working tough cases has me needing an escape from my adult life more frequently, but over the course of the last few years, I've found it more and more difficult to connect with Daddies for scenes at our local premium BDSM club.

Part of that is the reputation I've developed as a brat. I can't help it if I enjoy being cheeky and if I like being punished from time to time. But 'time to time' seems to have become 'always' in the eyes of the Daddies that know me, and when I ask for something sweeter or more intimate, most of them think I'm joking.

I know that I've woven this noose for myself. I know that I'm the one who has spent the majority of my kinky exploration pushing boundaries and begging for Daddies to discipline me.

I don't need a degree in psychology to point out that a lot of that was a cry for attention.

And I loved the attention it got me.

I still do on occasion.

But lately I've just wanted to be cuddled. I've wanted a Daddy to play with stuffies with me, to kiss the top of my head and feed me my meals (preferably while making airplane sounds or choo-choo train noises) and read bedtime stories to help keep the nightmares at bay.

The freaking nightmares. Ugh.

I've always suffered from them in times of stress.

And, naturally, they are usually accompanied by bed-wetting which as a Little is fine, but as an adult? Not so great. Especially when there's no discernible medical reason for them. It's all in my head.

Yes, I have seen a therapist. No, there is no magical cure. Yes, I'm still trying to work on it. No, it's not going well.

Also, I am aware that it's not healthy to avoid sleep because I'm afraid of both the nightmares and the bed-wetting, but I'm sick and tired of waking up scared, alone, and wet.

I want a Daddy so badly.

I'm done trying to convince myself that I don't need one. I've tried that for years and look where that's gotten me! Alone, with the reputation of a bratty scene player, and spending way too much time and money laundering my bed sheets.

Right now, I've just wrapped up a super disturbing case at work (there was a body in an oil barrel…it was gross and the mental images will fuel my excessive nightmares for months, I'm sure) and I've come to The Grove on a Tuesday night to finally relax. And there are no single Daddies. None. Not one. Nobody's even flagging as interested in playing, even if they are in relationships.

Already well on my way to regressing, I can feel the desperation and disappointment welling in my chest almost like it's a physical thing. A big balloon of pain and sadness inflating, making it hard to breathe and even harder to keep the tears at bay.

I sit myself in front of the Play Doh table and focus on my breathing, willing myself to calm down. I blink rapidly against the stinging and the moisture building in my eyes, and I prod uselessly at the lump of bright yellow Play Doh I selected. It mocks me with its cheerful color.

All around me, Littles play with their Daddies and Mommies, squealing and chattering delightedly. I feel like a living cloud in the middle of their sunshine, the balloon inside me darkening with an impending storm.

And then, just when I think things can't get worse, my friend Matt plops down beside me, his distinctive tattooed arms bare beneath the bright orange onesie his Daddy, London, has dressed him in. When I spare a closer glance, I realize that the onesie is covered in tiger stripes and bears the slogan "I'm Grrrr-eat."

I'm fairly sure that's copyright infringement in action.

"Hey, Josh," Matt says, grinning beneath his epic beard as he reaches for his own lump of Play Doh. "What you doin' here?" He cocks his head in genuine curiosity, his usually infectious Little space not doing much to encourage mine today. "We coulda' hads a group play date." He says 'gwoop' and 'pway' in a way that suggests he's hit deep Little space tonight. I'm immediately jealous of him. Even more so when London ruffles Matt's shaggy, graying hair, squats to press a kiss to Matt's forehead, and then whispers something undoubtedly sweet and supportive into Matt's ear.

My heart aches.

I want that.

Why can't I have that?

Not with London, obviously, but…when's *my* Forever Daddy gonna come and smother me with kisses and sweet nothings, huh? Everyone else in our social circle has met their Happily Ever After person. Where the hell is mine?

Breathe, Josh. Breathe.

I try to remind myself that it wasn't so long ago that Matt felt much like I did now. Hell, he was considering leaving the whole kink scene behind because all the Daddies he met kept telling him that he was too old and too buff to be someone's Forever Little.

I'm just as buff as Matt. And I'm in my thirties now.

I can't help but feel like I did not give Matt enough empathy or consideration when he felt this way. Hell, I brought him here for his birthday and, in a move that makes me cringe with mortification, I left him on his own to go and be bratty for a cute Daddy I knew.

Yes, that was the night Matt met London and one could argue that it wouldn't have happened if I hadn't been an oblivious dick, but I still feel really bad for abandoning my friend when he felt Little, alone, and unwanted.

Maybe this is my karma. My universal penance for doing shit like that my whole life.

Maybe being a brat wasn't *all* an act. Maybe years of doing stuff just like that has earned me the lonely, Daddy-less existence I'm living now.

"Joshie?" Matt prods me with an extended index finger, and it takes me a second to realize that I never answered him.

My lump of yellow Play Doh lands on the table with a thud as I drop it. "I didn't know I was gonna be here," I tell him, not quite little enough to fully lapse into the same kind of speech patterns. "I thought I'd come look for a Daddy."

Matt's smile turns knowing and his eyes sparkle with mirth. "*Oh*," he drags the word out, "do you need to be naughty?"

I bite my bottom lip before it can wobble and I shrug. "I don't know. Maybe."

He cranes his neck around, unabashedly taking in the small crowd assembled here tonight. Our table is set in the inset 'play pit' in the middle of the large, carpeted room which spans the length of the front of the large warehouse building that happens to be home to The Grove. On the other end of this massive, high-ceilinged space, there's a bouncy castle where a few Littles are currently having the times of their lives. Along the wall near us, there are couches for the caregivers to sit and stare out over the space, 'supervising' us Littles at play. It's all brightly colored and welcoming, but I still feel sad and alone despite all of that.

I watch as Matt's face falls when he makes the same realization I did. "Damn," he says softly and full of empathy. "No Daddies tonight. Well, not unless you wanna see if Emmett wants to play?" Matt gestures towards a familiar figure.

The man is hot, I'll give him that. He looks like Idris Elba, but he's built like Shaq. I'm not short at 6'1", but Emmett Reid is a mountain of a man who makes me feel small in all the best ways.

And now I'm fighting the urge to cry again. As if Emmett would ever be interested in me! And it's a bad idea anyway, considering he works for Charlie.

I force another shrug and shake my head, managing to get

the word "Nup" out without giving away how close I am to losing it.

"Oh well," Matt says brightly, "you just play with me." Once again it's 'pway' and 'wiff'. It's cute, but I'm still nowhere near that mental space.

But Matt's one of my closest friends, so I force myself to fake it, plastering a bright smile on my face and clapping my hands together. "What first?"

Chapter Two — Emmett

The Grove is quiet tonight. That's the first thing I notice as I step into the Playroom. It's mostly couples or throuples gathered together in groups, the majority of whom I recognize either through my frequent visits here or through my work at The Little Community Center as a kink-friendly counselor. I raise my hand, the bands on my wrist flagging my status as an available Daddy, to wave at those who acknowledge me, but I don't approach anyone.

I generally like to take a seat on the couch and just watch for a while. I love people watching. I enjoy seeing how individuals interact, especially with their guards down. It's part of what drew me to being a Daddy in the first place: seeing how vulnerable and unguarded Littles are in their Little headspaces is equal parts fascinating and liberating, and there's certainly something to be said for being trusted to look after someone when they are at their most open and honest, too.

As I settle in on the end seat of the couch closest to the

middle of the recessed carpeted play area, my attention is drawn to the two Littles playing with Play Doh. I recognize both instantly because they are a part of my social circle.

My boss at The Center is Charlie, a former police officer whose career ended abruptly due to injuries sustained in a shooting somewhere between six and seven years ago. One of his two younger brothers, Josh, is also a cop. But, more relevant to this moment, Josh is also one of the pair of muscular men currently bowing their heads together and giggling over the obscene things they are creating with the modeling dough. The other is a man closer to my own age, with heavily tattooed arms and a bushy graying beard. He looks more biker than Little, but Matt is one of the sweetest, most softly spoken people I've met.

Over the course of the past few months, I've gone from knowing these men as acquaintances through Charlie, to becoming more integrated into their friendship circle, comprised of Age Play enthusiasts heavily involved in the lifestyle. This is in no small part due to the friendship I made with Kade, a Little I met here close to a year ago now, whose Forever Daddy, Chance, is close friends with Charlie. Since developing a friendship with Kade, I have found myself hanging out with the entire group in its various iterations more and more frequently. It has been different and refreshing to be part of such an open, non-judgmental group socially.

Still, I don't move from my seat as my eyes land on the two boys. They're engrossed in play and I don't want to interrupt. I'm content to sit and watch my friends relax and lose themselves in their Little personas, though I do find myself casting my gaze across the room, searching for Matt's Daddy, London. It hasn't escaped my notice that the younger man doesn't like to be too far out of reach when his boy is in his Little headspace.

Sure enough, I find the young Daddy leaning against the far wall, chatting to another Daddy animatedly. His eyes still drift over to Matt every so often, but his relaxed posture suggests that he's in no rush to interrupt Matt's playtime. The pair of them are well attuned to each other and seem to have a fantastic grasp on communication, something I privately applaud them for. Relationships are hard work, communicating effectively through kinks and kink negotiation even more so, and they make it seem almost effortless. It's always heartwarming and uplifting to watch them interact.

My eyes are drawn back to watching Matt and Josh sculpting penises out of brightly colored dough and my lips lift in the corners. They're adorable together, and it's always fun to see Matt come out of his shy shell when he's Little. But it's Josh I'm curious about.

Even before I met him in person, I'd been informed that he was a brat and a scene Little. Age Play is an occasional thing for him and not a lifestyle like it is for his older brother. However, none of my interactions with Josh have led me to believe that those assumptions are correct.

Oh, sure, he's cheeky, and sometimes downright naughty, but he's not malicious or deliberately defiant. He might enjoy being bratty to get a bit of attention, but he is far too sweet and thoughtful with his friends for it to be the driving force behind his desire for Age Play. Too many times over the past few months, I've watched him hover at the edges of our social gatherings, his brown eyes filled with abject longing as he watches his friends frolic and play. At Kade and Chance's recent surprise engagement get-together, I noticed that he slipped away from the festivities not long after Kade proposed to his Daddy. If I were to make an educated guess, I'd say he wants a relationship like theirs for himself.

Don't we all?

Humans are not designed to be solitary creatures. We're pack animals; social and generally motivated by attention, affection, and positive reinforcement. Even if Josh started his journey into the kink community through scene play, it's unfair of those around him to just assume his needs and desires stayed that way. People evolve, kinks evolve, and I feel like it's more than obvious (to me, at least) that Josh is a lifestyle Little trying to keep his need for Age Play masked and contained.

I lean back against the plush couch cushion and settle in, my thoughts now tunneling, as they are prone to do. I suppose that Josh's choice of career plays a big part in why he plays up the brat card, and why he hasn't spoken out about wanting a Daddy and a relationship like the ones his friends have all fallen into. He's a cop. A Detective now. It's a job where he holds authority. Where he likely feels he has to uphold a strong façade. Where he has to be steady and mature and unruffled.

It's not exactly the sort of job that screams 'Little'.

And, to look at him in street clothes or a uniform, you would never guess that the six-foot-tall wall of gym-sculpted muscle enjoys playing with stuffies or being diapered. He's buff and oozes masculinity, confidence, and charm.

But when he's Little, he's different. Softer. Sweeter. Vulnerable.

Well, unless he's cruising for a spanking. Then he's boisterous and cheeky, determined to push boundaries, but still undeniably sweet.

23

I have not had the pleasure of being Josh's Daddy for a scene, though. My observations are purely social. And tonight, as I watch him play, I can't help but let myself wonder whether he'd be interested in a scene with me. Or, if my suspicions about what he really wants are correct, maybe more?

I'm one of few men larger than him. Hell, I'm taller than Charlie's 6'3", and broader, too. No, I don't have the finely toned body that either of the Walker brothers in my orbit do, but I'm hardly what I'd call unfit, either. I'm strong enough that I could probably lift Josh up if I wanted to. I could carry him short distances on my hip and treat him like a Little in a way I don't expect he's had much experience with.

I wonder if he'd like that.

This is not the first time I've had thoughts like these. I don't advertise them —especially not to Charlie or any of the other people in our social group— but I wouldn't be surprised if Cherie, another colleague and member of the same circle of friends, has picked up on my interest in Josh. She's sharp like that.

It's not that I'm ashamed of my interest. Sure, I'm twenty years Josh's senior and I worry that it might give him pause, but age is just a number and I look damn good for fifty, if I do say so myself. I'm not even that concerned about the professional implications, because he's not a client, nor is he related to one. He's my boss's little brother, but he's also a man in his thirties and no blushing virgin, either.

Not that there's anything wrong with being a blushing virgin.

This is perhaps the crux of my issue: my interest in Josh makes me stupid. I think stupid things. I get lost in stupid daydreams. I start having stupid fantasies about potential futures that I have no reason to think might ever happen.

Yeah. So. My interest in Josh? It's a crush.

And I'm not used to having crushes.

It's easier to try and stay removed from it. To pretend my analysis of Josh's behaviors are clinical or borne of friendship at most. It's safer for me, because I'm not used to feeling untethered the way I do when I give in to my sillier crush-y thoughts.

Now, I am a professional therapist, so I know that the above statement is not entirely healthy. Neither is my deep-seated discomfort over being a fifty-year-old man with a crush on a thirty-one-year-old Little. If I were one of my clients, I would suggest being kinder to myself, to consider why this thought makes me so uncomfortable and to work on accepting my feelings because they are valid and there is absolutely nothing wrong with them. But I'm not my client, and I refuse to listen to my own psychobabble.

Instead, I'll just sit here and watch my Little friends play. That seems to be my safest option.

Chapter Three – Max

"Another day, another dollar," my partner, Vince, laments with a sigh as we start our patrol down the quiet city street. He tosses the dregs of his takeaway coffee into a trash can as we pass it and chuckles to himself. "Or fifty cents once the tax man gets his share, am I right?"

I die a little inside. We have this exact same conversation at the start of every shift. We have done for the past three years. I could probably predict by rote recall how the rest of it is going to play out. But I don't. I just nod, force a light laugh, and say, "Damn straight."

How is this my life?

Don't get me wrong. I love being a cop. It's all I ever wanted to be growing up. My dad was a cop, like his dad before him, and his before him and so forth. The thin blue line is in my family's veins. And I love the job. I love helping people. I love being in the thick of action. I love being an integral part of society.

I don't love having mundane repeated conversations with

my boring as fuck partner.

He's a nice guy, and I feel a little guilty for my negative thoughts, but I can't help the fact that if we have this start-of-shift conversation one more time, I might slam my head into a brick wall.

I've been a cop for close to twenty years now. At forty-five, I never imagined that I'd be anything else. Before he passed away two years ago, Dad expressed his disappointment that I hadn't yet attempted to climb the chain, but I'm happy as an Officer. I don't need the stress of being a Detective, and I certainly don't see myself wearing a Sergeant's or Lieutenant's bars or anything higher up the command than that, either.

Which might come as a surprise to some.

As a Dom, you might assume that positions of power excite me. That having people under my explicit control is exactly where I want to be. But it's not. At least, not in my career.

In my private life? Well, that might be something different altogether . Not that being a Dom is about the control or power. If that's how a Dom looks at it, they need to take a step back and re-evaluate.

No, being a Dom is about taking care of one's subs. Working out what they need and pushing them to the edges of what they can handle. Making sure that they are safe physically, emotionally, and mentally. The misconception that being a Dom means being aggressive and controlling is irritating.

On the surface, it might look like I have all the power in a D/s relationship, but it's like any other kink. My subs and I are partners, going into any scenes or interactions as equal members of the power exchange. If anything, my subs control the scenes more than I do, even if I'm the one holding the floggers, or chains, or whatever their particular brand of submission entails.

So…yeah. I guess I'm not exactly power hungry in my private life, either.

But at least my private life isn't boring the ever-loving hell out of me.

Vince prattles on as we walk, and I find myself reminiscing about my last long-term partner. Charlie Walker was a great cop, but also a good friend. The day he got shot on duty still haunts me. It's a lingering ache in the back of my head and heart because I still feel guilty that it happened. Not that I would tell my mandated psychologist that. They likely never would have let me return to work if I'd admitted that I still blame myself.

In the almost seven years since Charlie's shooting, my friendship with my former partner has become more of an acquaintanceship. Where once we were thick as thieves, brothers on the force, now we exchange texts every few months and maybe meet for beers twice a year. It's not for lack of trying on Charlie's part, mind you. No, it's all me.

I can't look at the guy and not feel riddled with guilt.

It's my fault that he's not walking the beat with me. It's my fault that he's got a permanent mild limp. It's my fault that he had to ditch his dreams —the same dreams I am still living for myself— and had to work out a new life for himself as a civilian.

He's done amazing work for himself and the community, though. Building a kink-centric community center from the ground up is nothing short of inspirational. Every so often, he'll reach out to me for help with someone who has walked in off the street, or he'll give me a heads up on potential trouble makers that have crossed his path, but he's otherwise created a safe haven for people from all walks of life with very little fanfare. It's commendable.

But he still should have been walking the beat alongside me. Or even progressed to Detective like his kid brother, Josh, did.

Josh.

Fuck.

If I thought I'd fucked up big time with Charlie, it's nothing compared to the way I screwed up with Josh.

When Charlie was shot, Josh was still green. He was a kid, all of maybe twenty-five if he was a day, and so lost without knowing his big brother was okay. And what did I do? Instead of being a supportive friend, I took advantage of his vulnerability. I mean, hell, I knew the kid had a crush on me, and I used that to my advantage, too.

I'm a Dom and not a Daddy, and the night I spent looking after Josh in his Little space should never have happened. Especially not when it was my fault that Charlie was in the hospital to begin with.

Then Josh kissed me and I did the worst thing I could have possibly done. I walked away.

I left a hurt, scared, stressed-out Little in an empty hospital room on his own, because I was too cowardly to explain myself to him.

Josh has every right to hate me. We still work at the same precinct and cross paths a lot, but he's a bigger man than I am because he doesn't ever acknowledge that night or the following day. Even though he outranks me now, he just nods, half-smiles, and goes about his day like normal, while I fight the instinct to grovel and apologize and explain.

Not that there's all that much to explain, and Josh is a smart man. He has to have looked back over the situation and realized that I should never have taken advantage of the position he'd been in. He has to know that I was out of line to have offered to be his Daddy for a night. I'm his colleague. At the time, I was his brother's partner. It was highly inappropriate for me to be anything other than a supportive friend.

So…okay, Josh might also be part of the reason I've let my friendship with Charlie waste away over the years. And if Charlie ever found out what I did, he'd hate me even more than he should for letting him get shot. I can't have that. Even though I'd deserve it, I'd rather keep the very tenuous friendship that we have.

I'm selfish that way.

Chapter Four — Josh

After my failed night at The Grove, it's back to work on Wednesday. At least my time spent with Matt in some semblance of Little space gave me a boost, so I'm no longer afraid that I'll stress out and start regressing at work. I can kiss my career goodbye if that shit ever happens.

Today is spent making sure all of my reports have been completed properly, that procedures have been followed to a T, and that there's absolutely no chance in hell that anything my partner or I did will compromise the integrity of our investigation or the subsequent charges laid against the bad guys.

It's actually kind of a relief to spend the day at my desk, not that I would ever admit that to anyone. That would certainly make them suspect that I'm not like them. I mean, who the fuck likes paperwork?

Nearing the end of my shift, I lean back in my crappy rolling desk chair and stretch out my back with my arms above my head, yawning widely.

"That about sums up my feelings," Dana, my partner, chuckles ruefully, tossing her pen onto the desk in front of her. She makes a show of clenching and unclenching her fingers while she grimaces, then shakes her head, little wisps of blonde-turning-gray hair escaping from her tight bun with the motion. "Ugh. I hate this part of the job."

See? If I disagree, she'll look at me funny, so I just nod and grin. "But we got the bad guys and this," I lurch forward again in my chair, ignoring the way it creaks ominously, and tap my dated computer screen, "makes sure it's all airtight."

"Still, I'll be happy when we're back out there," Dana waves vaguely behind us, towards the Captain's office which looks out onto the streets below, "and not being glorified desk monkeys."

I snort and fight the urge to do my stellar impression of a chimpanzee. Somehow, I don't think that would go over well with my cranky partner. It's also probably too close to letting my Little side out than I'd like.

When I yawn again, she shoos me towards the break room, telling me to grab a coffee and wake the hell up. I'm still chuckling as I grab a mug from the cupboard beside the refrigerator, and I turn and walk straight into Max.

"Oomph," he says as we collide, and I'm just glad that my mug is empty, because it would have spilled all over him if it hadn't been.

"Shit, sorry," I rush to apologize, already feeling my pulse pick up.

I haven't had a proper conversation with Max in years. If I'm being honest, the last time was when Charlie was in the hospital, and I'm not so dumb that I can't put two and two together. That short time spent with him had been magical…

and had also destroyed what little friendship we shared. And yet, my crush on the guy has never quite abated.

If anything, I can still recall with clarity just how amazing he was when he took on the role of temporary Daddy. His strong embrace when he cuddled me to sleep after I had tearfully begged him. The smooth, firm pressure of his lips against mine, however briefly, when I'd kissed him.

No, even if we've only exchanged one or two words every time we've since seen each other, that night at Max's place all those years ago pushed my crush into overdrive. You'd think after nearly seven years I'd be over it, but I swear that time and separation has only made me want him more.

He reaches out to steady me by the biceps before he registers that it was me who bumped into him, and he drops his hands as though they burn. I try not to think about how much that stings. Then he takes a step backwards, and that hurts even more.

"No harm done," he says stiffly, and I have to swallow back a complaint.

'Look at me!' I want to demand. I want to stomp my feet and cry. 'I want Maxxie back!'

It's ridiculous. I only had that side of him for one night. A few hours at most, and almost seven years ago at that. How can I be so attached? How can just the sight of him bring my Little space roaring back so close to the surface?

I pride myself on my usual control. I've been even more proud that, in the years since Charlie got shot, I've been able to keep my feelings and reactions about Max an additional secret. Anyone observing our minor interactions over the years would be surprised to know that all I want to do is be Little for the guy again. Even the people who know that I'm a

Little would never guess it.

Though they haven't exactly guessed that I'm more lifestyle Little than scene player, either, have they? And I can't help but feel like I've pretty much spelled it out for them all lately.

But why would they bother paying attention to me when they're all wrapped up in their own Daddies and boys?

I'm being a little dramatic and unfair, I know.

I know Charlie's noticed something's up, but he's doing his usual big brotherly 'wait for Josh to come to me' thing. I appreciate that he respects me enough to give me space, but he's supposed to be some kind of Daddy guru. Shouldn't he realize that I'm never going to bring the topic up with him? That I need to be guided and supported by someone in a more mature headspace?

And I suppose the other Littles in our circle are trying to get me to talk, too, but…well, have you ever tried having a deep and meaningful conversation with a bunch of people who are mentally aged five and under?

Yeah. Exactly.

I'm starting to feel that same impending meltdown feeling from last night again and I stop, close my eyes, and take deep breaths to push it back. I've kept my Little headspace under wraps at work for so long, I am not letting it out now.

A touch to my arm makes me almost jump out of my skin, though, and I open my eyes to find Max's blue pair eyeing me with concern. "Are you okay?" he asks lowly.

What is it about that question that can destroy any and all composure? Tears sting my eyes and my throat goes tight as soon as he asks it, but still I nod and try to swallow the building meltdown back again. "Fine," I answer, probably a bit too gruffly, but it's all I can manage.

Max's gaze narrows. *"Joshua—"*

"No." Stepping back until I run into the refrigerator, making its contents rattle, it's only panic I can feel. How dare he use that voice now?

He's too late.

Over six years too late, in fact. But it still affects me the way it did the last time he used it, and I hate that. I hate that I can't control my reaction to him. I hate that I want nothing more than to sink into Little space and have him take away all my stress and worries. "I'm fine. Back off."

There's nobody else in the break room, but Max still checks over his shoulders before he closes in on me. His worry is almost palpable. "You're not fine, Josh. You look like you're going to cry."

My face flames and I look down at the floor, mumbling, "As if you'd care."

"What was that?" he demands, but I still don't look up at him.

Maybe I'm more of a natural brat than I thought because I can feel the petulance set in and I just shrug.

"Joshua," he repeats firmly.

Fucking Daddy Dom voice.

"I said," I make myself look back up at him, setting my jaw, glaring at him as hard as I can, "that it's not as if you would care."

Max's handsome face falls and he raises his hand as if to reach for me, and then seems to think better of it. He drops it back to his side. "Josh…" He sounds defeated and pleading.

That is *not* how a Daddy Dom is supposed to sound.

Oddly enough, that helps me to push back the encroaching headspace until I'm feeling like my Big self again. Thank God for that.

"No, I know, so spare me," I skirt around him, still clutching my mug tight. I go to fiddle with the pot of sludgy station coffee, more to occupy my hands than to actually drink the stuff. "It's been six years; I should be over it."

I'm proud of myself for not saying 'over you'.

"Josh…"

I hold up my hand. "It's fine. I'm fine. I just had a moment, but I'm good."

I don't know if he believes me, but I find I don't really care. Instead, I grab my half-filled mug of grossness and stalk out of the break room.

I guess I'm going to visit The Grove again tonight.

Chapter Five – Emmett

I'm surprised when Josh shows up at The Grove alone on Wednesday night. I'd spent last night just people watching, and my plan for tonight was to try and find a Little in need of a scene partner.

I did not anticipate that Josh might be one of the only available Littles in the Playroom tonight.

He enters wearing a different outfit to the one he wore yesterday. This one is younger than last night's shorts and t-shirt combo. This one is a blue long-sleeved footed onesie covered in puppies dressed in police uniforms. It looks soft to the touch and clings to his body, and I'm surprised to find that it looks like he's wearing briefs and not a diaper beneath the material, because I've seen him Little socially enough times to know he prefers the latter. To complete the look, he has a pacifier attached to the neckline, dangling via a bright blue saver ribbon.

I observe him as he scans the room, watching his expression dim as he clocks peoples' flags. Then he notices my wrist first and steps forward with an almost nervous energy, his eyes traveling from my wrist where it rests on my thigh, up my abdomen and chest, and finally to my face.

Recognition flares in his brown depths immediately, but he doesn't seem disappointed. He does hesitate for a brief moment before he continues towards me, and I watch as he seems to slip further into his Little persona on his way. His shoulders loosen and sag, and his face loses some of the tension and stress around his eyes and mouth.

"Hi, Josh," I greet him smoothly, keeping my voice low and lulling. I stay seated, letting him set the pace for this unexpected meeting.

A cute blush spreads up his neck and beneath the scruff on his cheeks. He nibbles his lip and sways side-to-side from his hips. "Hi, Emmett."

Christ, his Little voice is adorable. Higher pitched to his usual way of speaking, sweeter and slightly more cautious. Shy, maybe.

"Are you here just to play tonight?" I ask him, and he looks down towards his feet and shrugs.

I won't have that.

"Joshua," I start, relishing the way he shivers at the tone and then looks at me from under his thick, dark eyelashes. "Use words, please."

Not answering immediately, it looks like he's steeling himself before he takes a deep breath and rushes out *"I'm-looking-for-a-Daddy"* as though it were a single word.

I nod. "Any particular Daddy?"

Josh shrugs again, then his eyes widen and he speaks before I can correct the behavior a second time. "No. Nobody 'ticular."

The cuteness overload is going to kill me. How can anyone

think this boy is all brat?

"Do you want just a scene partner, or—"

"I just wanna be Little and lov...um, let go for a bit." His cheeks turn a darker shade of pink beneath his eyes as he holds up his thumb and index finger with a smidgen of space between them. Then, to my horror, his eyes brim with tears and he sniffles, "I don't wanna be bad. I just wanna be...be... be..." He dissolves into hitching sobs and I wonder how long he's been holding this breakdown back, because I don't think I've ever seen him distressed. Certainly not like this.

"Oh, honey," I'm on my feet and tugging him in for a hug before I know it. "You just want to be looked after for a while, hmm? Let someone else deal with all the big boy problems for a while?"

He smooshes his face into my shirt, nodding emphatically while he cries.

"Can I do that for you, Joshie?" The nickname slips out without thought and his fingers tighten in the fabric at my back.

"Pwease," he says. "I be good."

"Of course you will be, honey. You're a good boy, aren't you?"

My heart clenches when my words only make him cry harder.

Just how starved for positive reinforcement is this boy?

I don't care that we're starting to draw looks from the other people in the room, but I know Josh well enough to think that he might. So, thinking quickly, I ask him if he'd rather come home to my house where we can have a proper playdate with no time limits.

"There's absolutely no pressure, Josh. Standard safe words

can be used at all times, and you're going to set the pace. But I think you might benefit from being somewhere private tonight, hmm?"

He nods and pulls back to wipe at his red, puffy eyes. I bend to press a kiss to his forehead and that almost seems to set him off again.

"Is your bag in the locker room downstairs?" I ask him.

Trying to get himself back under control, he takes some shaky breaths and nods. "Yeah."

"Okay. Let's get that and go. Unless you'd rather stay here and play?" It's important that he knows he has a choice. I'm not taking him away from here if there's any chance he'd rather stay. "I'll be happy doing whatever you want to, honey."

"Your house," he insists, then looks up at me through big, wet eyes. "Pwease."

Oh dear. I think I'd prefer him as a brat. I'm going to struggle to say no to those eyes, crush or no crush.

I use the tip of my index finger to bop him on the nose, eliciting a watery giggle. "You got it. Let's go get your stuff."

We leave the large room and travel down the carpeted hallway towards the grand staircase and elevator that will lead us back downstairs to the main club floor. We pass a couple of people along the way to the locker rooms, but nobody pays us any mind. At least, not until Josh is slinging a black duffel bag over his shoulder and we've almost reached the soundproof door to the little reception room.

Under the loud, thumping bass of the nightclub music, I can still hear the concerned "Josh?" coming from the blonde guy approaching us.

He's an attractive man, a few inches shorter than Josh, with a lean, toned, athletic build and neatly trimmed blonde hair which is slicked back with gel. In the dim lighting, I'd guess he was in his early forties maybe, but looks can be deceiving. Something about him seems familiar, but I can't place him.

He's wearing shiny leather pants and a black vest with nothing beneath it, and his wristbands have him flagging as a Dom.

My protective instincts flare, even though I know there's not a huge technical difference between his role as a Dom and mine as a Daddy. He eyes me with suspicion as he gets closer, especially when he takes in Josh's red, puffy eyes.

"You've been crying," he says with dismay, before he nudges in between me and Josh, heedless of the space I take up just by existing, and puts his hands on Josh's shoulders. "I knew you were upset this afternoon."

Josh shrugs out of the concerned hold and glares at the blonde guy. "I is *fine*, Max."

I almost give myself whiplash as I swivel my attention back over the guy I now know is Max. Charlie's former partner. We've met a few times through work, when police assistance has been required, but he looks completely different out of uniform.

"Sorry," I apologize to him, sticking out my hand. "Emmett Reid," I introduce myself. "We've met through The Center. Through Charlie. I'm a counselor there. I didn't recognize you at first."

Max shakes my hand, but continues to cast concerned looks at Josh. He sighs. "Josh, please. Can we talk?"

"He's in Little space right now," I warn, still feeling protective of the man I promised to look after tonight. "And, yes, he's upset, so I'm taking him back to my place where he can relax properly."

Something in Max's expression tightens, though I don't think it's a jealous expression. Not really. I want to prod and ask questions about what that look means, but it's none of my business. Right now, Josh is my business.

Then Max, with all the finesse of a raging bull in a china shop, turns to Josh and asks, "Can Maxxie come, too?"

* * *

As I'm buckling Josh into the passenger seat of my car, I remind him that he can change his mind about anything at any time, can safe word out without question, and if Max being with us while he's in Little space is a problem, I'll gladly ask the other man to leave.

Josh nods his understanding and then nibbles at his lip in that way I'm coming to realize means he's debating saying something. So I wait patiently, and he fiddles with his fingers in his lap as he blurts, "Maxxie was my Daddy once. Kinda'. One time." He holds up his index finger before he looks back down at his lap and returns to fiddling with his hands. "Was a long time ago."

Ooh boy, there's a lot to unpack there.

But it certainly explains some of the interaction I've just witnessed between the two men.

"Thank you for telling me, Joshie," I kiss his forehead again and he leans into the chaste touch of my lips to his skin. "We can talk about that some more if you want. *Only* if you want."

He relaxes into his seat and nods. "Maybe later. Wanna go play now." He cocks his head at me. "Do you have toys?"

"Do I ever!"

It doesn't take long to get to my place from The Grove. I live in a recent suburban development just on the other side of the city's industrial area, and there's very little traffic on the drive there. Max's headlights remain visible in my rear-view mirror the whole way, but I don't really pay them much attention, too busy concentrating on the road and telling Josh about my collections of stuffies and blocks and Legos.

He listens in rapt attention, asking questions about the stuffies and wanting to know if he's allowed to draw with them. I revel in his obvious enthusiasm for the simple, sweet things and assure him that he's definitely allowed to do that.

"An' I don't gotta be bad?" he asks just as I'm turning onto my street.

"No, honey. We can talk about bratty scenes and punishment another time if it's something you want to do. But tonight you can just enjoy being Little and having a Daddy look after you."

I almost expect another outburst of pure emotion from him but, aside from a tiny little sniffle, he doesn't react except to nod. "Otay."

I pull into my driveway and click the button on my garage remote, which is clipped to the inside of my driver's side sun visor, and wait for the paneled cream colored door to roll up. My house is a single-story brick and tile ranch style home. It was built about five years ago, and is modern and inviting, or at least I think it is. The color palette inside is contemporary but comprised of warm, neutral tones, and my furniture is eclectic and lived in.

The internal door from the garage leads through to the laundry, which also has a door on the other side of the large, cream-colored marble bench that runs around the short wall, leading to the back yard. When we walk out of the laundry, the open plan kitchen/dining/living areas are off to our right, with another set of sliding glass doors that lead out to the back porch. If I walk around the living area and turn left, I hit the wide hallway that takes me to the front door and to the bedrooms and bathrooms off to the right from there.

Knowing that Max has pulled into the driveway by now, I do just that, heading to the front door to let the guy in. I can't help but think he looks just a little out of place in his sexy Dom outfit, standing in the middle of my suburban foyer. He lifts his own black duffel bag, which I notice matches Josh's, complete with the police department's seal on the side, and asks if he can use my bathroom to change.

I point him down the hallway to my right and tell him to make himself at home, and if I watch his ass as he goes, I'm only human.

I head back into the living room where Josh is waiting for me on the couch, jiggling his legs with nervous energy.

"Did you want to come and see the nursery?" I ask him brightly. "That's where all the stuffies are. But we can bring them out here to play if you're more comfortable in an open space."

Josh's eyes go wide and genuine excitement spreads across his face. "Nursery?"

I am beyond proud of the room I designed back when the house was being built. It's essentially a second master suite complete with attached bathroom, the whole area large enough to house the specialist furniture and floor space for playtime. I didn't have a Little in mind for its use, just a hope that one day I'd be able to share it with a boy for more than a few nights at a time.

And, even if Josh is only going to enjoy it for the one night,

I'm excited to share it with him.

I take him by the hand and lead him down past the front door and into the other half of the house. We pass the two standard guest rooms, separated from each other by a small lounge room complete with TV and a powder room consisting of a shower, toilet, and single sink. I can hear sounds behind the door of the powder room, and I surmise that's where Max is currently changing out of his Dom clothes.

Further down the hallway, the two master suites are situated side by side. The first door on the left is the nursery. The second is my bedroom. Josh peeks into the open doorway to my room, taking in the lengthy space and California king bed.

"I'm not a small guy," I explain when he turns back to look at me with a cheeky expression, "and I like to be comfortable."

He nods, then looks back at the bed one more time before casting his curious gaze over the closed door to the nursery. He gasps when I turn the handle and push it open.

This room is a Little's paradise if I do say so myself. The carpet is soft and plush, a bright yellow that makes the whole space seem happy and welcoming. The walls are a softer yellow, with decals of the alphabet, teddy bears, and building blocks decorating their surfaces as they wrap around the space.

The first half of the room is dedicated to play. There are toy chests brimming with anything a little boy could ask for, and bookshelves, and a giant Costco teddy bear propped up in the corner of the room to the left of the door, with beanbag chairs on either side of him. The space beyond is designed to accommodate a Littles' other needs. A purpose-built change table sits near the door to the bright white bathroom, stocked with diapers, barrier cream, pacifiers, and powder. Tucked into the opposing corner is my favorite piece: a custom-built adult sized crib with a working sliding side rail. It's the size of a twin-sized bed, raised off the ground enough so I can deposit a sleepy boy on the mattress without too much struggle, or can drop the side rail and lift him out just as easily. The timber of both the changing table and crib is strong and sturdy and painted a glossy sky blue. There's also a small walk-in wardrobe next to the bathroom, but I haven't had a Little for whom to buy outfits, so it's sparse right now, save for some generic emergency outfits in a variety of sizes.

"*Whoa*," Josh exhales as he steps tentatively into the room, spinning around slowly to take in as many details as he can in his current headspace.

"Do you like it?"

He nods quickly and enthusiastically. "It better than da Gwove."

He's lapsing deeply into his headspace again, which is a great sign. I feel a little of my own tension melt away and I smile at him. "That is a big compliment, thank you."

I stand back and let Josh explore, running his fingers over the spines of the books, peeking into the toy chests, then toying with the ear of the big, floppy brown bear in the corner.

"You can play with whatever you like, honey," I remind him when he hesitates, seemingly overcome by indecision.

He casts a look of longing back over the giant bear before he heads over to the first of the two toy chests, the one containing the stuffies. He's just starting to dig through it when Max pops his head in the doorway.

I watch as Max takes the space in with his own wide-eyed awe. He walks over to where I'm still standing, just off to the side of the play space, and nudges my bicep with his shoulder.

Now that he's dressed in jeans that grip his ass and thighs just so, and a dark red Henley, he's more recognizable. I'm mildly startled to realize that I'm attracted to him in this state as well. Doms have never been my thing.

"This is something," he murmurs appreciatively, gesturing around the room with a roll of his head. "Design it yourself?"

I nod, smiling softly. "Yeah. Had the furniture custom made, but I did everything else myself." I let the pride seep into my tone with the admission. Knowing that the Littles I bring here enjoy something that I created for them myself makes me feel like a good provider. A good Daddy.

"You've built something magical here," Max compliments, then turns his attention back to Josh. A series of complex emotions seem to wash over his face, but his expression smooths out into a melancholy sort of fondness. "He's loving it."

Sure enough, Josh has grabbed a big, fluffy white teddy bear from the stuffie toy box, and has plopped down on the carpet to play with his find. He's holding the toy by its soft waist, dancing it from side to side. All of the distress and upset from the club seems to have leeched out of him, and what remains is a Little in relaxation mode, completely uninhibited.

We haven't negotiated anything, though I feel confident that I made it clear to him we're not going to attempt any specific scenes that might make him uncomfortable. He can play with toys, or draw, or we can read stories and cuddle, but that's as far as I'll let anything go today. Once he's back out of his Little headspace, we can talk about progressing from there if he's interested in doing so.

"So, uh, do we...join him?" Max's question pulls my attention back to him. He cocks his head. "I've never really

47

done the Daddy thing. I mean, spanking I can handle, but—"

"Is that what you did for him before?" I feel ashamed for asking. As soon as the question blurts its way past my lips, I want to take it back. It's unprofessional and none of my business, and I know Max is thinking those exact things because his blonde eyebrows go upwards. I wince. "Sorry. None of my business. Josh just mentioned that you, uh…"

Uh? Since when do I stammer and lose control of my sentences? My crush on Josh makes me stupid, I know that. But I'm talking to Max, not Josh. Why am I getting flustered?

Unexpectedly, Max's handsome face falls. He closes his eyes and sighs. "It wasn't like that. Josh was hurting, and he needed some Little time —not all that dissimilar to tonight, actually— and I volunteered to look after him. It was a mistake."

"You're a Dom, not a Daddy," I nod my understanding. "You didn't like it?" Even as I hazard the guess, I know I'm off the mark.

Max shakes his head, his smile rueful. "I kind of loved it. It made me feel good, taking care of him. Being needed. But," once more his exhalation is heavy and weary. "I feel like I took advantage. The kid had a crush on me, and he was vulnerable, and—"

I don't want to ask my next question, but I feel like I have a duty of care to do so. "When you say you took advantage," I start carefully, "did you do anything that made him uncomfortable? Did you cross any lines? Subvert your previous negotiations? Was there dubious consent or even a lack thereof?" Usually I would be far more direct, and I don't know why I'm beating around the bush now. Nevertheless, it's a relief when Max shakes his head vehemently anyway.

"No. Nothing like that. I just…" He trails off and looks

back over at Josh, who is in his own little world, now having grabbed a book to read to the bear. "I know he wanted a Daddy. I know he wanted *me*. And even though I was in no place to be that person for him, I still gave him that night. All we did was basic stuff, nothing sexual, but I still feel like I gave him hope when I shouldn't have. I had no intention of being more for him, I didn't —*don't*— deserve to be more for him, but I was too selfish to walk away before I made things worse."

I blink at the onslaught of information, then frown. Because none of that sounds at all like he did anything wrong. "Max," I start in the understanding but firm voice I use with clients who need to really think about the root of their issues, "did Josh ask you for more than one night?"

"Well, no, but—"

"Okay. And did you give him support and help when he needed it?"

"I guess, but—"

"And did you make sure he was safe and looked after until he was back out of Little space?"

"I…yeah. But—"

I fold my arms and stare down at him. "Then, honestly, I don't see what the issue is. It doesn't sound as though you took advantage of anything, and I certainly don't think you were selfish."

"It was my fault he was hurting," he hisses at me, and pokes at his own chest for emphasis. "Mine. I got Charlie shot, I—"

"*Whoa*," I shake my head and place a calming hand on his shoulder. "You did not get Charlie shot, Max. Charlie says you saved his life." I only met Charlie a few years ago, when I joined the team at The Center, but he's open about his career on the force and how it ended, and his story has never wavered.

I feel my eyebrows knitting together. "You're not telling me that you're still blaming yourself for that, what, five years down the track?"

"Six," he corrects. "Coming up on seven. And, yeah, because I should have seen it coming. I should have pushed him out of the way. I should have—"

"For fuck's sake," I mutter and pinch the bridge of my nose. "From what I understand of the situation, it happened fast and neither of you had a chance to react any other way than you did."

Max is silent for a moment, and I wonder if he's going to argue with me, but he just shrugs. "Whatever. I can't help that this is how I feel."

I'm torn between amusement at the sheer petulance coming from a man who is both a cop and a Dom, and frustration because "Yes you can." He rolls his eyes and I glare. "As a psychologist, I know what I'm talking about. You should probably consider talking to someone about this and working on your guilt complex because, I assure you, nobody but you blames you for what happened. And Josh," I point towards the man in question, "probably turned to you because he saw you as a safe space, and because you cared about Charlie as much as he did. And the way he spoke about you being his Daddy for that one night was almost reverent, Max. I promise you; he doesn't see it the way you do."

Max gives me a sideways glance and chuckles darkly. "You're good at this."

"I'm a psychologist. It's my job."

"No," he rolls his eyes again. "You're good at the Daddying thing. I mean, you just Daddy lectured a Dom. And it's hot."

I blink, surprised and taken aback by the open admission.

"Uh...good?"

He looks me over, a slow exploration from my feet to my eyes, making his appreciation obvious. "Very good."

My cock stirs in my business pants. Even though I freely acknowledge that I thought he was attractive, I didn't see this coming.

Well. Damn.

Chapter Six – Max

Flirting with this behemoth of a Daddy serves dual purposes. One, he drops the uncomfortable line of conversation. Two, it revs me up with the excitement of exploring something new to me.

Under the warm, yellow lighting of the cute nursery he designed, Emmett's dark skin seems to glisten with hints of gold. His soulful eyes also glitter with hidden shades of amber, drawing me in like a moth to a flame. He's huge —at least half a foot taller than me, and at least twice my breadth— and his sculpted face is handsome as sin. He is most certainly not a sub.

I've never been drawn to any one body type or gender. I'm into personalities, and the more interesting and complex someone seems, the more attractive they start to appear to me. But I have never been interested in someone as dominating as this man.

He's forthright, which I appreciate, and clearly has no problem questioning me or calling me out. I want to say that it's frustrating, but I'm too turned on to actually have an issue with it.

Part of me wants to know if I can push back, if he would ever submit to me, but I'm surprised to realize that even if he wouldn't be interested in that, I'd still be turned on by him.

I can't help that my thoughts start to drift towards how sex between us might work. I prefer to top, but I can't say that I'm not insanely curious about the monster he's packing in those tightening business pants of his, and what it might feel like moving against me or even inside of me.

Then I stop my thoughts because that is not why I came here tonight. I came because of Josh. Josh, who was upset at work. Who was then even more upset when I bumped into him at The Grove. Josh, who I still can't get out of my head, even though I was only his pseudo-Daddy for a single night years and years ago. Josh, whose puffy red eyes made something inside of me snap.

It was a split-second decision to invite myself along to Emmett's place. A split-second decision to finally face the music and talk to Josh like I should have done six years ago. And now here I am, pining over both men, and making the situation even more complicated than it needs to be.

I clear my throat and break the tension building between Emmett and me. "So, um, do we go play with him, or...?"

Emmett appears confused for only a brief second before he understands the meaning of my question and nods. "Yeah. Yeah, we should." Then, without further prompting, he crosses the space between us and Josh and smiles down at the boy. "Can we play with you?"

Josh cranes his neck back and positively beams up at Emmett. "Yes pwease. I weeding." He holds up his book to illustrate his point.

"It's very nice of you to read to the teddy," Emmett tells him, sinking to the carpet with surprising grace for a man his size. He stretches his long legs out beside him and leans in to give Josh his rapt attention. "Does the teddy have a name?"

"Wanger," Josh answers without hesitation. "Cos he's white like ice."

Emmett can't make the connection, but I do. I snicker and sit down on Josh's other side, folding my legs beneath me. "Like the New York Rangers," I acknowledge. "That's clever. I like it." I smirk across at Emmett. "NHL." Then I turn back to Josh and pout exaggeratedly. "I thought you were a Bruins fan."

"Boo-in da Bear is a stupid name," he tells me matter-of-factly.

"Fair point," I concede, trying not to laugh.

It's a whole new experience seeing him like this. When he was Little with me before, he was wrung out and sad. But this version of him is cheeky and playful.

Word around The Grove is that he's a brat, and while I can see that he'd be good at it, he's not being overly bratty now. If anything, this kind of behavior feels like standard Little regression, not that I have any experience to go by outside of Google searches and conversations at the club.

"Um, Da...er," Josh looks between Emmett and I with consternation, biting his lower lip before he settles on Emmett and tries again, "Memmett?"

I swear the big, strong, physically imposing man on Josh's other side melts into a puddle of goo. "Yes, honey?"

I'm also one hundred percent certain that Josh realizes the effect he has on Emmett, because he bats his lashes and brings the ear of his bear up to partially cover his face, enacting a full-on cuteness assault. "We draw now?" Once again, his 'r' is a 'w'.

I'm pretty sure that he could have asked for the moon and Emmett's answer would have been the same. "Of course, honey. Whatever you want."

So much for the dominating Daddy type.

Maybe stern lectures are reserved purely for people who aren't adorable Littles.

We all get up from the floor and I remind Josh to put his book away, but he clutches Ranger tighter against him, a pout pushing out his bottom lip. It even freaking trembles!

"It's okay," Emmett soothes, and now it's starting to feel a little like the old 'good cop, bad cop' routine and I know exactly which role I've been cast in, "Ranger can come with us."

Josh sags with relief. Then, after Emmett turns to lead the way out of the room, Josh pokes his tongue out at me.

"Why, you cheeky little…"

"*Max*," Emmett's voice is back to that stern, 'take no shit' tone and he frowns back at me over his shoulder.

Josh still has his back to Emmett and grins at me with smug satisfaction. His brown eyes dance with mirth. Now that I'm onto his game, I'm amused and impressed.

"…monkey." I finish my thought almost lamely, giving Josh a look that says he wins this round, but I'm not going down without a fight. He giggles. The sound makes my stomach flip.

The three of us wander back through the house and into the main living/dining area. From a sideboard in the dining room, Emmett pulls out a Tupperware container full of crayons and a brand-new artist's sketch pad. He sets both on the dining table.

He helps get Josh settled, putting Ranger in the seat beside him as requested. "Start drawing, honey. I'll get some snacks." Then he gives me a look of warning, which is about ten different kinds of amusing, and even more kinds of hot.

I take a seat on Josh's other side and prop my elbow on the table to support my chin while he picks up an orange crayon and starts to scribble on the first page of the sketch pad. He pokes his tongue out as he draws, and I'm so immersed in what he's doing that I startle when a can of soda is slid in front of me.

"Thanks," I say, glancing across the table to where Emmett has now sat down, leaving Ranger in his spot directly beside Josh. He's also put a blue sippy cup and a plastic plate of apple slices down in front of Josh.

Josh looks up and grins, reaching for the sippy. "Fanks," he says, taking a few hissing drags from the cup before smacking his lips and placing it back down a touch too heavily. He munches on a couple of slices of apple. "Nummy."

It's adorable, but I am far more interested in the way Emmett once again visibly melts. He's got it bad for Josh, of that much I'm certain. But he's still shown interest in me, too, and I don't know what to do with that.

Because I'm still feeling indecisive, I opt to do nothing about it at all. Instead, I chat with him and Josh about what's happening in Josh's drawing, and I make outlandish decisions about the sorts of things Josh should include. Josh giggles and shoots down my suggestions of three-legged aliens and deep-sea monsters, and I'm not unaware of Emmett's appraising gaze during these interactions.

After a little while, Josh grows bored of drawing and Emmett suggests that we move over to the large, soft couch in the living room to watch a movie. Josh isn't showing any sign of coming out of Little space, and I'm not going to leave things the way I did six years ago, so I agree to go with the flow.

I sit on one end of the three-seater couch and Emmett sits on the other. Josh sandwiches himself between us and then gripes and complains until we're all cuddled up together. I'm pretty sure I see his eyes gleam with mischief during these machinations, and I tickle him and whisper that I'm onto him, which makes him shriek with glee. Still, I can't complain about how good it feels to be wrapped up so domestically with these two very attractive men.

Emmett scrolls through Disney+ and puts *Toy Story 3* on at Josh's urging, then we snuggle back together as if this is an everyday occurrence. We're about twenty minutes in when Josh starts to yawn, and Emmett pauses the movie and gives him a little nudge that reverberates into me.

"Okay, honey, bedtime."

Josh has been so cute and compliant all night that his reaction startles me.

"No!" he yells, leaping from the couch. He crosses his arms tightly over Ranger and stomps his foot. "No bedtime!"

A glance across to Emmett says he's just as surprised by the swift change in mood as I am.

"Joshua," he starts, not exactly using Daddy voice, but his tone certainly implies that he's not going to take a temper tantrum sitting down.

"No!" Josh repeats himself, and his eyes brim with tears. He steps backwards towards the TV, shaking his head. "No bed. Don't wanna sleep."

57

"Okay," I bargain gently, while Emmett frowns at him. "What about a story?" I remember how much he relaxed the night Charlie was shot. I push it a tiny bit further than I did back then. "We can get a bottle, and—"

His expression has turned horrified, which I don't understand at all. "No! No bottle! No sleep!"

I look to Emmett for backup. Emmett stands and holds up his hands in a placating gesture. "Calm down, honey," he says, and I can hear that he's just as concerned about the sudden, frantic panic that seems to have taken over the previously docile Little. "Bedtime's not—"

Whatever he was going to say is cut off by Josh's cry of, "Red light! I'm not...I can't...Not here. I don't want to sleep, damn it!"

In the ensuing stunned silence, Emmett and I have both frozen in place, respecting the safe word for what it is. Josh takes off towards the door at a run, his footie-pajama covered feet slipping on the tiles. I'm on my feet now, too, exchanging worried, confused glances with Emmett because safewording out of something as innocuous as bedtime has alarm bells blaring in my head.

"Do you know why..." Emmett starts, then stops himself and shakes his head. "No. Why doesn't matter right this second."

I'm still racking my brain for answers, though, worried about Josh and what the hell just happened. Emmett hurries off after him, and I go through possible reasons in my head, ranging from awful, terrifying ideas like this being the aftermath of sexual assault, to more palatable things like a (still concerning) freak out over having two Daddies here instead of just one.

Hell, this could even be my fault, triggering a fear that I

might pull the same kind of shit I did six years ago.

Well, whatever it is, I'm not letting him leave in the state he's in. Not this time.

Chapter Seven — Josh

I slip and slide across the tiles in the hallway as I make my way to the front door. I look around for my duffel —which contains my wallet and phone, as well as my adult clothes— but I can't find it anywhere. I don't give a shit about my clothes, but without my wallet or phone, I can't arrange a ride back to my car, which is still parked at The Grove.

"Fuck," I mutter, pacing in front of the closed front door. "Fuck, fuck, fuck."

The abrupt crash back into my adult headspace is disorienting and upsetting. *This* is what I get for not negotiating before launching into kinky role-play with a new partner. *Partners*. Fuck. Even if it seemed like harmless regression on the surface, how had I not thought about bedtime being a trigger for me?

The bed-wetting is an issue I am not coping with. I'm not wearing a diaper right now, and if Max and Emmett had let me fall asleep on the couch while we were watching the movie…I shudder to think about the embarrassment *that* might have led to.

"Josh," Emmett's voice, deep and soothing, has me pausing in my pacing.

He's been so good to me tonight. Both he and Max have been. They've been exactly what I needed, and now I've gone and fucked things up by panicking and safewording and trying to run away and they deserve so much better than me and my issues.

"Josh," he repeats, stepping closer with his hands raised like he's a hostage situation negotiator.

Oh, God, that makes me the guy holding the hostages.

"I'm sorry," I tell him, feeling guilty for putting him in such a position. "We should have talked about expectations and triggers. That's…this is all on me. My fault." I clamp my mouth shut, then look around again, as though my duffel might have magically materialized. "Do you know where my bag is? I'll just get changed and get out of your hair."

"I don't think that's wise," he says slowly, shaking his head. Genuine concern is etched across his handsome face. After hours spent being Little for him, I just want to rush into his strong arms and let him comfort me, but I can't let myself go there. "You just pulled out of your headspace pretty hard and fast. I wouldn't be surprised if you drop in a few hours."

I make a face. "I can drop at home," I shrug. The urge to tell him I usually suffer through sub drop on my own is strong, but I don't think it'll reassure him like I want it to.

"I don't think that's—"

"Emmett," I firm my tone into my work one. I'm not backing down on this. Shame is roiling my gut and ruining the magic of the night we'd all shared. I need to get out of here. I hate the words I pull out next, but I can't let the temptation of being doted on by Max and Emmett lure me into making a choice I'll come to regret. "You said I could safe word at any time. I did. And now I'd like to leave, please."

His handsome face falls and I hate that I'm the cause of that bereft expression, but he nods and backs up a step. "Your bag's in the living room, I think. I'll go get it." Then he turns around and heads back into the room where we had all been snuggling on the couch together like one big happy fucking family.

God damn it, why do I have to be so messed up? I had a good thing going in there. But there was absolutely no way in hell I was going to fall asleep around anyone else, especially not two people I have to see again. People with close connections to my big brother, at that.

Ugh.

Part of my insistence on scene play over the years has been to protect myself from the embarrassment of my little problem. I don't do sleepovers. I'll play with a Daddy, have some sexy fun and then leave. No muss, no fuss, and my secret stays safe with me.

I came too close to fucking that up tonight.

Max is with Emmett when he returns. "I'll grab my bag and drive you back to your car," he says, and his tone brooks no argument, so I sigh and nod. He ducks into the hallway that leads to the bedrooms and comes back with his duffel which matches mine.

I reach out with my right hand and take mine from Emmett, slinging the strap over my shoulder. I want to apologize again. I want to reiterate that this is all my issue, nothing that he or Max did wrong. But all I can manage is to look at my onesie-clad feet and offer a weak, "Thank you for tonight."

"Anytime, Josh," Emmett says emphatically. "I mean it. And keep Ranger, okay?"

I look down to my left arm, surprised to find it still curled protectively around the bear I'd chosen from the toy chest. He's big and soft and cuddly, and I'm stupidly attached to him even in my adult headspace. I should protest and give him back, but instead I hold him a little bit tighter and nod. "Thank you."

I wish I could say more, but no other words will come.

Emmett hesitates for a moment before he casts his gaze to the ceiling, mutters something that sounds like 'fuck it', and then crowds into my space to place a super chaste, incredibly sweet kiss on my lips.

"You are welcome here any time, Josh. You've got my number. Use it." Then he surprises Max and me both when he turns to Max and kisses him, too. "You too, Max. Tonight was..." he seems to search for the right word and eventually settles on, "special. I liked having you both here and enjoyed what we shared tonight. Take from that what you will."

Because I can't help myself, my brain betrays me with all the possibilities those words could conjure up. I imagine repeating tonight's events and more – exploring this fun chemistry that seems to exist between the three of us. The flirty vibes between Max and Emmett are super hot and picturing myself in between them makes me want to throw caution to the wind and stay over despite my fears of discovery.

If we stayed awake all night having sex, I wouldn't sleep. And if I don't sleep, I won't have nightmares. And if I don't have nightmares, I won't wet the bed.

Sadly, these men are Daddies and doms. I don't see them

letting me get away with an entire night of no sleep, so the whole idea is a pipe dream.

I could also just play wetting off as deliberate…but I could only keep that act up for so long before they cottoned on to me.

No, it's easier to just walk away and deal with it myself, the way I always have.

Oblivious to my thoughts, Max's lips pull into a rakish grin and he nods at Emmett. "I liked it, too. I'll see you around, Em." His features soften and he can't quite hold his concern when he looks at me. "Come on, Josh. Let's get you home safe, yeah?"

* * *

The drive back to my car is not as awkward as I thought it would be. Max doesn't bring up anything that has happened tonight, nor does he want to talk about the night Charlie was shot. Instead, he puts the radio on and lets me sit in silence for the short drive.

Just before I climb out of the passenger seat, though, he reaches out and puts a hand on my thigh, stalling my movements.

"I'm sorry about what happened," Max says softly, and his blue eyes are imploring me to believe him.

With how raw I feel, I don't have the energy to argue with him, but I don't need him thinking that he was at fault for anything that went wrong tonight. "It was all me," I reiterate. "I've got some stuff I'm trying to work through."

Max shakes his head. "I don't mean tonight. I mean last time."

In the darkness, with only slivers of moonlight and the scattered floodlights over the parking lot behind the warehouse, I can't pretend to be looking anywhere else but at him. I sigh. "It was a long time ago, Max. It doesn't matter."

"It does," he insists. "I need to explain."

"There's nothing to explain. I asked too much of you, and then I made things weird by kissing you." I shrug. "I get it."

He surprises me by gripping my thigh a bit more firmly and giving it a frustrated shake. "It wasn't like that at all. I…Josh, Charlie got shot and it was my fault. And then you were so messed up and I feel like I took advantage of the situation."

I can only stare incredulously at him.

He continues, "Then I walked away from you after that kiss because you deserved so much better than the old asshole who couldn't keep your brother safe…and I kicked myself for that, too, because as a Dom I know better than to leave a sub stranded and upset."

"You…I…what?" I can't form a coherent question. My eyebrows draw down into a frown and I try to process exactly what he just said. "One: *nobody* ever blamed you for Charlie getting hurt. Nobody. You're not telling me you still feel responsible?" He averts his gaze and I resist the urge to lean over the center console and strangle some sense into him. "Jesus fuck, Max. We're revisiting that when my brain is better equipped to handle it." I scrub my palm over my face, still struggling with my disbelief. "Secondly, how do you think you took advantage? If anything, I overstepped by launching into Little space with no prenegotiation. I thought that I had taken advantage of you, not the other way around." A blush burns my cheeks as I recall kissing him. "Then I kissed you and fucked our friendship up."

Max hangs his head. "I fucked it up, Josh. Not you. You were a kid—"

"I was twenty-five! I might be a Little, but I was an adult. I wasn't some innocent kid."

"I was still fourteen years older than you," he huffs out a self-deprecating kind of scoff. "Old enough that I felt like I was leading you on while you were in a vulnerable state. A state that I had caused."

And we've circled back to his guilt over Charlie again. I can't believe this has been eating at him for so long. If I had known —if *Charlie* had known— we would have nipped that in the bud years ago.

"Charlie wouldn't be alive if you hadn't reacted like you did," I remind him, wondering how many times he needs to hear it before it sticks. "And the only person responsible for how I felt back then was the guy who pulled the trigger, not you. You were exactly what I needed that night, Max." I turn back around and reach for the door handle again. Lowering my voice, I can't help but add, "And you and Emmett were both perfect for me tonight, too."

I climb out into the inky darkness and shut the car door behind me before he can respond, gripping both my duffel bag and my new teddy bear tightly.

Chapter Eight — Emmett

Wednesday night's events take up too much real estate in my brain for the rest of the week. I'm distracted at work, but thankfully my appointment schedule is light enough that I can focus when it counts. I avoid Charlie as much as I can because if he asked me what's going on, I wouldn't know what to tell him. I don't believe in lying, especially not to friends, but he's Josh's older brother and I don't have any answers to the questions I know he will ask me if he finds out.

And when I'm not thinking about Josh, I'm thinking about Max.

I can't believe I kissed them both. Chastely, yes, but it's unlike me to make a move like that without thinking everything through first. It's been a long time since I've been in any kind of relationship, and I basically made my interest in being with both men obvious. Would a throuple relationship even work for us? Because, in the heat of the moment, that's what I wanted. It's what I still want. I haven't been back to

The Grove because I have no interest in playing with anyone else now.

It was only a few hours spent together, but Wednesday night was like a taster event that put all sorts of hopes and ideas in my head. Max and I worked well together as Daddies to Josh, and I didn't imagine our chemistry. Max and Josh have a history, but their chemistry is also obvious. And Josh and me? I'm pretty sure that's a given as well. All together it just felt *right*. We didn't even do anything sexual: it was a purely innocent and sweet evening, and it was the most satisfying night I've had in ages.

I can't help but think I'm being ridiculous. Wanting a relationship with not one but two men is an indication of just how lonely I've been. Am I overcompensating? After all, how could I possibly be lonely again if I had two lovers? Two lovers who are both police officers with erratic schedules. Even so, logic dictates that at least one of them would be accessible at all times.

Yeah, I'm mostly focusing on my own needs. But there's nothing wrong with wanting a connection with someone. Or, in my case, two someones. There's nothing wrong with wanting to love and be loved in return.

And I think we could make it work between us all.

Josh certainly seemed to benefit from having two Daddies doting on him. Well, until he safe worded and fled my house.

I will never begrudge anyone for safewording, but I wish he hadn't felt so spooked that he'd left completely. That made my guts clench and my heart hurt. Not because I felt rejected, but because I unintentionally triggered him to the point where he no longer felt safe with me.

I'm worried about him and about what happened. I want to

know how to prevent it from happening again, assuming he ever feels comfortable enough to regress with me again.

I'm also worried about him experiencing sub drop on his own.

Over the past few days, I've been tempted to reach out and see if he's okay. To make sure he didn't drop too hard and to let him know that I care. But I haven't. He safe worded. I don't want to push boundaries with him and accidentally make him uncomfortable again.

You'd think as a psychologist and counselor I would be better equipped to handle this situation, but I'm not. I'm just like any other person, at war with my own insecurities and feelings. Trying to tell myself to accept the advice I would give any clients in my situation works on paper, but the second my heart gets involved, being rational is harder.

I can only hope that Max, working at the same station, has at least been able to keep an eye on him. Even if it's from a distance, I'm sure Max is sharing my concern.

It's Saturday now, and I've just finished up at the gym, my thoughts still cycling around Josh and Max even as I tried to distract myself with cardio and then weight training. I wonder if either of them are working this weekend or whether they might go to The Grove.

I don't want to go to meet new people, but I am tempted to try and bump into one, if not both, of the men I'm now so fixated on. I didn't exchange numbers with Max, but I could pull it up in the system at work. That feels like crossing a line, though.

Who am I kidding? It *is* crossing a line!

No, I told them both to reach out to me and I can't push the issue. I put the ball in their courts and it has only been a few days. I can't let my eagerness ruin any potential there is for something to happen between us again.

So instead of going out, I opt to stay at home.

Against all odds, it turns out to be the right choice.

Chapter Nine — Max

I'm just coming off my shift when the call comes in about an officer taking fire. Already out of uniform, I pause in the bullpen and frown, my brain trying to recall who is working right now. We're not a huge precinct and we work rotating shifts, but that doesn't account for people working overtime or switching out at last minute for whatever reason.

"...Walker's being taken to Southside Private for treatment," I hear the Captain saying and I swear my heart plunges into the pit of my stomach.

I turn on my heel so I can join the conversation. It's no secret that I'm still friends with Charlie, even if our contact has been more sporadic in recent years, so my concern for Josh isn't going to surprise anyone.

"Josh got shot?" I demand, my heart rate picking up.

It feels like déjà vu of the worst kind. First, I couldn't prevent Charlie from being shot, now Josh?

Captain Briggs sighs. "Grazed, but yeah. Apparently the guy he and Robards put away last week has friends in one of the local gangs and someone wanted revenge."

Oh God.

I feel sick.

The idea of Josh having a target on his back isn't one I can handle, apparently.

"Did we get them?" I'm seeing red, wanting every last one of the people responsible to suffer. "Are they gong to go after him again? After Robards?"

Briggs shrugs. "Robards collared the shooter. Who knows whether more will be stupid enough to come at us."

It's not *us*, I want to scream at him, it's *Josh*. But I bite that back and nod sharply, then pat down my pockets, checking for my keys, phone and wallet. Finding them all, I thank the Captain and hurry out of the station.

* * *

Charlie and his husband, Asher, are racing through the doors to Emergency just as I round the corner from the parking garage. Charlie's taller than Josh and eight years older, with blue eyes instead of Josh's deep brown, but he's otherwise the spitting image of the younger man. I feel a stab of guilt at his limp, though, as I hurry to catch up with the couple.

"Charlie!" I call after him. He stops and turns, concern melting into recognition and appreciation as he sees me. I don't think I deserve the latter.

"Max," he says as I catch up to him, and he pulls away from his husband to hug me in greeting.

I don't deserve that, either.

After Charlie lets me go, I turn to Asher, who also yanks me in for a surprising hug. We've crossed paths a few times over the years, but I can't say I know Charlie's husband all that well. He's roughly a decade Charlie's junior, with a slender athletic build and a mop of unruly curls on his head.

Ash is also a Little like Josh, only he's more fluid in his headspace. I'm assuming having his brother-in-law in hospital with an injury similar to the one that ended his husband's career might be enough to push him into a more regressed state of mind, so I hug him back and greet him softly.

Charlie gives me another appreciative smile for that.

"What happened?" Charlie demands of me as I release Ash back over to him. "I just got a call saying Josh had been involved in a shooting and was being brought here."

I'm not oblivious to the way Ash whimpers and grips Charlie's hand tightly, so I try to sound optimistic when I explain what Briggs had told me. "Just a graze," I reiterate, "nothing life threatening. He probably needs a couple of stitches and some pain meds, but they'll let him come home tonight." I smile genuinely now. "Of course you're his next of kin: I couldn't imagine him having them call your mom. Not," I rush to add with my hands raised in surrender, "that she's not a lovely person, but—"

"She's a lot to handle, yeah," Charlie chuckles ruefully. "She would drive Josh insane, for sure."

"Come on," I jerk my head towards the desk and reach for my badge, "let's get some more answers."

It feels almost like old times to have Charlie at my side as I flash my badge and ask about Josh. The pretty young woman at the desk blushes when I turn up the charm, and she taps away at the keyboard to get me the answers we're looking for.

It's only a few minutes before we're being led back into the general emergency treatment area, where two rows of curtained off beds line the walls. Josh is in the very last bed on the right side of the room, still in his usual outfit of dark jeans, a business shirt and tie, though the right sleeve of his shirt has been cut off and a large gauze pad covers the side of his impressive bicep. His trademark black leather jacket is nowhere to be seen. He looks pale and shaken, and Ash pushes past me and Charlie to throw his arms around his brother-in-law.

"Don't scare me like that," he sniffles at Josh. "When they said you'd been shot—"

"I know," Josh nods and squeezes Ash with his good arm. "But it was just a scratch. Burned a lot, but they've given me some of the good medicines and stitched me up good as new." Now he pulls back to grin. "Kinda like the time your favorite bear needed to be sewed back up."

Ash frowns and pouts. "That was 'cause you were playin' tug of war with him and he got torn."

Josh has the decency to look apologetic. "I said I was sowwy."

"It was years ago," Charlie sighs as he interjects. He looks at Josh with a furrowed brow. "Are you feeling Little right now?"

Josh shrugs and looks away.

Charlie throws me a startled glance. "He doesn't usually regress. He's a scene Little."

Now it's my turn to frown. All of my past experiences with Josh suggest otherwise. But, as I open my mouth to say as much, Josh shakes his head imperceptibly at me.

My concern only deepens.

How can the people he's closest to not know how badly he needs Little time when he's stressed? And why is he so intent on keeping it from them?

The puppy dog eyes he sends me stop me from asking the

questions, though, and his relief is almost palpable.

"It's probably the pain meds," I eventually tell Charlie. "They have a way of loosening inhibitions."

Charlie lifts his eyebrows and nods. "True. Good point." He rubs the back of his neck. "Well, Joshie, the doctors aren't going to let you go home by yourself while you're medicated like this."

Josh sighs and shrugs again. "I know," he pouts.

"But you can come home with me and Ash and have a play date," Charlie continues with forced cheer. "How does that sound?"

Josh bites his lip. "Play date and then you take me home to sleep? Alone?"

Charlie shakes his head. "They're going to want us to monitor you overnight."

Josh's panic is immediate. "No!" He cries, and Ash immediately hugs him again, shushing him and murmuring calming words. Josh ignores them, but he does lower his voice. Shaking his head vehemently, he insists, "No sleepover."

"It'll be fun," Charlie tries to cajole him, but it's obvious he's losing patience with his younger brother. "Ash loves his bedtime routine and—"

From the moment Charlie says 'bedtime', I see it coming. Memories of Wednesday night hit me at the same time as Josh's lower lip quivers. "No bedtime," he interrupts Charlie emphatically. "No sleep. I can't sleep." He looks at me with big, wet eyes. "Tell him. Tell him, Maxxie. No sleep. No bedtime."

Charlie turns back to face me with an unreadable expression. It's expectant, curious, concerned, and God only know what other cocktail of emotions. "Yes, *Maxxie*," he drawls, and I hope I'm imagining the undercurrent of 'watch yourself with my baby brother' that I'm picking up, "please tell me."

Straightening my spine, I lift my chin and prepare to be honest, but Josh seems to realize what he's done and he cuts back in.

"Maxxie knows 'cause I just told him," he justifies with all the logic of a three-year-old.

Clever boy, I think to myself.

The additional regression, or appearance thereof, is enough to have Charlie pinching the bridge of his nose and making a sound of comprehension. "Right," he says in the dismissive tone Josh just manipulated out of him. "Well, even so, you're going to have to come home with us, Josh."

Josh's lower lip quivers again and he looks to me for help.

And, because I'm already wrapped around his little finger, I give it. "Why don't I take him back to his place and crash on his couch?" I offer. "If he's going to be more comfortable in his own space, it makes more sense."

"But he's Little right now," Charlie argues. "You're not a Daddy."

"But I'm a Dom," I shrug, "and I'm not worried about switching roles to something more nurturing for a few hours."

"I don't know…" Charlie looks back at Josh, who points at me.

"I wanna go with Maxxie."

I lift a shoulder, then let it drop. "If there are any problems, I'll call you."

Lies. I'll call the other man I haven't been able to stop thinking about since Wednesday. In fact, once I have Josh in my car, I'm going to try and convince him to give me and Emmett another chance to look after him.

If I could only work out what the sudden, unexpected issue

with sleepovers is, maybe we can even circumvent it.

Six years ago, Josh seemed fine with having a Little bedtime routine. He'd even had me diaper him, which was…okay, it was strange, but not something I disliked. I'd read him a story, we'd cuddled, and I slipped away to let him sleep by himself. He was big again by morning, taking himself off to the bathroom after he woke up.

"Fine," Charlie says, as though he actually had a choice here. Then he turns to Josh and asks, "do you need to go potty before Max takes you home?"

Josh blushes and squirms, then nods. "I go myself." He resolutely avoids my gaze.

It's like a light bulb flares to life above my head, because I suddenly recall Josh's awkward shuffling down my apartment hallway almost like it was yesterday. And the diaper he'd put in the trash after emerging from the bathroom with pink cheeks had been heavy and sodden, landing in the can with a dull thud. I hadn't thought anything of it at the time, but it was obvious that he had wet during the night.

I remember because I recall thinking about how jarring it must be to wake up in an adult headspace with a wet diaper, but he'd seemed so uncomfortable and embarrassed that I hadn't wanted to ask him. Especially not while I was still feeling guilty about putting Charlie into the hospital and setting Josh's stress off myself.

Now I'm starting to wonder if the wetting hadn't been a deliberate thing. What if it hadn't been part of his kink? What if he doesn't want anyone knowing about it? God knows bed-wetting is not the sort of thing I'd want people to find out if I was dealing with it.

With my brain turning over the past few minutes, analyzing

Josh's panic and determination to avoid sleep, or at least sleepovers, and I'm almost certain that my suspicions are correct. And if it's been going on for at least the past six years...

Oh, poor Josh.

Chapter Ten – Josh

I chose the lesser of two evils, or at least that's what I tell myself when I'm finally climbing into the passenger seat of Max's dark blue Toyota sedan. It's a newer model than the one he'd been driving six years ago, but there's a strong sense of déjà vu in leaving the hospital with him. Only this time it was me who got shot (barely grazed, so I don't think it counts) and I'm already coming back out of my Little headspace.

"You can just drop me off at my apartment," I tell him, forcing myself to be big. "The drugs are wearing off and I'm not an invalid."

Truth be told, my arm aches a bit, and I really could use the comfort I know Max can provide, but I also want to avoid him discovering my secret *problem*.

"Nope," he shakes his head and keeps his eyes on the road. "For one, you've got more meds to take in," he checks his watch briefly, "half an hour. For another, I think sneaking in a bit more Little time will be good for you. You were shot – if that's not stressful enough to warrant a full night of kink indulgence, I don't know what is."

I blink back tears at the obvious care in his voice. "Max..."

"Don't *Max* me, Joshua."

God, has he been practicing Daddy voice? Because it's enough to entice my brain back towards that wonderful, floaty Little headspace.

"Now," he says, "I know I said I'd stay at your place, but I've had another idea..."

I widen my eyes, anticipating his suggestion before he even says it.

"I think we should go to Emmett's again if he's not busy."

Yep, there it is. The words I'd been hoping he'd say and also wish that he hadn't.

Being with Max and Emmett on Wednesday night had been magical. It had been the first time in a long time that I'd fully regressed and truly enjoyed my headspace for no other reason than relaxation. They had given me a perfect evening of being doted on by two Daddies and I had spent the rest of the week trying to tell myself to never expect that kind of luxury again.

And now Max is dangling that temptation in front of me like a carrot on a stick.

I take too long to protest, and Max takes that as a sign that I'm open to the idea.

"So we'll go to your place, pack an overnight bag, grab Ranger and—"

"Not overnight," I shake my head and look down at my hands in my lap, realizing that I just agreed to everything else. I can't deny that I want it.

Out of the corner of my eye, I watch Max firm his lips. "Can you talk to me about why overnight stays upset you?"

My cheeks flush and I clamp my lips shut. There's no way in hell I want to talk to him about my issue.

"Josh…"

"No."

He's quiet for a few minutes, and I don't look at him. Instead, I stare out of the window and watch the familiar scenery zoom past.

"We are going to talk about it," he tells me as we pull up outside my apartment building. I live on the outskirts of the city proper. The building is six stories tall with two apartments on each floor. It's an older brick building, but it was well priced when I signed my lease and I'm happy here. Much happier than when I was living with my parents and younger brother, anyway. "But it can wait until we get to Emmett's place."

I close my eyes and wonder if maybe I should have just gone home with Charlie. I probably could have sneaked away from him and Ash, after all. But I'd seen Max and craved the connection between us. So, really, this is my own fault. Some part of me wants him to know my deepest most embarrassing secrets. That same part says that he'll look after me and give me the validation and support I'm desperate for. (Especially if he does it side-by-side with Emmett.)

That part of me is a ridiculous optimist.

Well, that part of me is going to get its way now, apparently. And as much as I daydream about that part of me being right about Max and Emmett, I'm so afraid that they're going to think I'm a freak.

I'm a grown man who has nightmares every night. Who wets the bed every night. At some point, that's going to become tiresome to them. It's certainly tiresome to me. And if I hate

81

it, I'm pretty sure they'll hate it, too.

"Fine," I huff petulantly.

Max's hand reaches out and squeezes my shoulder. When I look up, his face is painted with empathy. "I promise, Josh. It's going to be okay."

He can't possibly promise that, but I nod anyway. Then I let him accompany me upstairs to my third-floor apartment and wait while I pack a bag and grab my new favorite bear.

Here goes nothing.

* * *

Emmett is surprised when Max and I knock on his front door, but he looks extremely happy to see us. He seems even taller and broader than I remember, but that could be my Little headspace threatening to kick in at just the sight of my two temporary Daddies together. It could also be the pain meds Max insisted I take before we got back into his car, though they're not as strong as the stuff I had in the hospital.

Max briefly explains what brought us here and Emmett's concerned gaze zeroes in on my injured bicep.

"Poor baby," he coos, every bit the sweet, caring Daddy I remember, "come on in. Let's make sure you're okay, hmm?"

I'm powerless to prevent my feet from complying, and I cross the threshold ahead of Max, and Emmett presses a soft kiss to my lips and then to Max's and fuck if it doesn't feel right.

"I was thinking Josh could use another night like Wednesday," Max tells Emmett as he hands over my bag.

I'm already clutching Ranger close to my chest, and I'm wearing another long-sleeved footed onesie, too. This one is pale pink with a rainbow over its belly and has a hood with cute teddy bear ears. I'm pretty sure it's a knock off Care Bear onesie, and I love it.

Emmett's smile is wide and genuine. "I would love that." He turns to me. "You're on board? Same safe words?"

I nod. Max was right: after the day I've had, I need to regress for a while.

"But," Max interjects, his tone firm, "we're staying here all night. You can be big or Little, but staying is non-negotiable. Understood?"

Oh, God, they're going to find out.

I shake my head. "I'll be fine to go home. I—"

"Yeah, that's not happening," Max interrupts, leaning against the wall, his eyebrows raised as if daring me to argue with him.

I frown. "Max," I start in warning, and he holds up his index finger before his whole countenance softens.

"Come with me," he says, taking my hand and leading me towards the bedrooms, apparently not giving a shit that he's just made himself at home in Emmett's house. He takes me back to the amazing nursery and to the change table. Reflexively, I cuddle Ranger tighter. "Go on," he jerks his chin to the table. "Climb up."

My heart picks up speed. He can't know, can he? How does he know?

Behind us, Emmett says Max's name warningly.

Max shakes his head at him, then looks at me expectantly. "What's it gonna be, Josh? Are we going to pretend this is not the issue? Because I can. But I know you need this. Let me help you. Let *us* help you."

Well, I guess that answers my question. My stomach

plummets. Shame expands in my chest and tightens my throat. "How…?" I croak.

"I mightn't be a Detective, but I'm still a damn good cop," he answers easily. Then he steps in closer and cups my cheek, searching my eyes before he brings our mouths together in a sweet kiss that says more than words ever could. When he pulls away, he says, "I shouldn't have given up on what we might have had six years ago. I should have talked to you."

I swallow roughly and nod. "Yeah, you should have." Not that I would have been comfortable confessing my issue back then, either, mind you. Not entirely. But for Max? In that moment? I would have.

Emmett clears his throat. "I'll, uh, give you some space. I'll just—"

"For fuck's sake," Max sighs. He eyes me firmly. "Stay." Then he walks around me and grabs Emmett, pulling him over to me and tugging the bigger man down for a kiss between them, too. It's ridiculously hot to watch. Then, while I'm still processing that, he manhandles Emmett until he's facing me and says, "Now you two."

Where kissing Max was sweet and meaningful, kissing Emmett is kind of world changing. Until Wednesday, I never saw him as more than a hot friend. I never even considered that he might be interested in me. But now that our lips are meeting for real, in something more than a chaste, sweet brush of skin against skin, I can feel his desire in the way he holds me. I can feel reverence in the tiny, cautious licks of his tongue at the seam of my lips. I sigh into it, letting his tongue explore my mouth, and it feels so *right*. Kissing both men is like coming home.

"Wow," I breathe when we part, and Max grins at us both,

his expression equal parts smug and turned on. Then he gives himself a shake and pats the top of the change table, and my stomach drops all over again because *he knows*.

"What am I missing here?" Emmett asks, looking between the two of us. He brings one of his huge, warm palms up to cup my cheek, searching my eyes for answers. "What can we help with, honey?"

I close my eyes and take a deep breath, preparing myself to make the admission I've only said out loud twice to two separate medical professionals.

"I've...I've got this...*problem*," I start, feeling my skin heat up. I look at the floor and shuffle my onesie clad feet. "I have nightmares. Bad ones. And I...I wet the bed. Like...um, pretty much like every time I sleep."

I can't look up, not wanting to see the pity or the revulsion on Emmett's face. But I hear neither of those things when he brushes his lips over the top of my head and softly says, "And that's why you freaked out last time."

"Yeah," I nod morosely, finding that now the flood gates (excuse the pun) are open, I can't hold the rest of my feelings back. "I'm trying to manage it. I was getting therapy when my doctor couldn't find a medical reason for it, and I've been trying to be less stressed, but that means being Little more... only all the Daddies at The Grove just want me to be bratty and do punishment scenes and that's not helping." And now I can feel myself hovering on the edge of tears again. "And I just want a Daddy of my own, like the other guys in our group have, but nobody wants me for me and I'm broken anyway."

I mean, who wants a relationship with someone who *has* to wear diapers to bed because they can't actually control their bladder overnight? When it's not a kink but a necessity, it's not fun. It's embarrassing and weird and gross.

I'm engulfed in a hug from both sides, strong arms wrapping around my shoulders and waist. It's warm and reassuring. I slump against Emmett, trusting his strength to hold me up.

"You're wrong," Max tells me. "You're not broken. And, no, you don't have *a* Daddy," he pauses, and I feel him move his head back to peer over the top of mine. Tilting my own head back, awkward as it is with my cheek to his chest, I watch Emmett nod in silent answer to whatever Max's expression asked of him. Then Max finishes, "You've got *two*."

Chapter Eleven – Emmett

I f you had told me, even as late as this afternoon, that I would find myself agreeing to try a three-way relationship with my crush *and* a Dom before the day was done, I would have laughed at you, and not only because I was sitting at home alone with no intention to visit The Grove or seek out the objects of my affection.

I don't rush into things. I'm usually slow and considered. I play the long game for everything. Every little life decision has been carefully measured. I compile lists of pros and cons. I do mental risk assessments. I am constantly weighing every available option.

But now? Ever since I bumped into Josh on Wednesday, I've been impulsive and have followed my gut through a rapid series of unexpected events and it has been nothing short of glorious. Even those few days of uncertainty between when this started and now can't dull that feeling of bliss and anticipation.

Josh's response to being told he can have two Daddies if he'll have us is to burst into happy tears, gripping us both as tightly to him as he can. I can feel his teddy bear, Ranger, smooshing into my back as he does, but it doesn't bother me. If anything, it elates me.

I have a boy. Josh is my boy.

My eyes meet Max's as I peer down over the top of Josh's head now that he's once again curled against my chest. That same elation fuels me to bend over and around my boy, dipping my head to kiss Max again. It's an awkward position with our height difference and Josh squished somewhat between us, but I don't care.

Our first real kisses having been too fleeting and over too soon for my liking. Max's mouth is minty fresh, and he's not soft and pliant like Josh was. He matches my fervent energy, kissing me back just as forcefully, one dominating partner to another. I love it. And, really, I have him to thank for this sudden change in circumstances.

How he knew what Josh's panic was about, I don't know. But I appreciate the way he approached the issue. He made sure Josh knew that he would help and support him. He made it clear that he was acting purely out of care, and not out of pity. He didn't show an inkling of discomfort or distaste. He let Josh decide if he wanted to discuss it or avoid it, but without shying away from his own position on the issue.

That level of confidence is sexy as fuck.

It's actually a surprise that Max isn't a Daddy Dom. His instincts scream 'Daddy' to me. And, somehow, that just makes him even hotter.

But then, that's wrong, isn't it? No, not thinking he's even hotter for it. Thinking that he's not a Daddy Dom. Because he *just* told Josh he'd be his Daddy. One of his Daddies. Plural.

Speaking of...

With reluctance I end the kiss with Max, sending him a smoldering look full of promise before concentrating on the boy sandwiched between us. Josh's tears have subsided, and he's snuggling in against my chest.

I rub his back. "So," I start carefully, "can we sit down and talk this through?"

I want nothing more than to just encourage him to ease into Little space. I want to diaper him and dote on him and put him to bed knowing that, when he wakes, he doesn't have to deal with the aftereffects of his nightmares on his own.

But to just assume he'd be comfortable with that is wrong of me, and if Wednesday's events proved anything, it's the necessity of talking through our limits and triggers. We should also address Max's inexperience with Age Play and what that might mean in terms of how he wants to approach this new dynamic we've leapt into together.

I'd also like to discuss what that means for his primary kink. He's still a Dom and asking him to set that aside in preference of Josh's and my kinks isn't fair. If we're actually going to do this as a threesome, we need to compromise and negotiate so we're all having our needs met.

In addition to all that, and what is arguably the most important issue to discuss, there's the fact that Josh was shot at today. I don't want him making rash decisions because he's traumatized, for one. For another, I want to make sure that he knows he's safe with me and Max in every possible way. I don't want him to feel pressured to be Little if he doesn't want to be, or to agree to a relationship if it's not something he's actually looking for.

After Josh nods, we all tromp back out into the smaller

lounge area between the two guest bedrooms. The couch here is only a two-seater, but Josh just plops down on the floor facing it, leaving me and Max to sit beside each other.

Max takes my hand in his, then reaches out for one of Josh's, rubbing his thumb over the backs of Josh's knuckles. My eyes are mesmerized by the sweet gesture, until I give myself a little shake and hold out my free hand for Josh's other one. He lets go of his bear, cradling the toy in the pocket of space between his legs, then takes my hand, completing the circle. Well, triangle, really.

Semantics.

Both men look at me expectantly.

I guess that answers the unasked question of who is kicking this conversation off.

I start with the usual preamble we're all familiar with in various ways, reminding them that we need to be clear about our hard limits and our triggers. I squeeze Josh's hand when he cringes and tries to pull away, and then list my own to start.

"No rape play or CNC for me," I open with, which is probably not a surprise to either man. "No cheating fantasies, either. Oh, and while I'm on the topic, how are we going to manage this between three of us? I'm okay with the two of you having sex without me, but is that an issue for either of you? Assuming either of you want this to be sexual in the first place." I look between them both. They then look at each other and shrug.

Max turns his head back to me and answers, "As long as we're open about it happening, I don't think pairing off when one of us is otherwise indisposed is an issue. My problem is when people get secretive or try to hide it. That, to me, suggests a problem." He smiles softly. "But, yeah, I want this to be a sexual and romantic relationship between all three of us, in case all that kissing earlier wasn't enough of a message."

I nod. "One hundred percent agreed." I turn back to Josh. "Are you okay with it, though? If you're not, then we'll agree to only kissing or sleeping with each other when all three of us are present." Then I pause. "Unless you're just looking for sweet Daddy/Little interactions without sex. Then Max and I can negotiate our own limits outside of what we do in terms of the Age Play."

Josh shakes his head. "No, I'm not just looking for aromantic Age Play. I want the sex and romance, too. But Max and I are cops, Em. Our schedules can be erratic. We might never all be in the same room again," he jokes, but I can tell that, behind the humor, there's an honest fear that we might struggle to find time together as a threesome. "So, yeah, I'm okay with pairing off as long as we're open about it happening."

I squeeze his hand again. "Okay, good." I turn to Max. "Hard limits?"

His are even fewer than mine, though he does scrunch up his nose and say, "I don't do food play in bed. Actually, I don't like food coming into bed at all. Crumbs in the sheets and crap like that bother me. But I'm happy to spread you out over the dining table and turn you into a sundae there."

Josh nibbles his bottom lip and tugs at Max's hand. "Are bottles okay?"

Max's expression, which had turned predatory, switches over to soft and sweet in the blink of an eye. "Of course, baby."

I turn to Josh and ask him for his limits. He squirms. "I've done pretty much anything and everything," he admits, "but obviously the sleep thing is a trigger. It's because I can't control it, y'know? Like, if you want me to do a scene and be a brat who refuses to ask to go potty until it's too late, I'm not going to freak out about peeing my pants because it's a choice I've made for the scene, and it was pre-agreed upon. But…I'm embarrassed that I can't stop it overnight. That if I forget to put on a diaper or convince myself that I'm an adult and I shouldn't need one, it's gross and humiliating…and not in a kinky humiliation way."

"It's not gross, honey," I tell him firmly. "But if you want me…*us* to remind you to wear a diaper at night, we can. We can do a rewards chart or something. Not focusing on whether you wake up dry or not, but maybe focusing on whether you remembered on your own, or didn't fight us on the issue?"

Josh nods slowly, considering my suggestion. "I like rewards," he admits shyly. There's more lip biting before he says, "I do like to be a brat sometimes, though. There's a reason I have that reputation."

"I'm more than happy for you to explore brat play with me," I tell him. Then I tilt my head, gesturing towards Max, and smirk. "But I think your other Daddy will have fun punishing naughty behavior. I think he might be more creative than me in that regard." At least, as a Dom, I hope he is.

Josh squeaks excitedly, then his gaze seems to go a little distant when he repeats 'other Daddy' with blatant awe.

Max chuckles a little and gives my hand a tug until I look at him and we share a fond glance at Josh's expense. Then I sober a little and ask, "And while we're on the topic of punishments, what do you want from us in order to still indulge your Dom side?"

That gets Josh's attention quickly. Max doesn't rush to answer, though. He's quiet and contemplative, and I appreciate that he's actually giving the matter real thought. When he finally starts to talk, he surprises me with just how brutally honest he is.

"I don't know," he admits. "We're going to have to revisit it as it comes up. I've always been pretty flexible with the kink. I don't have a preference for any particular D/s practices. I dabble in it all, depending on what my subs need. So...maybe punishing Josh's bratty behavior will be enough? But, I will say, the idea of tying you up, Emmett, and having you spread out for me is incredibly appealing."

Immediately, I can picture it in my head and it's not at all a turn off. I swallow. "Like shibari? Or...regular bondage?"

His eyes take on that hungry sheen from earlier. "Whatever you want, sweetheart."

"Fuck, that's hot," Josh moans.

Max chuckles. "You think anything's hot as long as people are naked."

Josh cracks up, and his delighted laughter dissolves any remaining tension from the conversation.

"So...we're doing this? The three of us? Exclusively?" I ask, looking between my two new partners, still a little mystified that this is even happening.

They both nod.

"Okay," I say definitively. "Open and honest communication is going to be key to making this work. Standard safewording practices apply at all times. And if any one of us is at all uncomfortable or unhappy at any time, we need to get together and talk about it."

"Yes, Daddy," Josh answers with a hint of the cheekiness he's best known for.

"Mmhmm, yes sir," Max winks.

I grin, then I turn back to Josh. My expression sobers.

"Before we go any further, we need to also talk about what happened to you, today."

He immediately waves me off. "I'm fine. It was a graze. I barely even needed stitches."

I eye the bandage on his arm skeptically. "Well, I'll be checking that wound tomorrow, but someone shot at you, honey. You're bound to have feelings about that."

Josh rolls his eyes. "I'm a cop. It's part of the job description."

"I'm also a cop," Max reminds him dryly, "and GSWs are not an everyday occurrence, baby." His tone softens. "Charlie getting shot messed me up. When I heard you took fire today, it took me right back to that afternoon. If you'd been seriously hurt—"

"I wasn't," Josh doesn't sound dismissive now. He's as serious as I've ever seen him, squeezing Max's hand tightly. "Thank you for coming for me. For having my back with Charlie." He dips his chin, and adds, "And for bringing me here. You're right: being shot at was scary. And I will talk about it properly, but can we do that tomorrow? Right now, I really just wanna be Little again and forget for a while. Can we do that?" His brown eyes are wide and pleading, and he turns them on me. "Please, Daddy?"

Well, how can I say no to that?

* * *

After a night spent just like Wednesday, Josh asks to go potty before it's time to get him diapered and in bed. He seems a little nervous, but nowhere near the distressed mess he was when we mentioned bedtime the first time around.

This time, we've discussed the issue in advance, and neither

Max nor I have any problems dealing with a wet diaper or wet sheets. Max even admitted that he's curious about the humiliation aspect of Josh's earlier hypothetical bratty scenario involving deliberately wetting himself, which only seemed to amuse Josh rather than trigger him.

Josh also made it very clear that, even though he's got two Daddies now, he's emotionally wrung out and not interested in doing much exploring of our sexual chemistry tonight. He's insisted that Max and I should, though, if we both want to.

Considering the day he's had, including being grazed by a bullet and confessing his biggest secret to two people, I can't exactly blame him for not being in the mood for anything other than relaxation. But to insist that Max and I go ahead without him was a surprise. After all, it will be our first night spent together, and I don't know how I feel about not including him.

"He's stubborn," Max shrugged when I looked to him for support. "And, if he wakes up later and changes his mind, there's nothing to say we won't be up for round two."

I refrained from scoffing and reminding him of my age. My refractory period is not what it used to be now that I'm in my fifties.

After Josh comes out of the bathroom, I lift him up and carry him on my hip to the change table. His eyes are wide when I carefully set him down, and his cheeks are pink where I can see skin above his beard.

"Wow," he says as I carefully lay him back. "I never had a Daddy carry me before."

Max steps up beside me and hands Ranger down to Josh, distracting him as I unclasp the onesie around his legs and crotch and pull down the training pants he's been wearing beneath it. "Sorry, baby," he says, as I reach for a diaper, "but only Daddy Emmett can do that." He leans over and, in a stage whisper, adds, "Because he's a *giant*."

I snort and Josh giggles, then plants his feet and arches his hips up for me so I can slide the diaper beneath his muscular butt. He is absolutely gorgeous, all golden skin and plains of chiseled muscle. He's also waxed and shaved within an inch of his life, because there's not a single hair on his torso. Not on his chest, or stomach. Not on his ass, or over his balls or around his cock.

"You are gorgeous," I tell him as he drops back down into position, because he is like a Grecian statue, not an imperfection to be seen. If I hadn't already noticed the way he looks me up and down with obvious interest of his own, I might feel a little self-conscious about the soft swell of my belly, or the salt and pepper in the hair that covers my chest and around my cock and balls.

"You too, Daddy," he says. Then, because he really is a sweetheart, he looks at Max and says, "And you too, Daddy."

Max bends and drops a kiss on Josh's lips while I apply a layer of barrier cream over the smooth, golden skin of his butt and genitals. "Thank you, Joshie."

After wiping my hands clean on a wet wipe, I finish fastening the tabs on the thick, white diaper and start getting Josh dressed back up in the lower half of his onesie. When he's all done, he cuddles Ranger close to his chest under one arm, the thumb of that hand sneaking into his mouth while his other hand makes grabby motions at me.

Max steps aside so I can pick Josh back up and carry him over to the bed. I take my time crossing the short space, enjoying the way he nuzzles his head into the crook of my neck, and knowing that he's savoring this new experience, too. Then I carefully lower him to the crib's mattress and run my hand through his hair, smiling down at him before bestowing my own kiss on his lips.

As discussed, change time was my moment, and Max is taking over story time.

I sit at the foot of the crib as Max slides in next to Josh, the book we chose together already in his hand. They get themselves comfortable, with a pillow beneath Josh's head and the covers tucked in around him, and then Max starts to read.

Despite his pain meds and the long day he's had, Josh doesn't actually fall asleep. He listens to Max read and snuggles up close, but at the end of the story, he grins cheekily.

"So, I was thinking..." he starts, sounding more like his adult self than his Little one.

Max still reaches down to tickle his sides. "That sounds dangerous," he teases.

Josh squeals and giggles, squirming away from Max's fingers. "Daddy! Stop!"

The look of wonder that crosses Max's face is one I wish I could take a photo of. And he had the audacity to accuse me of being a pushover with our boy! "Sorry, baby," he offers. "Go on."

"Well," Josh draws out the word and then tilts his head down, looking back up at us from beneath his lashes, fluttering then for maximum effect, "I'm not really in the right headspace to have sex, but," he licks his lips, "maybe I could watch you two?"

Oh, fuck yes.

My dick is on board before my brain fully computes the

question. I look to Max, whose grin is slow and wicked.

"I'm very okay with that if you are," Max tells me.

"More than okay," I respond, sounding breathy even to my own ears. I clear my throat. "Any rules or conditions? Either for me and Max, or for Josh?"

Max shakes his head. "Not tonight. If he wants to touch himself while he watches us tonight, that's fine by me. We can experiment with edging and orgasm denial another time. Tonight should be just about what feels good." He tilts his head, "Unless either of you feel differently?"

Josh and I shake our heads as if we'd choreographed the move. We all laugh.

"Well, alright then," I avoid kicking the descended crib railing with the backs of my heels as I push to my feet, "let me show you my bedroom."

I gesture for Max to lead the way out of the nursery and I follow him. Josh is only a step or so behind me, and as awkward as this might feel under most circumstances, it doesn't feel strange at all with these men.

When we're out in the hallway again, though, it feels kind of momentous.

Max and I stare at each other silently for a second or two, and then it's like something in the air *snaps*, and we're on each other in a heartbeat. I crowd him against the hallway wall, slamming my mouth down on his, giving into the urges that have been building all night.

Just like before, his energy is every bit as dominating as my own. His tongue fights mine for control in the sexiest way possible, his hands gripping at my sides and at my ass as he tugs me closer to rub up against me, pressing his hard cock into my thigh. Mine is doing its damn best to burst through the confines of my pants, jutting hard into the side of his lean belly.

I want to take my time with him, learning his body, discovering his personal erogenous zones, but I know that's not going to happen tonight. Tonight is going to be hard and fast, because we've been dancing around our attraction since we first stood next to each other in the nursery on Wednesday evening. This hot, heavy, feverish meeting of our mouths and bodies was inevitable.

We can do gentle and sweet later, preferably with Josh included. Something tells me that, as bratty as our boy says he likes to be, he's going to love being in the middle of two men intent on worshiping him.

I pull away to look over at Josh, who is leaning against the opposite wall, watching us with a hungry expression. But when I reach for him, silently double checking that he's not feeling left out, he smiles and shakes his head.

"I'm watching, Daddy," Josh says, Ranger still dangling at his side, the toy's paw held in his hand. "And I like what I'm seeing a lot."

"Safe words still apply," I remind him. "If you need us to stop…"

"I know," he nods, then makes a 'get on with it' gesture with a roll of his wrist.

If I wasn't so desperate to kiss Max again, I'd give Josh a talking to about his slightly bratty behavior.

But then Max is pulling me back down for another rough, hungry kiss and I forget about Josh's cheek.

Somehow, Max and I fumble our way into the bedroom, leaving the door open and shedding clothes along the way.

I'm dimly aware of Josh grabbing one of the two armchairs

from the bay window and hefting it over to a spot near the end of the bed, facing it on an angle so he can watch the show properly.

Max's hand wraps around my cock. He hums and then, with a smug smirk, asks, "Sir, can I see your license and registration for this weapon?"

I can't help wincing and groaning at the awful joke. "Max," I say his name like I'm lamenting all the choices that led me here, "that was terrible."

He chuckles and nips at my lips with his own. "Hmm, maybe. But, damn, Em. You sure it's not a third leg?"

I can feel my cheeks heating and I try to shrug it off. "I'm in proportion, is all." If I'm honest, I'm a little self-conscious about just how well-endowed I am.

Max senses that immediately and he loses all sense of teasing, even as he continues to slowly stroke up and down my considerable length. "You're perfect. You get that, right?"

In the chair, Josh makes a sound of agreement.

I cast my gaze up to the ceiling and lick my lips. "I've...I've had flings in the past which, uh, haven't gone so well once my pants have come off. People —and Littles especially— don't... um..." Brilliant. Now I'm back to being flustered around Max. Some of that could be due to the hand jerking me off at a slow pace, though.

"They can't handle having you inside 'em?" He guesses softly.

I nod, feeling embarrassed that I'm complaining that people think my dick is too big. First world problems, right? "If we even get that far."

"Well," Max presses an open-mouthed kiss to one side of my chest, then the other, "I'm probably gonna need a hell of a lot of prep to take it, but I'm game."

I pull back my head to blink at him in surprise. I don't subscribe to the generalization that all doms are tops and all subs are bottoms, but it does surprise me that Max is vers, or that he would be at all comfortable with my cock inside him.

"Come on, now," he teases as I stare down at him, "you can put your mouth to better use than just gaping at me."

I don't need to be told twice. Getting us settled on the bed (because, at my age, the mattress is better for my knees than the carpet, no matter how plush my flooring is), I get Max to lie back and I trail my way down his toned body with my mouth. He writhes and gasps as I hit presumably ticklish spots, and I try to remember them for future exploration.

From behind me and to my left, I can hear Josh moan softly, too. The sound eggs me on.

When I reach Max's cock, it's straining up towards me for attention, flushed a desperate pink color and pulsing with the beating of his heart. A drop of precum beads at the tip and I watch as it spills over and then trickles down the veined underside of his shaft before I bend to lick the entire thin trail of it up from base to tip.

"*Ohhhh*," Max moans, throwing his head back on the pillow and arching his hips up. "Yes. Fuck. *More*."

I want to make him beg and plead, but I'm not sure I have the patience to get him there tonight. The fact that he's not trying to run this situation and that he's willingly letting me make all the decisions says more about how earnest he was once I told him about my size issue than words ever could. It's actually sweet and I'm not going to ruin the gesture by turning this into a power play.

So, instead of torturing him, I do as he asks, and I lick another broad stripe from his balls to the head of his cock, savoring the slightly musky scent of him, and the hint of salt from his sweat.

Even just that small action has his thighs trembling with anticipation, and I want to chuckle just a little. The big, tough Dom so easily brought to submission.

I bring my hands into play now, sliding one up to fondle his balls which are hidden in a thatch of golden curls, and the other to the base of his cock. I enjoy the contrast of our skin tones against each other —him, pale and blonde, and me, dark with peppery hair— before I start to pump his erection while I nurse on the head.

"God, fuck, Emmett..." he curses, but it's most certainly a compliment, "so good. So fucking good."

I fondle his balls, then his taint, pressing two fingers into the stretch of skin there, massaging back up towards his balls, thoroughly enjoying the low moan of pleasure the action earns me, as well as the taste of more precum escaping his slit into my waiting mouth. I repeat the motion a few times, then return to playing with his balls, allowing him deeper into my mouth.

"Your mouth, Em. Fuck, your mouth. It's...*ungh*." I've returned my fingers to his taint again, teasing him, trying to milk more precum from him. I want every moment of this to feel intense for him, because it sure as shit feels intense for me.

From the chair, I'm reminded of Josh's presence again, his heavy breathing and quiet whimpers telling me that he's enjoying the show so far.

Between my legs, I can feel my own cock, heavy, aching, and dribbling down onto my sheets. I'm rutting my hips into nothing while I suck and tease Max, but I'm still feeling the pleasure coursing through me almost as if our positions were reversed.

"Lube, babe," he demands, breathing heavily. "Lube and a condom. Now."

His urgency mirrors mine, and I grin while I continue to bob my head up and down his length, only pulling off when he whines and repeats his demand, warning me that he'll come too soon otherwise.

Those words elicit a heady feeling, and I scoot across the mattress on my knees to rifle through the top drawer of my bedside table, nabbing the ever-present bottle of high-end lube and a foil square as instructed.

Max arches an eyebrow when I hold them up for him to see. He whistles. "You go for the good stuff, huh?"

"There are certain things in life a person should never skimp on," I inform him.

He smirks and nods towards my cock, which is bouncing in the air between us, glistening with its own juices. "Well, I s'pose when you've got a monster like that, it makes sense." To soften the unintended sting those words cause me, his smirk turns into a more salacious smile. "Now, put it all to good use and fuck me already."

That's an offer I can't refuse and he knows it, but he pushes my buttons further when he cranes his neck to look down the bed towards Josh.

"You want to watch Emmett fuck me, don't you, honey?" he asks our boy, and Josh groans his agreement.

I swivel my head to look over at him and swallow roughly at the vision that greets me. Josh is still fully clothed, the fabric of his onesie clinging to the curves of his hard, muscular body. His strong legs are spread wide in the bucket seat of the armchair, and he's rubbing his teddy bear over his padded crotch, thrusting slowly up to meet the movements. It's almost obscene for him to look so adorable and be doing something so debauched. My cock throbs harder at the sight.

"Focus, babe," Max says, and it takes me a moment to realize that he's talking to me. I look back at him, finding that he has rolled onto his hands and knees and has stuck his beautiful ass up for me. He wiggles it, and I salivate. "Fuck me," he repeats his previous demand.

I shuffle over into position between his spread legs, drizzling the lube over two of my fingers generously before pressing them against his hole. I start by massaging the outer ring with firm but slow circles, urging his body to relax and let me in. It doesn't take long, and I keep my eyes on what I can see of Max's face the whole time, as well as the set of his shoulders, looking for signs of discomfort.

He grimaces a little when I first breach him but urges me to keep going.

"It's been a while," he tells me, rocking his hips experimentally against my probing, scissoring fingers, "but it's good. I promise. I—*fuck—yes—more!*"

The run-on cry is wrenched from him as I locate his prostate and massage it with the pads of my fingers. He throws his head back and I can't help leaning over his back to kiss him again, even though the angle is awkward. It's a sloppy kiss, uncoordinated and messy, but just as intense as our earlier ones. I continue to pump my fingers in and out of him, stretching, crooking and twisting them while our tongues and mouths are joined.

By the time I've added a third finger, Max is practically slamming his hips back against my probing digits.

"Now, Em. I'm ready," he pants, and I trust that he knows his body well enough to be the judge of that.

I withdraw my fingers and glide the condom over my leaking, aching dick, notching the head at his hole once I've lined myself up.

"You'll tell me if it's too much," I say, refusing to move until I know for sure that he's not going to just grit his teeth and bear it. He nods, and I push in slowly, getting the tip through his tight pucker.

"Holy fuck," Max exhales and makes an obvious attempt to relax, "that's...*whoa*. Keep...keep going."

He's so hot and tight around me, keeping up a snail's pace is just as much for my benefit as his. I sink into him in tiny increments, withdrawing a fraction and pushing back in a tiny bit further each time, trying to focus on his reactions. At the first sign of serious pain, I'll pull out. I don't want to hurt him.

I hold his hips as I go, but I'm not gripping down hard. If anything, my touch is a caress, my hands petting him soothingly as he takes me bit by glorious bit.

After what simultaneously feels like forever and no time at all, I'm bottoming out, my balls slapping against the lower curve of his cheeks. I close my eyes and relish the overwhelming sensations, almost unable to remember the last time I enjoyed sex like this. That someone could take my cock so easily.

"You okay?" I ask him when I'm sure I can speak properly.

"More than okay," he replies. "I've never felt so full. *Fuck*, babe." He tries to rock forward and back. "I love your cock."

I curl my bigger frame over him, reaching under him for his dick. He's only half-hard, which isn't really a surprise, but he starts to plump up again as I stroke him. He lets loose a needy whimper when I start gently rolling my hips in tandem with the movement of my hand.

"Yes," he encourages me, his head hanging low. I can see that he's closed his eyes, a blissful expression on his handsome face. "Harder, babe. Fuck me like you mean it."

A strangled whine sounds out to my left and back a bit, and I remember our audience. I turn my head, and Josh is well and truly fucking up into his teddy now, grinding the stuffed bear over his crotch on every upwards thrust.

His eyes are wide open, his desire obvious as his gaze connects with mine.

"Please, Daddy," he begs, jutting his chin downwards towards Max, "fuck him. I need…I wanna see…"

Experimentally, I pull back and then swiftly piston my hips forward again, and Max cries out at the same time as Josh moans.

"Like that?" I ask them both.

"Fuck yes," Max answers, pushing back into me eagerly while Josh encourages, "Again, Daddy!"

I lock my eyes on Josh as I start to fuck Max in earnest, setting a hard and fast pace that falls just shy of punishing. I want him to feel me tomorrow, but I don't want to hurt him.

Josh's assault on the teddy syncs up with my pace, and I revel in watching him inch closer and closer to orgasm. He maintains eye contact with me as he fucks his toy, his sensations possibly inhibited by the diaper he's still wearing. Or maybe the cotton and plastic mix lends extra friction? I don't know, but Josh isn't complaining.

"You gonna come for me?" I ask, and once again I'm addressing both men.

"So close," Max admits, and in a spur of the moment decision,

I lean forward over his sweaty back on my next inward thrust and wrap my arm around his chest, pulling him up so that he's kneeling and sitting on my cock.

It takes some maneuvering, but I shuffle us around until Max is facing Josh face on and I'm looking over Max's shoulder at our boy.

"Oh, fuck, Joshie that's *hot*," Max says, finally seeing what I've been watching while I drilled him.

"That's our boy," I growl into Max's ear and piston my hips sharply. "He likes watching us, don't you, honey?"

Josh nods almost frantically, his mouth lolling open. His fingers are gripping tightly around Ranger, the soft, stuffed insides giving way, the white fur curling around his digits, practically swallowing them. Beneath the pale pink fabric that clings to him like a second skin, Josh's thighs have drawn tight.

"Gonna…" Josh says, still not tearing his eyes away from me and Max, who is now using the muscles in his own legs to bounce hard and fast on my cock. "Oh, oh, *ohhh.*"

"That's it," Max urges him, wrapping his own fist around his weeping dick so I can hold him upright against my chest. "Come for us, honey. We'll change you after and get you all clean again."

The imagery Max's words put into my mind proves to be my undoing. I go from being close to the edge to flying right over it, shouting as I fill the condom with the intense bursts of my release. Max hisses out low curse words of his own, and a splattering of warm fluid finds my arms across his chest. But I'm still watching Josh.

Josh's eyes blow wide and then slam shut, and he holds Ranger down over his covered cock and grinds hard, until his thrusts stop and his legs shake, a litany of 'Oh fuck, holy shit, fucking fuck's escaping his kissable lips. He slumps back in the chair, boneless and flushed. "Wow," he declares.

Max chuckles. "Wow indeed," he agrees.

I carefully slide out from inside Max, releasing my hold around his chest to grip the base of the condom as I do. Climbing off the bed, I head into my private attached bathroom, dispose of the condom in the trashcan, grab a couple of washcloths, run them under the hot water and then pad back into the bedroom where Max and I clean off. He winces as he runs the cloth over his ass, and I frown.

"Did I hurt you?"

He shakes his head. "No. It's just been a while, like I said." He grins. "I'm gonna be feeling you for days."

"Mmmph," Josh murmurs from the chair, his eyes half-lidded, "my turn next time."

Warmth fills me from the tips of my toes all the way to my heart.

Next time.

I like those words.

Chapter Twelve – Max

T his is the greatest life choice I have ever made. Hands down, no argument, nothing I've ever thought about doing even compares.

Okay, so that might be the orgasm endorphins talking.

But still…wow.

I might need to rethink my stance on only bottoming occasionally, because Emmett just rocked my world. And watching Josh get himself off as he watched us? That's just chef's kiss perfection right there.

He looks so fucking sexy when he comes.

I wish I could have seen Emmett, too. Maybe I'll volunteer to watch next time. Or we can invest in a mirrored ceiling or something. All I know is both these men are mesmerizing and they're mine right now. We're exclusive to each other.

How'd I luck out like that?

Emmett heads into his walk-in closet and comes back out tugging up a fresh pair of boxer briefs. They are bright red and hug his ass and thighs enticingly. He scrunches his nose at me.

"I'm sorry, I don't think I have anything that will fit you."

I just smirk and stretch out with my arms behind my head. "What? You have a problem with my nakedness?"

Dark eyes do a slow sweep from my toes to my eyes. "Not at all." He cocks his head. "You prefer to sleep naked?"

"I do, actually."

Emmett's lips pull upwards, his smirk mirroring mine. "I can work with that."

A loud yawn from the chair redirects both of our attentions to Josh, who is currently attempting to curl his bulky body up on the armchair while his head droops.

He's adorable, but there's no way I'm letting him sleep like that. I feel a pang of guilt for wearing him out even further after the day he's had. And should I be concerned that he was on pain meds? Is consent in question right now? No, Josh seemed completely alert and sober when he requested this.

Climbing off the bed, I crouch in front of him and give his knee a gentle shake. He grizzles and bats me away with Ranger, who has also been through a lot tonight.

"Nuh-uh, baby," I insist gently. "Come on. I've got to change you before your sticky mess dries, remember?"

Josh grumbles and tries to nestle deeper into the armchair.

I look to Emmett. "Can you carry him?"

My co-Daddy smiles that soft smile that seems to be reserved for Josh's Little space and bends to scoop our boy up with only the most minimal grunt of exertion. He carries him with Josh's knees over one arm and Josh's back supported by the other, the sleepy Little looping his own arms around Emmett's neck for additional leverage.

Josh smiles up at both of us when he's placed back on his

change table. "I really like bein' carried like that," he states, then yawns widely again.

I'm willing to bet it's a whole new experience for him. He's a big guy himself, and there aren't many Daddies of Emmett's size and strength out there.

"Nothing wrong with that," I tell him. "I'm sure Daddy Em loves carrying you, too." I start unzipping his onesie from the footed end, wrangling his left leg out of the other side and exposing his lower half like Emmett did earlier.

It's not until I'm undoing the tabs on the diaper that the reality of what I'm actually doing hits me.

This is only my second time changing him, and the first time in six years at that, but to this point it has felt natural. I've followed instinct, and watching Josh splayed out before me, his legs akimbo and his thumb stuck in his mouth, it feels good. Right. I'm giving him something he needs, and he's relaxing back into his Little headspace while I do. The level of trust he's showing me right now gives me a bit of a head rush.

"Daddy Maxxie," he says around his thumb, seemingly unconcerned that I'm having a mild revelation while changing him, "You called Daddy Memmett 'Daddy Em'. But that's confusing," he pronounces it 'con-foo-zing' and I smother a grin, "because your name starts with M, so there's Daddy M and Daddy Em."

"Well, you just solved that by calling me Maxxie, didn't you?" I ask him in return, now peeling back the front of the diaper. Emmett hands me a wet wipe and I warm it between my palms before I wipe over Josh's sticky, flaccid cock.

I can see how this change time thing can become sexual, too, and I consider the fun I could have with Josh laid out like this in front of me. I'd need a step stool to get to the right height to comfortably fuck him, seeing as this was clearly designed with Em's height in mind, but the image in my head is a hot one.

I will have to ask my men how they feel about sex in Little space. I know some people are uncomfortable with the concept, but judging by the way my pulse races at the idea, I'm game to try it.

Tonight, though, Josh is falling asleep even while I get him to lift his hips so I can slide a fresh diaper underneath him. It's been a long day for him. I'm honestly surprised he had the energy to rub out an orgasm at all, but then he is much younger than me, and even younger than Emmett.

I try to hurry through the process of doing up the side tabs of the plastic-cotton contraption, running my index fingers beneath the leak guards to make sure the whole thing is sitting right. Then I wrestle our boy back into his onesie and Emmett hoists him back off the change table.

Emmett glances at the adult sized crib before shaking his head and marching us back out of the nursery and towards his bedroom again. The bed in there is definitely large enough for the three of us to fit comfortably, and I think it's only right that we do share it.

Josh stirs as Emmett gently lowers him to the mattress and tries to roll him towards the middle.

"What if I…?" our boy asks, his cheeks turning pink. He doesn't have to finish the question for either of us Daddies to understand his concern.

"Diapered," Emmett reminds him with a soft smile. "And the mattress protector is waterproof anyway."

Nodding, Josh allows his thumb to migrate to his mouth. It's so adorable, and such a contrast to the wanton behavior we indulged in earlier. I slide beneath the covers on the far side of the bed, and Emmett slips into the remaining space.

We huddle together and Josh turns over so he's spooning my side, his leg hooked over my hip and cradled between both of mine while I lie on my back. At Josh's back, Emmett is curled around him protectively.

I'm once again blown away by how easy this feels, and the comfort of it soon has me drifting off into dreamland.

Chapter Thirteen — Josh

The first thing I notice when I wake up on Sunday morning is that I am not alone. Warm bodies —two of them— press in on either side of me, making me feel cocooned and cared for. The next thing I notice is that I've woken naturally, not from a nightmare but from my body's clock telling me it's time to get up. And, finally, perhaps most remarkably, I'm dry.

My bladder insists that this is an actual issue I need to deal with, but I revel in this experience. I savor waking up in my adult headspace without feeling the familiar rush of shame and embarrassment at being unable to function like most people.

I was afraid that the nightmares would be worse after being shot at. After being grazed by a bullet which had been intended to kill me. But being taken care of so well by the two men who want to be my Daddies, accompanied by a mind-blowing orgasm and then a night of snuggling together in a dogpile seems to have been enough to keep the nightmares —and, thus, the bed-wetting— at bay.

I want to bottle this moment and keep it forever because I know that my issue hasn't been cured. Delayed for a night, sure, but I'm not stupid enough to believe I'll wake like this after every sleep.

My bladder is screaming at me now and I wonder how I'm going to extricate myself from the strong arms and legs holding me in place. I don't want to wake either of them just because my body isn't used to waking up with a full bladder.

I wriggle carefully, attempting to sneak down the middle of the mattress, but Emmett holds me tighter.

"Where you going?" he asks sleepily, and his voice is a rumble that travels up my spine in the most delicious manner.

"Gotta piss," I explain.

He props himself up on his elbow and leans over me so I can see his face. "You're still diapered, honey," he murmurs softly, obviously just as aware of Max snoring softly on my other side.

My cheeks heat, but there's no expectation or judgment in his dark brown eyes, so I explain, "I'm dry, which is kind of new for me. And I'm big. So…"

Emmett's smile softens into understanding. "You don't want to ruin that. I get it." He carefully pulls his arm out from underneath me and helps lift Max's from around my waist. Our third just grizzles and rolls over, snuggling into the blankets he's hogged during the night.

Emmett climbs off his side of the bed and I follow him, and then I pad into his attached bathroom, unzipping my onesie as I go. I take the whole thing off and remove my diaper, do my business and then wash my hands. Then I sigh down at the onesie because I'm not in my Little headspace anymore, and I don't relish climbing back into it.

Thankfully, Emmett knocks lightly at the open bathroom door, my duffel bag slung over his shoulder.

"I thought you might want this," he says, slipping it down his arm before extending it towards me. "You're free to shower or whatever if you want, too. There are new toothbrushes under the sink, and you can use whichever toiletries you need."

"Thanks, Daddy," I say, even though I'm in my adult headspace. Watching Emmett's face brighten and then morph into one of those sappy looks that I've only ever seen directed between my friends and their Littles makes me want to keep repeating the title at any given opportunity.

He leans forward and kisses my forehead before leaving me to my own devices. As I shower, I still can't quite believe that any of the past twenty-four hours has been real. Not that it's even been that long. But this time yesterday, I was getting ready for work. Now, I'm on leave until I get medical and psych clearance to return because some lunatic pulled a gun on me and got a lucky shot off.

I haven't really processed how close I came to being seriously injured. Especially when the events that followed were even more surreal.

I've gone from being lonely and trying to deal with the prospect of never finding a Daddy, to suddenly having two. To being in a throuple. A throuple with Max and Emmett, at that.

Maybe I hit my head when I went down yesterday, and this has all been a hallucination.

Except my bicep protests when I move my arm, and I remember almost too late that I'm not supposed to get the dressing wet if I can help it, so I have to aim the shower head away before I ruin the emergency doctor's hard work.

Washing without getting the gauze wet is awkward, but I manage it, and then I scrunch my nose against the brief pain when I slide my arms into the sleeves of the Henley that I packed last night. I should have chosen something less clingy, not that I own many loose shirts. I mean, come on: have you seen my arms? Why wouldn't I want to show them off?

By the time I pad back into the bedroom on bare feet, Max is sitting up in bed, looking deliciously rumpled. His blonde hair is all mussed up and the covers are barely covering his naked hips, displaying his toned abdomen with pride.

Emmett's nowhere to be seen, but Max gives me a lazy grin and says, "Morning, baby. Em's making breakfast. Don't know how we managed to rope him, but we got damn lucky."

Ignoring the thrill of being called 'baby', I grin back and nod. "I think I'm getting the best deal here," I acknowledge. "I get two hot Daddies. You have no idea…" I'm horrified that my voice cracks. I was trying to be flirty and playful, but just saying it out loud has the wave of emotions rolling over me unexpectedly. I clear my throat and try again, mustering a cheeky smirk that doesn't quite cover how overwhelmed and happy I am. "Two sexy, dominating men to pamper me? Yes please."

Max climbs off the bed, not at all concerned that he's completely nude, and saunters over to wrap me in a hug. It feels so good to just be held.

"We're going to pamper the fuck out of you," he says, kissing my cheek. "You deserve that, Josh. I'm sorry it took me so long to get my head out of my ass."

I shrug. "It just wasn't the right time for us back then. Now… " I look towards the doorway and a goofy smile takes over my face. "This feels right. The three of us, I mean."

117

"Em does seem to balance out our personalities," Max agrees with a smile of his own. "And his dick is a thing of beauty, too."

"Mmm," I swallow at the memory from last night. Of watching my two sexy men fucking in front of me. Putting on a show while also connecting and learning about each other. "It's *so* my turn next."

Max swats my denim-clad butt as he moves towards the bathroom. "Behave, or we'll make you wait for it."

I doubt he'd follow through on that threat, not when he'd be depriving himself pleasure at the same time, but I'm resolved not to be too naughty or bratty for my Daddies so soon into our relationship.

Relationship.

That word is definitely going to take some getting used to.

* * *

Breakfast is better than anything I could have imagined, and I'm not just talking about the food. That's not to say that Emmett's cooking isn't amazing, because holy hell that man can whip up a spread! But it is just the experience of having both of these beautiful men with me, making conversation while cutting up my food as though it's second nature. It is having Max squeeze my thigh and Emmett kiss the top of my head as he reaches for the orange juice.

Even though this is so new for all three of us, we interact easily, without any awkwardness. Even better is watching Max and Emmett relate to each other. Despite them both expressing their interest in each other last night, some part of me was still a little concerned that they might just be doing this to be with me and keep me happy.

I know that sounds conceited, and it's not meant to. But this is so new for me, and I know I'm the common connection between them. I have a prior relationship with each of them, whereas they were acquaintances at best. Physical attraction can only take a relationship so far, you know?

But those worries are put to rest as I listen to them banter and flirt over their coffee cups. For as long as I've known him, Emmett has been cool and composed. I've tried to ruffle his feathers before to no avail. But Max seems perfectly able to get under his skin, teasing him until he's flustered and chuckling ruefully.

"What do you mean you don't meal plan?" Emmett asks Max in horror. "How do you grocery shop if you don't meal plan?"

Max shrugs, and the twitch of his lips tells me that he's playing this up deliberately. "I just buy what looks good at the time."

"What? Without a list?"

I'm beginning to suspect that Daddy Emmett is a little anal-retentive.

"Well, yeah." Max grins. "I can always go back if I forget something, or—"

"Wait," Emmett puts down his fork and stares at our third partner as he cuts him off, "you at least shop aisle by aisle, right? Not all randomly?"

Max reaches across me to pat Emmett's hand. "*There there*, big man."

With a strangled groan, Emmett looks at me. "Tell me you're not a grocery store savage," he pleads.

I give him my sweetest, most innocent smile. "Nope, I'm

not like that at all."

He sags with exaggerated relief. "Thank God."

Max snorts and nudges me, "Tell him *why*, Joshua."

Emmett frowns and his expression turns expectant.

I look down at my plate of breakfast goodness and mumble under my breath.

"What was that?" Emmett prompts.

Pasting the 'butter wouldn't melt' smile back on my face, I brightly repeat myself. "I live on takeout. Mostly. And cereal." Emmett's scrunched up forehead has me rushing to extrapolate, "Unless I'm visiting home or Charlie's. Which is actually a lot more frequent than you'd expect."

Emmett groans and shakes his head. "We're changing that, honey."

It's not like I don't follow a balanced diet. With the hours I put in at the gym or jogging with some of the other guys, I wouldn't want it to derail my efforts to maintain my physique. And, yeah, that might make me sound a bit vain, but I do it purely for myself. I'd obviously never judge or belittle anyone else's lifestyle habits. Not that I feel like Emmett is judging or belittling me. In fact, there's something heartwarming in Emmett's declaration. It's *very* Daddy of him, and that gives me a little thrill.

"Yes, Daddy," I give him a cheeky smile and he turns to putty in my hands.

"Good boy," Emmett says warmly, his eyes practically molten.

Max snorts and waves his fork at Emmett. "You're going to need to work on your poker face with this one," he tells him, jerking his fork in my direction. "He just played you like a fiddle."

I bat my lashes. "Would I do that?"

Emmett narrows his eyes and looks between me and Max before settling those dark orbs back on me. I aim for innocence, but I can't hide the way my lips pull upwards under his scrutiny. He groans, but there's amusement and affection in his voice when he says, "Yeah, I'm going to work on that."

"Who knew you'd be such a pushover?" Max teases him before digging back into his meal. "Put a cute boy in front of you, and that stoic façade just dissolves, doesn't it?"

"Shut up," Emmett argues back, but he's still smiling.

It really is the best breakfast ever.

* * *

"I can't believe you were *shot* and you didn't tell me!" Mom's shrill voice echoes out of my phone when I answer her call later in the evening. Even though she's not on speaker, I can hear her without having the phone pressed to my ear.

I wince.

"It was a graze," I tell her, trying to sound as dismissive and carefree as possible. "They shouldn't have even called Charlie."

"Your brother knew about this?" she demands.

I frown. "I assumed he told you." I was even plotting my revenge. Probably a good thing we cleared this up before I acted on it.

The couch beside me moves as Emmett sits down and then pulls me against him, careful not to bump my injury. Being enveloped in his larger embrace is instantly soothing, and some of the agitation I feel from talking to Mom evaporates.

I've spent the day here at his place, the three of us getting to know each other better in between my new Daddies' not-exactly-subtle questions about how I'm dealing with everything that happened yesterday. That part's actually sweet, and I've been quick to assure them that the Little time helped me cope with the stress of it all. It's not a magic cure, but I do feel a lot more stable having spent last night with them than if I'd gone to Charlie's place.

Anyway, we made a game of learning about each other, asking ridiculous ice breaker questions which launched into proper conversations.

I learned that Max likes dogs where Emmett prefers cats, and I surprised them both by expressing my desire for a pet ferret. (They also told me no, but it's early days, yet.) Emmett likes to read psychological thrillers and murder mysteries, while I've become interested in shifter romance novels. Max doesn't like to read at all.

Unlike me and my large-ish family, both Max and Emmett are only children. I already knew that Max was from a long line of cops, but when Emmett explained that he was adopted and that both his parents were accountants, it was a surprise to hear. Even more surprising was when he pulled out his phone and, after some searching through his Facebook albums, showed us photos of his parents.

In the photo, a younger Emmett towered over the couple almost comically. His dad, the taller of the pair, only came up to Emmett's shoulder. But his mom was tiny, the top of her hair barely reaching his pecs. Emmett spoke with pride when he gestured at them, telling me and Max that his dad was Irish and his mom was Japanese-American.

"They used to joke that adopting me was like those stories you hear about people who adopt a tiny puppy that grows up to actually be a bear," he'd said fondly.

Max and I had grinned because, yeah, Emmett's got 'bear' written all over him.

Unfortunately, both Emmett's parents have passed on, so we won't ever get to meet the people he speaks so warmly about or thank them for raising such a wonderful man.

And whoa. Meeting the parents? Am I really thinking that after one night of officially being in a relationship?

Reel it in, Walker.

Mom's voice in my ear brings me back to the conversation at hand. "...who heard it from her cousin, Lance, told me when I bumped into her at the store," she's explaining, and I scrunch up my nose.

"Lance wasn't even on shift yesterday." *And he should have kept his big mouth shut. Asshole.*

"*That* is hardly the point," Mom complains. "You should have called. I'll be having words with your brother. Put him on the line. Has he at least been looking after you?"

I close my eyes and count to ten. Emmett pets my hair in a soothing gesture. I let my breath out slowly. "I'm not at Charlie's, Mom. I'm," I hesitate, not wanting to share details of my new relationship so soon. I mean, there was a reason Charlie put off introducing Ash to our crazy ass family. "I'm at a friend's place, but I'm fine. It was a graze. I barely even needed stitches."

I feel Emmett tense up against me and I fight the urge to groan. I'm going to have to explain this to him. It's honestly not him, it's me and my ridiculous mother. The fact that he was so close to his parents might make it harder for him to relate to, but hopefully he's heard enough stories about Mom from Charlie that maybe he'll get it. Besides, he's a counselor at a kink-friendly community center. I can't be the only person he's ever spoken to who has a less-than-ideal family dynamic.

Don't get me wrong: my mom is a good person. She is. But she doesn't always approach things the way most people would expect or appreciate. She's intense, oftentimes meddling and very high maintenance. I love her, but in small doses.

"*Stitches*, Joshua," she repeats, sounding horrified. "Who is this friend?"

"Mom, I am thirty-one. I am a cop. A *detective*. You do not need to vet all of my friends."

She huffs dramatically over the line and I roll my eyes.

"Don't give me that look," she says, and I can't help laughing.

"That is freaky," I tell her.

"I just know you well," she sniffs. "At least come home for a meal so your dad and I can see that you're okay in person."

"Jesus, Mom. Do you need me to send you a photo of me holding today's paper, too? Proof of life and all that crap?"

Emmett gives me a little shove and brings his mouth to my ear. His breath ghosting over the shell makes me tingle all over in pleasure, as does his low, whispered, "Language, Josh. That's your mother you're talking to."

Even though we don't have a rule about me swearing, Emmett's admonishment stirs my cock to life and I have the sudden, desperate urge to get Mom off the phone immediately.

"Lunch tomorrow, Josh," she says, ignoring my snarking entirely. "And bring your *friend*." The emphasis she puts on the word leaves no question about her suspicions. I can't even tell her she's wrong, because saying that Emmett is my friend isn't a lie, per se. Denying that he's more than that would be a lie, though, and I won't outright lie about our relationship. But I don't want to leave Max out of the equation, either.

"Mom," I whine plaintively, "he has to work." A thought

that has made me feel increasingly morose as the weekend has come to an end.

"Then your dad and I will have you all to ourselves. Be here by eleven." Mom doesn't give me a chance to argue or weasel out, ending the call before I can even try.

I pout.

Emmett pinches my thigh. "No sulking, baby."

"I can't help it," my reply is petulant, a hint of the bratty behavior that I'm known for. But this isn't part of our role-play, and I'm not doing it for fun right now. My mood is souring, and the urge to regress and be cuddled and comforted is itching at the back of my brain. My lower lip quivers, so I bite it.

"Oh, honey," Emmett pulls me in for a tighter hug, "you've been through a lot this weekend, huh? It's okay to let go and be Little again if you need to. I'll get Ranger."

Relief washes over me and I move over on the couch so he can do just that. By the time he comes back, all I want is to snuggle up against him.

"I don't want the weekend to be over," I murmur into the crook of his neck, surprised to find my throat constricting and tears threatening behind my eyes. "I want more time with you and Max."

"I know," he soothes. "I know."

I sniffle. "It's not fair."

Max had to leave for work earlier. I'd complained about that because he was supposed to be off for the next two days, but with me out with an injury and two others calling in sick, he had to cover. I cling to the memory of him promising to make it up to Emmett and me later, the smoldering look in his eyes telling me that I'll enjoy his penance a lot.

"No, it's not," Emmett agrees. "But we will make this work, Josh. I promise."

Wrapped up in his big arms, his warmth spreading into me, I close my eyes and let myself believe him.

Chapter Fourteen — Emmett

The next couple of days at work are torturous. I want nothing more than to sing from the rooftops that I've found a boy and a Dom, but because Charlie is Josh's brother and Max's former partner, I keep my exciting news to myself.

It's not that I want to keep this new development from my employer-come-friend. But Josh asked me and Max to keep it to ourselves for now. It's been less than three days, so I see his point. Even though my gut says that what we have is more than just a fling, making announcements so early on might be overkill.

But I still can't help the desire to tell people. I've been quietly interested in Josh for a long time, never thinking that the beautiful younger man would go for a Daddy like me. And, even though Max is a wild card I never saw coming, he completes our dynamic perfectly.

I can be stern when I need to be, but having a Dom step into the role of Daddy beside me takes a weight off my shoulders that I didn't even know was there. I know I'm good at meting out punishments, but I've always preferred the cuddlier side of the kink.

Watching my boys relax and play, providing them a safe, welcoming space to regress, knowing that they trust me enough when they're so vulnerable...*that* is what appeals to me most about being a Daddy. Setting boundaries and giving discipline is part of that, sure, but with Max content to take on the main disciplinarian role with Josh, I get to focus more on spoiling both my men rotten.

In what has to be a blessing of timing, Max is working the early shifts this week. I was originally surprised to learn that his and Josh's precinct has their staff on a rotating roster, knowing that most cities tend to have set shifts for their police officers. However, Max explained that their precinct's system began as a trial unit, the theory being that rotating shifts meant better work-life balance and a feeling of 'fairness' spread over the whole unit.

From a psychological perspective, I can then make the links between employee satisfaction leading to better productivity and performance.

But I digress.

Max is working early shifts, which means he will be home before I finish work today. He's going to swing by his place for some clothes and essentials, will then head to Josh's to pick our boy up, and then they'll both come back to my house for more time dedicated to exploring this new relationship between us.

Already, just over the course of the weekend, I feel like we've set the foundations for something special. It's not just about sex, or even just about the kinks we like to indulge in. We all seem to get along, despite differences in the ways we approach everyday tasks, or our varied tastes in music or television shows.

Obviously, there's more to successful relationships than proving we can get along for a few days, but I can't help that the pros and cons list in my head is mostly stacked with pros right now. We haven't indulged in more sexual exploration yet, but that's because we agreed to try and get to know each other properly first. That said, the tension has been building, and every time we kiss or touch casually, it feels like a slow tease.

"Earth to Emmett," Charlie waves his hand in front of my face. I blink out of my thoughts, feeling my skin heat when I realize that I had zoned out. He grins, looking so much like his younger brother that I can't help grinning back. "Where'd you go?" He asks, head cocked. "It's not like you to drift off."

"Sorry," my grin turns sheepish. "I had a date over the weekend, and I guess I'm still floating on the high of that."

Now Charlie's smile turns knowing. His eyebrows arch up and his eyes glint. "I'm assuming it went well then?"

"Very," I agree, doing my best to not let my thoughts cycle back around again.

Charlie claps me on the shoulder. "Glad to hear it, man. I'll be sure to tell Ash – he's still on a matchmaking kick, and I'm pretty sure you were next in his line of sight. Well, you or Josh, but…" His face falls as he trails off.

Now I'm stuck in a hard place where I already know exactly what's going on with Josh, but for me to admit as much would be letting the cat out of the bag. "But?" I prompt.

Charlie shakes his head and scrubs his hand over his bearded jaw. "I've been worried about Josh lately. I've been trying not to push, you know? But I think he's lonely. And he had a near miss at work the other day, but he refused to come home with me and Ash and..." With another shake of his head, Charlie leaves the sentence hanging. "I'm just worried about him. I tried calling yesterday, but he didn't answer. I know he's okay, though, because he's active in the group chat."

After getting off the call from his mother, Josh had not been in the mood to talk to any more of his family. He explained that he finds them a bit overwhelming, despite knowing that their intentions are good. While I couldn't relate, I understood where he was coming from.

"He's a Little," I tell Charlie, carefully riding the line between being Josh's Daddy and Charlie's friend. "Yes, from what I've seen, Josh is pretty independent for a Little. He's not a Middle, but he has Middle tendencies. That probably comes from his job and the headspace he has to be in for most of the day. I get that. But he's still a Little. He's probably not going to open up to you as his big brother or as a caregiver without gentle prompting. To put it simply, in these dynamics, you're the 'adult', Charlie."

I'm generalizing, and I'm glossing over the issue, but Charlie nods anyway. "I just don't want to push too hard. I know how stubborn he can be." He sighs. "I guess I was hoping he might talk to the other Littles, but he hasn't even opened up to Matt, and they're quite close."

"I can't speak for Josh, but is it possible he feels pigeonholed into being the carefree bratty Little of the group?" I suggest gently. I'm comfortable offering my perspective on this, at least, because I've been included in a few group events and seen how the guys all interact. "He might feel as though stepping out of that role will see him ridiculed or not taken seriously."

I flash back to Wednesday night, to Josh tearfully telling me he doesn't want to be bratty, he just wants to play and be loved on. My heart clenches all over again.

Charlie leans against my office wall, folding his arms across his chest. He's built similarly to Josh but is a bit softer around the middle. "I've had my suspicions about that for a while, to be honest. Even before I met Ash, I thought Josh might want to be more than just a scene Little or a bratty boy. But I gave up pushing the topic with him because he insisted that he knew what he wanted, and I needed to trust that and stop projecting my own desires."

I nod. "Like I said, he's independent. And that was a long time ago, right? Maybe at the time, he really was content with life as he knew it. He would only have been in his early twenties."

"So was Ash, but—"

"As I understand it, Ash's situation was completely different to Josh's." I've heard the story of how Charlie met his Little husband, and I also know Ash. He's a nice guy, but he's a very different person to Josh. "Just because they're both Littles doesn't mean they both want to explore their kink in the same ways. You know that better than anyone, Charlie." I gesture vaguely around me, indicating the community center he established after his career as a cop ended. "That's why you opened this place up, isn't it? To give people a safe place to seek information and explore their kinks without having to go to a BDSM club or online?"

It's more than that, though. We help find emergency accommodations for people in the community who find themselves suddenly homeless. We offer counseling, FAQ sessions, and even mentoring programs. We hold themed events, charity auctions, and have even looked into starting up kink-specific speed dating events.

Charlie unfolds his arms and bobs his head. "Yeah, I know. I just..." he flounders for words.

"You just want your brother to be happy," I finish for him. "Which is completely understandable, but you can't force him to open up to you until he's ready. If he is going through something, remind him that you're there for him, but don't pressure him."

"Ugh, you're making it sound like I'm turning into my mother," he shudders dramatically.

I can't help chuckling. "She's a meddler?"

"Of the highest order," he agrees, but his tone is fond. He loves his mom, even if she frustrates him. Josh speaks of her the same way. He was exhausted when I spoke to him on Monday night after his lunch date with his parents, but he admitted that he was glad to have gone, even if his mother did nag him about his 'friend'.

Josh assured me that he has no intentions of keeping his relationship with me and Max a secret, but that he feels it's too early to go announcing it to his family. Like I said before, I understand his reasons and I don't feel compelled to push him, even if I do want to tell Charlie that Josh is in good hands.

"So, anyway, we're organizing a last-minute group thing at our place for Friday night," Charlie redirects the conversation. He cocks his head. "Did you want to join us? You can bring your date." He waggles his eyebrows suggestively.

I chuckle and shake my head. I can't exactly tell him that my date —or at least one of the pair of them— will probably already be attending. A part of me considers just bringing Max along, but that feels unfair on Josh. Like we'd be keeping him a secret.

This is suddenly feeling more complicated than it did over the weekend.

"Em?" Charlie prompts.

"Hmm?" I ask, still lost in thought, before I give myself a mental prod. "Sorry. Yeah, I'd love to come. But I'll take a rain check on bringing my date for now."

After he leaves my office, I text Josh and Max. This is something we definitely need to talk about.

* * *

"So, I've been thinking," Josh says over dinner, causing Max to chuckle with a forkful of pasta raised halfway to his mouth.

"Uh oh," he teases our younger lover. "That sounds danger-ous."

Josh pokes his tongue out at him. "Shut up. I'm being serious here."

Max chews and swallows the bite of food he'd taken before he waggles the fork at our boy. "Don't sass me, boy," he warns, "or you'll be punished."

A smirk tugs at Josh's lips and he appears to be considering his options. "Don't threaten me with a good time, Daddy."

Beneath the table, I nudge Josh's foot with mine. "Don't get distracted. What were you saying?"

Josh shovels the creamy pasta dish into his mouth and holds up his index finger, indicating we wait while he eats. Once he's swallowed, he replies, "I can bring Max to Charlie and Ash's place on Friday. Charlie knows we're hanging out since Max took me home after the whole bullet graze thing."

Out of the corner of my eye, I watch Max frown a little, and

I assume he takes issue with our relationship being dismissed as simply 'hanging out'. Meanwhile, I'm concerned with Josh's blasé attitude about being shot. Regardless of the fact that the injury he sustained was minor, he was still shot.

Maybe we need to discuss it again...

Josh looks between us and huffs. "I'm not trying to lie to them or anything. I just...I just want *us* to be special to us for a little while longer. Just until we've ironed out most of the kinks and we're all agreed that it's going to work out in the long term." He turns to Max beseechingly. "Charlie's not as bad as Mom, but he's going through an overprotective phase right now. Do you really want to be on the receiving end of one of his interrogations?"

Max sighs. "I'm not afraid of your brother, Josh. He was my partner for a couple of years. If anything, that should work in my favor. And this guy," he tilts his head, indicating me, "has worked with him at The Center for a while now. Charlie knows and trusts us both."

"Uh huh." Josh's tone is a little sarcastic. "You're both significantly older than me, this is your first time exploring Age Play, and I've never really been in a serious relationship." He lists potential reasons for Charlie's concern on his fingers. "And if this all goes to shit, it has the potential to screw up his working relationship with Emmett, too. So, yeah, I just want to keep it to ourselves a little bit longer if we can. Just..." he exhales, "just to be safe, okay? It's not like I think we're not going to work out, but it hasn't even been a week yet."

"I'm not lying to Charlie," Max insists.

I nod my agreement. "If he asks us outright, I won't lie, either."

Josh rolls his eyes and looks at the ceiling for a long moment before glancing back between me and Max. "I'm not asking either of you to lie," he says in a tone that is full of forced calm. "But if Charlie and the guys want to assume I've just brought Max along as a friend, I'm going to let them."

"Fine," Max says, but he sounds unimpressed.

I reach out and smooth my hand over his forearm soothingly. "It is only early days," I remind him softly.

He bobs his head, then sighs. "I can't help that I'm excited about *us*," he says, finally smiling softly. "This week has been so good. Just being able to text you both or coming back here for dinner and a movie…it's nice. It's better than nice. It's…"

"Comforting?" Josh offers. He's looking down at his plate, swirling his pasta around with his fork. "It's been like that for me, too." When he looks up, his expression is pained. "I'm not trying to *hide* this," he repeats. "But I'm not ready to let other people in on it. It's *nice* having something for just me."

I process that for a moment. Max and I were both only children, but Josh is the third child in his family, with one more born after him. I want to kick myself for not considering that earlier. I've spoken to so many people who grew up in larger families like Josh's. I should have realized that he might have some of the same hang-ups about his personal time, space, and belongings. And, really, it explains a lot about why he is known as a brat, too.

He's not the firstborn child. He's not the only daughter. He's not even the baby. He has probably been fighting for attention his whole life.

"We are all yours, honey," I tell him emphatically, fighting the urge to get up, walk around the table and pull him in for a bear hug, "I promise."

Chapter Fifteen – Max

E mmett is a big old softy. He looks the strongest and toughest of all three of us, but the man is pure marshmallow. How I ever felt intimidated or ruffled by him, I will never know.

We've spent a few days getting comfortable with each other. It helps that we already knew each other in some capacity prior to starting this relationship, but figuring out how we all click has been a priority. Strangely, though, we haven't really fumbled over it. There have been a couple of moments where Em and I have been on slightly different pages regarding Josh's discipline —not that our boy has been anything other than mildly cheeky— but we've otherwise just asked questions and communicated our thoughts. It's been easier than I expected, but not so easy that I feel like the rug will be pulled out under my feet.

Maybe the fact that Em and I are older and experienced with kink negotiation has played a bigger part in this whole thing than I first thought it would. We've been very clear with each other, and with Josh, about our intentions and feelings every time he has regressed. In turn, he's been just as open with us. He's told us when he wants to play or draw, when he wants to be cuddled and given a bottle, and when he'd like to be left to independence, most notably when he needs to go potty. He hasn't been bratty or demanding, and he's made the transition into being a Daddy feel remarkably effortless.

I've even felt comfortable enough to ask them about having sex while Josh is regressed, to which Josh just grinned and answered "I like grown up touches all the time, Daddy." Em had just shrugged and said he was comfortable as long as he knew both Josh and I were, and that had been that. We haven't tried it out yet, but it's not high on my list of priorities. Not when everything is still so new.

After dinner on Wednesday, we all snuggle on the couch. Josh tells us that he's got his appointment for medical clearance arranged for Monday morning, and I remind the guys that my weekend this week is Sunday and Monday, but then I'll be on night shift for the six days following that. After agreeing that we should go out on an official date on Sunday, we sit and discuss the times that we're all going to be free, and we find it's a lot more complicated with the addition of a third person, particularly when Josh and I aren't working the same shift cycle.

Nevertheless, it's not impossible, and once we're all on the same page, the snuggles slowly morph into touches and exploration of bodies. While sex during Little time mightn't be a priority, my body is saying that extending the exploration of our sexual chemistry in some way —literally any way— is.

"We should take this to bed," I murmur in between kisses.

Side note: three-way kisses are messy but incredibly hot.

"God yes," Josh agrees emphatically.

Emmett just chuckles. "Lead the way," he says, and I don't need to be told twice.

I separate from our pile of interconnected limbs and climb off the couch, reaching for Josh's hand first, then Emmett's. I tug them both through the house to the master bedroom.

"How are we doing this?" I ask once we're there, exchanging kisses and pulling off each other's clothes.

Josh bites his lip, casting not-at-all surreptitious glances towards the bulge in the front of Emmett's underwear. "Can I…" he starts, reaching out to touch.

Emmett closes his eyes and groans, throwing his head back when Josh's fingers graze over the fabric. It's ridiculously hot to watch. My own cock twitches at the sight.

"I have an idea," I offer before they go any further. The words have tumbled from my lips before I can stop them, and both of my new lovers turn to look at me expectantly. I swallow. "Only if you're okay with it."

"I trust you," Josh assures me, and Emmett nods his agreement.

Well then, there's no reason for me to backpedal now. I smile and look between them. "I'd like to blindfold and restrain Em."

Emmett's eyes widen while Josh grins and claps his hands excitedly. "I've never done anything remotely dominating before," our boy says before Emmett can react. "Can I help?"

I've been imagining getting the big man to submit to me in some way ever since that first night, but I won't do anything he's not comfortable with. I look to him in askance. "Are you okay with that? We won't do anything intense. A blindfold and some silk ties to restrain you while we pleasure you. Maybe a cock ring to extend the experience if you're down with that."

"Fuck," my older lover reaches down and adjusts his obvious erection, squeezing himself as he does. I salivate at the thought of sucking on his impressive length as he continues, "That sounds hot."

"You can safeword at any time," I remind him.

He nods. "Of course."

"Wait here," I instruct him, then I turn to Josh. "No touching him until I get back."

Our boy pouts. "Can I touch myself?"

"No," Emmett and I answer him in unison.

Josh huffs dramatically and his hand twitches as though the simple denial has made him want to disobey even more.

After slipping my shirt and pants back on, I hurry out to my car, pulling my duffel bag from the trunk. It practically lives in my car because I like to have it on hand for any impromptu trips to The Grove. Or, I suppose, surprise chances like this one now that I'm in a relationship again.

Despite neither of my new lovers being a sub in the style I am used to, they're both clearly happy to explore these new things with me in much the same way I want to explore the Age Play element with them. Being a Daddy to Josh's Little has just been a different expression of the D/s roles I'm familiar with. There are similarities between the roles, and now there are opportunities to bring in some of my own kink.

Heat prickles under my skin when I think of all the things we can do together. Not just tonight but going forward. If they like the mild restraint play, of course. And if they don't, we can experiment with other things. Paddles, maybe. Or cock cages. Orgasm denial. Some light humiliation play.

The options really are endless.

When I get back to the bedroom, Josh is standing in front of the bed in just his bright red boxer briefs, his cock straining against the soft fabric. He's chewing on his bottom lip and wiggling with anxious energy. It's adorable and sexy all at once.

Emmett is, as expected, calmer. He's also only wearing his briefs, that monster cock of his putting the material through its paces, but he only smirks at me when I walk towards him. Dropping my bag on the mattress, I smooth my hands over his chest, patting his furry pecs as I say, "Good boy."

He snorts and Josh whines.

"That's a no on the praise kink for you then, huh?" I ask Emmett, enjoying the way Josh squirms in my peripheral vision. He's desperate for my attention, and I revel in seeing how far I can push him.

"I'd much rather dish it out than receive it," Emmett replies with a shrug.

I nod. "I expected as much."

"*Daddy*," Josh complains.

I share a knowing grin with Emmett before I school my expression and turn to face our boy. I arch an eyebrow at him. "Yes?"

He shifts his hips from side to side, still chewing on his lip. "When are we going to play?"

"Patience, baby."

I get far too much pleasure from the strangled sound he can't quite contain.

Nevertheless, I'm the Dom here and I need him to realize it. "Do you need corner time while I get Em situated?"

Josh's eyes go wide and he shakes his head. "No. I'll be good. I just…I want to help."

"I know, baby. But we want to tie Em up safely, so you'll

need to watch me do it this first time, okay?"

With reluctance, he nods.

Drawing out the anticipation for him is the icing on the cake as I direct Emmett to lie in the center of his mattress with his arms outstretched up and along the headboard. It's pure luck that Em's bed is a solid timber construction, with thick, decorative beams of wood that prove perfect for the plans I have for him tonight. I doubt he's ever considered using his bed's aesthetic design for this purpose before.

"You can take his underwear off," I tell Josh as I tug my own shirt back over my head, giving him the task as a reward for his ongoing patience, "but don't touch his cock, do you understand me?"

Josh's Adam's apple bobs as he swallows roughly, but he hastily jerks his head up and down to show his agreement. I note that there's a growing wet patch on the front of his own underwear, testament to how turned on he is. My own dick is getting slick and sticky at the head, too. It's been a long while since I've indulged my kinks like this, and even longer since I had multiple partners for the scene.

The fact that it's Josh and Emmett bending to my will only makes the whole situation hotter. This is more than just a scene – this is an expression of our trust in each other, which is kind of mind-blowing to experience so early on in our relationship. But then we've known each other for a while, even if it was only in a professional capacity between Emmett and me. It doesn't feel as new as it actually is.

I get the lengths of soft silk from my bag and carefully tie Emmett's wrists to the beams of his headboard while Josh gets him naked. I double check his positioning, not wanting to put unnecessary strain on his shoulders or back, and make sure the ties aren't so tight that they'll inhibit circulation, but that they're tight enough he can't accidentally slip out of them or pull them undone.

"You're okay?" I check in with him, my dick twitching at the picture he presents, all spread out for me and Josh. At our mercy.

There's something overwhelmingly hot about a man so physically imposing submitting to me.

Emmett's cock is also dribbling precum, curving up towards his navel, so thick and flushed dark. It's a beast of a thing, and so beautiful to look at. It shifts under the weight of my appraising glance, and he chuckles.

"I'm more than okay," he answers me, jerking his chin downwards, "obviously."

I bend over him and take his plump lips in a sloppy kiss. "Good," I say, then add, "I'm going to leave your legs free this time. We're starting off mild here. I'll get the blindfold next. Then I want you to stay quiet. No sounds, understood? No matter what we're doing to you. And, obviously, no coming until I say you can."

He groans and closes his eyes. "What have I gotten myself into?"

Despite the question, a smile tugs at his lips. He's looking forward to this, no matter what his words suggest. I take this opportunity to remove my pants and toss them aside as I go back to my bag of tricks.

The blindfold I pull out is black satin, soft and comfortable, but it shuts out all light. I slide it over his eyes, remind him that he can safeword at any point, and then tell him the scene has begun.

Josh is practically vibrating out of his skin at this point, so I gesture for him to climb up onto the mattress and jut my chin at Emmett's body.

'All yours,' I mouth, but I don't speak. I want to keep Emmett guessing as to which of us is doing what to him at any point, even though Josh's beard will probably give him away before too long. Not that it really matters if Emmett knows whether it's me or Josh: he's still not going to know what's coming next.

Josh surprises me when he doesn't immediately go for Emmett's straining dick. Instead, he knee-walks up the mattress to Emmett's side and then bends to suckle at one of the dark, pebbled nipples on Em's chest.

Emmett's sharp intake of breath is the only sound he releases, and he tenses as he seems to hold it.

It's so fucking hot to watch Josh suck and nip at that perfect little brown bud, his hand teasing and pinching the other one while Emmett tries not to writhe beneath his ministrations. I can barely tear my gaze away, but then I realize that I can add to the delicious torture myself.

Still not heading for Em's cock, I fish the bottle of lube out from my bag and warm a drizzle of it between my fingers. I guide Emmett's legs apart and then tease his hole slowly, slicking up the puckered rim, massaging in slow circles to relax the tight muscle.

Josh pulls up from the nipple he has been torturing and looks over. His pupils blow wide with lust. I smirk, and mouth, 'Wanna swap?'

He seems to consider it for a moment before shaking his head. His eyes draw down to Emmett's leaking cock and he licks his lips.

'Go on,' I urge without sound.

Emmett's hips are slowly rocking. Whether he's looking for more attention from my fingers or silently trying to encourage one of us to suck him, his need is more than obvious.

Josh seems to have gotten the memo about dragging this out, though, because he shakes his head and then climbs off the bed, gesturing for me to do the same.

"This way he won't know who is doing what," he whispers in my ear as we stand at the foot of the bed, watching Emmett squirm. We take the opportunity to remove our underwear while we're up and off the bed, and I feel like this has got to be the biggest act of deprivation for Emmett, not being able to see our boy in all his muscled, naked glory.

The big man on the bed is breathing rapidly, his body tensed, just waiting for someone to do *something*.

It's intoxicating seeing him like this. But even more thrilling is Josh's participation. He's the most submissive of all three of us, but he's just as into this as I am. I guess the temptation to tease and torture one of his Daddies with pleasure appeals to his brattier side.

Grinning, I can't resist kissing Josh before we return to the bed. Our lips slide against each other as our tongues twirl, and he practically melts into my embrace with a moan as our cocks bump and grind together.

A desperate whine comes from the bed before Emmett can stop himself, and I smirk against Josh's mouth. Then I pull away from him and turn my attention to the bed.

"That's your first and only warning," I tell Emmett. "If you can't be quiet, you'll be gagged."

His throat works as he swallows roughly and nods.

Josh and I resume our original places on the mattress. I pinch the cheek of Emmett's ass as Josh hovers his mouth over

Em's now painful looking erection. He teases his Daddy with a puff of warm air over the wet, weeping head and Em's hips surge forward immediately. I place my hand over one side to still his movements, and Josh's hand comes down on Emmett's other hip.

Moments later, Josh slowly suckles at the head of Em's cock, the girth of it stretching Josh's mouth wide. A gasp is the only sound Emmett makes and I allow it, watching the corded muscles in his arms strain against his bindings.

Josh is a good boy and holds back his own moans, and I realize that's because he really does want to keep Emmett guessing as to who is doing what.

I'm not going to ruin this for him by mentioning the difference between the feel of his bearded face and my clean-shaven one. Not when he's having so much fun.

With a little more lube added to my fingers, I return them to playing with Emmett's hole.

I'm tempted to release my hold on his hip so I can stroke myself while I watch Josh suck Emmett off, but I don't. Instead, I have to bite back my own groan when Josh picks up the discarded bottle of lube with his free hand and, after releasing Emmett's hip to spread some on his own fingers, starts opening himself up.

This is easily one of the most erotic things I have ever seen, despite the scene itself being quite tame. It has to be the emotional connection I feel with these men. It's so much more intense to play like this when I care for my partners.

Josh's eyes flutter shut while he fucks himself on his own fingers, and I crane around to watch him stretching and spreading his puckered hole with practiced ease. He's still sucking earnestly at Emmett's cock, and I'm now perilously close to blowing my own load without even touching myself.

Before I can become overrun by lust, I lean back and snag a couple of condoms from the outer pocket of my bag. One day, I'll propose we get tested, because I want to see Emmett's cum running out of Josh's ass. I want to spill into both of my men, marking my territory in the most primal way. I want to feel Emmett do the same to me. But, for now, safety is key.

Emmett's writhing and gasping is increasing, and the way his thighs tremble when Josh pulls off him and I slide a condom over that thick, hard shaft tells me that he's close to breaking point. As much as I'd love to push him over that edge, I can't let his first time fucking Josh be while he's blindfolded and restrained. That would be beyond cruel, and this kind of play is not about cruelty.

"You've been extremely well behaved," I tell Emmett, my low voice sounding loud in the silence of the room, our panting breaths the only other sounds in the air. "So I'm going to release your arms and take off your blindfold, okay? You don't have to be silent anymore."

"Okay," his voice is rough with desperation as he answers, and I methodically untie him before slipping the blindfold from his eyes.

He squints and blinks against the muted light coming from the lamps on either side of the bed. Then he looks down to where Josh is still stretching himself out with four fingers and he groans deeply.

"Fuck, that's hot," Emmett says, then grabs at the back of my head and yanks me down for an intense kiss. There's nothing sweet or gentle about it. His tongue plunders my mouth, and he dominates the kiss, reminding me that his submission was an act of pure trust. He's just as domineering as I am, and my cock pulses at the reminder. When he releases me, his question takes my breath away, "Will you fuck me while he rides me?"

Chapter Sixteen – Josh

I'm pretty sure Max's eyes roll back in his head at Emmett's request. God knows I almost lose control and come on the spot at just the thought. I'm a strict bottom and I've never made a secret of that, but I can't say that the idea of being sandwiched between my two men isn't the hottest thing I've ever thought. Maybe next time we could mix it up a bit, and Em can suck me while Max fucks me? That could be a lot of fun.

When he gets his head back in the game, Max nods and then he pulls a couple of pillows from the head of the bed and slides them under Emmett's hips. "This is going to be a bit awkward," he says, "but I think we'll make it work." He turns back to me. "Can you wait until I'm inside him before you climb on him?"

I can't help the snicker of amusement that escapes me. "He's not a horse," I joke.

Max grins, "You're still planning on riding him."

"Touché."

"Uh, as adorable as your banter is," Emmett interrupts us, "*he* is still waiting."

"Extremely impatiently," Max observes dryly. "Did you forget who was in charge, Em?"

Emmett groans. I can't exactly blame him. We're all hard, but his epic cock is flushed so dark it looks painful. We have been teasing him for a while now, and he wasn't even allowed to make sound. I would have broken if those rules had been for me.

I bat my lashes at Max, aiming for sweet. "Daddy Maxxie, don't be mean to Daddy Em now. He *was* good before, remember?"

Max sighs, but his smile is fond. "You're both insanely soft and submissive, aren't you?" He cuts off any argument Em might have made by sliding two fingers inside him. Emmett moans and writhes on Max's fingers, begging for more.

God, my Daddies are hot.

I watch in rapt attention, imagining those same fingers sliding in and out of my hole, stretching me wide. My cock dribbles its desire to feel that happening. "To be fair, I think Em's more of a Switch than a Sub," I muse, my gaze not leaving Max's fingers. I'm pretty sure that if I stroked my dick right now, I'd come immediately.

When Max finally slides a condom over his shaft, my hole is clenching in desperation to be filled. Emmett's cock is one of the biggest I've seen and I can't wait to get him inside me.

Max pulls Emmett's hips up and slowly eases inside him. I have to grip the base of my cock to hold off the orgasm that threatens to overwhelm me. Watching these two gorgeous older men together, knowing that they're my Daddies and they're going to take care of me as well tonight, is heady as fuck.

"You good?" Max asks Emmett when he's fully seated, and Em nods. Max looks back to me once he's sure Em's ready. "Okay. Josh, baby, you're up."

He sounds strained as he says it, and both he and Emmett make matching sounds of pleasure when I sling a leg over Em's hips, hold Em's throbbing shaft with one hand while I brace the other beside his head, and then slowly sink onto him. The stretch is intense. Even though I'd opened myself up with four fingers, I'd underestimated how thick my bigger Daddy is. It burns almost unpleasantly, but his large, warm palms running up and down my sides help me to breathe through it.

Slowly —ridiculously slowly— I relax enough to bear down.

"That's it, honey," Emmett croons up into my face. "You're so tight. Perfection." The way I'm positioned, leaning over him with my arms braced on either side of his face so he can keep his hips raised for Max, I can't fight the temptation to dip my head and kiss him slowly and deeply.

"Fuck, you two should see this from my side," Max adds. His hands find my hips. Lust zooms through my body at the feeling of four hands caressing my skin like I'm something precious.

I relax enough to take Emmett the whole way and his eyes practically roll back in his head. "Oh, *Josh*," he exhales, and I feel Max move, the slow thrust moving Emmett's cock inside me, "*Max*, Jesus Christ..."

With the sheer size of the man inside me, it doesn't take a lot of maneuvering for him to put pressure on my prostate. My entire body feels lit up from the inside, a constant buzz of pleasure that zings down my spine and directly into my balls.

"*Fuck*," I moan, and Max slaps my ass. At least, I think it was

Max. I have my eyes squeezed shut and the two larger hands on my sides haven't moved. If anything, they're gripping me tighter.

"God, yes," Max growls out. His voice is even more strained now, almost like he feels just as close to the edge as I do.

Maybe he does.

With how tightly Em's holding on to me, panting heavily with every movement we make together, I can only assume he's feeling the same way, too. Not that I can blame him. He's arguably in the most intense position of the three of us, and it's no wonder he's letting Max drive our motions from behind.

Max sets a slow, indulgent pace at first. I'm glad for it, because I need the extra time to get used to the feeling of Emmett inside me. It also means I'm less likely to come straight away, with our rocking slow and the pressure on my prostate not as intense as a quick succession of thrusts would be.

Max is muttering praises and words that sound vaguely adoring, but I'm too busy focusing on not going over the edge to really pay any attention. Cracking my eyes open, I look down at Emmett and I'm surprised to find him watching me intently.

I would have thought he'd have his eyes shut against the onslaught of bliss, too, but those dark eyes are liquid pools of pure lust as they drink me in. My cock jerks and dribbles onto his lightly furred abdomen as I take notice of his attention.

"You're —*ah*— so beautiful, Joshie," he says, his voice a low rumble, despite the panted exclamation Max's thrust pushes from him. "You both feel so —*ohhhh*— fucking good. God, *Max*, do that again."

Max complies, and I crane around to try and catch my other

151

Daddy pulling out and then pushing back in with more force than before. The motion has Emmett pushing his cock back into me and I gasp as he once again nails my prostate with the movement.

Then his big, warm palm is no longer above my hip. It's wrapped around my shaft between our close bodies, stroking me in time with Max's thrusts. It's almost like we move as one, a well-oiled machine, if you'll excuse the lube pun.

Max starts to rock into Em faster, and, in turn, Em's movement inside me increases in speed. I rock back onto him, unable to be passive. I ride him with building energy, the jolts of pleasure inside me becoming almost painful as the wave of my orgasm crests.

The closer I get, the more I babble.

"Daddy...*Daddies*...I'm close! So—*ohhhh!*" I lose my train of thought for a moment, "Fucking...close..."

"Do it, baby," Max urges. "Paint Em with your cum. Mark him as yours. As ours."

"Oh!" I cry out, the deliciously dirty instruction pushing me over the edge. He hasn't even finished talking before I start shooting my load all over Emmett's stomach and chest, with some spurts landing as high as his chin. Emmett's hips jerk as I clench around him, and I feel his cock pulsing inside me as my orgasm triggers his.

"Fuck," Max bites out, and I can feel his movements becoming erratic as he pounds into Emmett now, "Fuck, you're both so hot. Oh, *God*." His last word is barely more than a moan as he stills, presumably finding his own release.

I flop over Emmett's chest, heedless of the fact that I'm smearing the cum between us. I feel blissed out and boneless, though I scrunch my nose against the mild discomfort of his withdrawal from my ass. With my eyes shut, I can only feel him moving as he removes the condom, wraps it in a tissue from his bedside table and tosses it God-only-knows where. Then Max is crawling up the bed to my right and tugging me down until I'm sandwiched between both men.

"We're going to have to clean up," Emmett says, not making a move to do so.

"Mmm," Max agrees lazily. "In a minute."

My own eyelids are heavy, but I know they'll get me up and take care of me when it's necessary. They're my Daddies, after all. That's what they do.

* * *

"Joshie!" Ash greets me with a wide grin when I waltz into his and Charlie's house, Max trailing behind me at a sedate pace.

Ash throws his arms around me, his mop of brown curls tickling my nose while we hug. When he steps back, I notice he is wearing a onesie with the tell-tale cuffs of a diaper poking out through the leg holes, cute little cartoon sheep decorating the whole ensemble. He has come a long way since I first met him, no longer the scared, embarrassed Little who had just found himself homeless through no fault of his own. Our group has been good for him. Now, he's more than confident with his fluidity between his headspaces, and he doesn't hide his enjoyment of letting Charlie take care of him, diapers and all. That part, in particular, makes my big brother extremely happy. It's a whole thing with him.

In their living room, which is just to the right of the main entry space, some of the others are also dressed and ready for play. There's Matt, my biker-looking best friend, wearing his favorite Eeyore onesie and blue play shorts, Zephyr in one of his pretty rockabilly-style dresses, wearing a face full of makeup today, his dark skin practically glowing where he has highlighted his striking cheekbones and the long, smooth line of his nose, and Kate, wearing cut-off jean shorts and a pink, belly exposing crop top with *Barbie* emblazoned over her ample breasts. Her round cheeks are also bright pink, and her long dark hair looks as though it's only half-styled, with one side braided and the other side loose. Her happy smile is infectious as always.

Matt once told me that Katie found it hard to find Little clothes that suited her vibrant personality because she's plus-sized. Before Zee joined the group, I used to play dress-ups with her, because finding Little dresses to fit me was just as difficult. We made a game of it, even if femme play wasn't my thing. But in recent years, Zephyr —and now also Kade— have made it their mission to find (or create) outfits for her. Now she practically glows with happiness when she's Little, wearing her new clothes with pride, and it's just one more thing that makes me love our friendship circle even more.

"Zeph's doing Katie's hair," Ash tells me as he leads me into the room. He looks over my shoulder at Max. "Daddy's out by the grill."

I snort. "You could say hi to D...*Max* properly, you know." God only knows Charlie would give him a lecture about his manners. It would be all 'Little lamb, is that how we treat our guests?' with threats of corner time as a reminder. Especially when Max has spent the past few years avoiding as many of Charlie's get-togethers as he could out of his misplaced sense of guilt. I know Charlie wants him to feel as welcome as possible, to avoid any of that guilt from making a reappearance.

Plus, Ash hates corner time.

Ash blushes, missing the way I stumbled over Max's name, and nods. "Sorry. Hi Max. Don't tell Daddy I was rude."

I miss Max's reply, though, too busy noticing the way Matt is looking at me. Even in his Little headspace, the guy is sharp. Sure enough, when I plop down beside him —still dressed in my jeans and loose T-shirt combination— he asks, "Did you just almost call Max *Daddy*?"

I promised myself and my Daddies that I wouldn't lie about our relationship, but I haven't even been here five minutes. Surely I can keep a secret for a little longer than that!

I shrug. "Yeah, I did."

My lack of denial makes him blink. Then his eyes drift to the gauze peeking out from beneath my sleeve and understanding dawns. "Oh!" He says, his shoulders relaxing. "He's been looking after you after…" Matt's face falls. His lower lip quivers, which should not be as cute on a big, bearded, tatted up guy as it is. "You got shot, Joshie."

I sigh and shake my head. "It was a graze."

"Beside the point," Matt argues, and I'm aware that he's slipping back out of his Little headspace to berate me. "Someone aimed a gun at you and fired, and I had to find out about it in a group chat?"

I do feel a bit guilty about that, but the hours (days, even) following last weekend's events were a whirlwind. I try to laugh his admonishment off. "You sound *just* like my mom, Mattie."

"Because I care about you, you dick."

"Hey! Do we call our friends names, sweetheart?" London has timed his entrance perfectly.

Saved by the Daddy, I think to myself smugly, watching the man himself stalk over to his boy and stare down at him with an unimpressed expression on his face.

London's about my age, substantially younger than Matt who is just now hitting his fifties. He's shorter than me, stocky and clean shaven where his boy is a big, bearded bear of a man. His black hair is, as always, styled up into a coif that makes me think of Elvis, even if it's not quite as dramatic, and his squared jaw is set with his displeasure.

"Why is it," he asks calmly, in that strict tone that has all of us Littles sitting up a bit straighter, "that any time Matt's naughty, I find him with you, Josh?"

I hold my hands up in surrender, pasting on my most innocent smile as I cock my head up at London. Matt was (and remains) London's first Little, but the man is a natural caregiver, and a natural disciplinarian. "I didn't do anything," I tell him honestly.

Behind him, I can see the other caregivers have made their way inside, and Max is frowning at Charlie's side.

Ruh roh.

I don't want to give my Daddy any reason to think I was being naughty. Especially when he can't do anything about it until we're in private. That's unfair on him.

"I swear, London. Matt was just chewing me out for not telling him about being shot…which, I admit, I should have done." With an apologetic pout, I look back at my best friend. "I didn't want you to worry, you know?"

"I always worry about you," Matt's response is exasperated, but the corners of his lips are lifting under that salt and pepper bushy beard of his. "You're a cop. We're all aware of the risks that involves."

I glance around and find everyone nodding their agreement. Usually, I like being the center of attention, but right now it feels overwhelming. Maybe because this is far too emotional, as opposed to the attention I usually strive for.

Ducking my head to hide my blush, I nod. "Yeah, okay. I'm sorry."

"Did I just hear Josh *apologize*?" Chance's jokingly bewildered voice breaks the weird tension building in the moment, and I've never been more relieved to see my ginger friend. He and his Little, Kade, must have just let themselves into Charlie and Ash's home, because they're making their way in from the same direction I did.

Chance and I have gotten a lot closer over the past year or so. We never really seemed to have much in common, so all of our original interactions were basically just banter. But ever since he reconnected with his childhood best friend, that has changed. I get along really well with Kade, so I spend a lot of time at their home, watching sports or even playing with Kade when he's in his Pup space. He tends to prefer that over his Little headspace most of the time.

Chance is the most Daddy looking man in our whole friendship group, if you ask me. He's of average build and height, with a soft belly and a warm smile under his copper-colored beard. He's a bit of a smart ass like me, and I am so glad to have him here to bounce off and break the weird 'I love you, you love me' vibe that was building.

Grinning back at him, I shake my head. "Good luck getting me to repeat it," I tease. Then I look to Kade. Tall, slim and blonde, he's still one of the prettiest men I've ever seen. He and Zephyr together could bring hundreds of men to their knees if they ever joined forces for (sexy) evil purposes. I smile at the thought, then ask, "Is Puppy Kade playing today? Or Little Kade?"

Kade snorts. "That was a smooth change of topic, man. Nobody noticed a thing. Very subtle."

"Shut up," I roll my eyes, doing my best to ignore Max's cough, which has come from the kitchen-facing side of the living room. "Pup or Little? I have money riding on this, Kaden."

Obviously, I don't. But I wouldn't be me if I didn't talk shit.

He shakes his head with disbelief painted over his pretty features. "Pup." His pink lips draw into a wide smile, and he looks adoringly towards Chance. "Daddy bought me a new bodysuit, ears and collar." His left hand travels to his neck, the platinum band he wears as an engagement ring glinting in the light.

Not all that long ago, his happiness made me a little jealous. To be honest, all of my friends' Happily Ever Afters did, each one stinging just a bit more than the one before it. But now, I don't feel jealous or resentful when I look at Kade's ring, or when I see the loving glances he and Chance exchange. It doesn't make my gut churn or my heart ache to watch Ted walk over to press a kiss to the top of Zephyr's head, or to watch Katie throw herself into Cherie's arms, almost bowling her petite Mommy over.

Instead, the longing I feel is directed towards Max, and I'm second-guessing my decision to keep our change in relationship private for now. That only increases when Spencer, his Little, Tony, and Emmett traipse through from the entryway.

"Look who I found," Spence declares, clapping Emmett on the shoulder. Spencer is also a tall guy, but he's built like a beanpole in comparison to the mountain that is my second Daddy. "Can you believe he was going to press the doorbell and wait?" He tsks, looking at Em with amusement. "Haven't you learned anything from this group yet?"

Emmett purses his lips. "Excuse me if my parents taught me to respect boundaries," he teases lightly.

Tony nods. "Don't worry," he says, not quite meeting Em's gaze, "I'd press the doorbell and wait, too, if I could. But Daddy insists Charlie and Ash are okay with us just barging in on get-together days."

"Well *I* can barge in whenever I want," I practically sing-song, falling back into my cheekier persona with ease. The guys expect this of me, and I know that they all worry when I don't act the way they're used do. I smirk in my brother's direction, avoiding Max's eyes. "Baby brother privileges."

Charlie tilts his head back, addressing the ceiling as he playfully groans, "I begged Mom and Dad for a puppy, but I got you instead."

"He could take Pup lessons from me, then you get the best of both worlds," Kade suggests, and it's sweet of him to try and defend me from the perceived insult in Charlie's teasing, even though I know there's no malice in Charlie's words.

My brother laughs. "Could you imagine Josh as a Pup? He'd be destructive and loud and disobedient."

"So, no different to Josh as a Little?" Chance jokes.

I roll my eyes, but I can see Max's frown deepening. Behind me, Emmett clears his throat.

"Yeah," I goad Chance back before either of my Daddies can say anything, letting them know that I'm okay with this conversation. I might have been sensitive about being seen as 'the brat' before, but since I've been with my Daddies, I

159

feel lighter again. More myself. Which is why I smirk and threaten, "and I'd piss in your shoes, too."

A chorus of 'Ewwww's and giggles erupt from my Little friends. Whether they're currently Little or not, toilet humor is always guaranteed to make them laugh. I give myself an imaginary pat on the back for the effort.

"Gross, Josh," Charlie admonishes, but even he's fighting a smile. It only widens when he looks over to where Ash is still giggling on the carpeted living room floor. "I'm about ready to fire up the grill, Little Lamb. You can keep playing, or you can come help. Your choice."

I love get-togethers with the group for this very reason. Nobody cares which headspace you're in – you can join the scene or just hang out with a beer and chat. Even when it was just Ash, Matt, and me, there was never any pressure to be Big or Little. I appreciate my big brother for fostering this kind of atmosphere, both here at home and at The Center.

Ash scrunches up his face and wriggles his nose from side to side, considering his options. "Can I play some more? The others only just got here." He looks up at Tony and Kade. "You gonna play?"

Kade nods and holds up his bag. "I'll go get changed now."

It still takes Tony some time to warm up in a group setting, but he gives Spence's hand a squeeze and nods silently, going to sit beside Ash. "I'm, um, already dressed," he says quietly, wiggling his butt.

Diapered, then.

I'm super proud of Tony for that. He doesn't use them during group play, but there was a time where he'd been too embarrassed to even wear them around us. I'm glad that he's comfortable enough with us now to do so. These get-togethers are supposed to be liberating and relaxing, and our group is all about supporting each other.

"Are you getting changed?" Matt asks me, cocking his head. I do feel a little out of place in my jeans and t-shirt, but I don't really feel like fully regressing today.

I shake my head. "Nah," I tell him, "I'm going to play, but I don't need to be super little today."

Nobody bats an eyelid at that. I've always maintained that I'm a scene Little, so it's not likely to be surprising that I don't feel the need to regress. But that's not why I said it.

I've had plenty of time in my Little headspace lately. More than I'm used to, in fact. For the first time in years, I am relaxed and happy. I want to play, but I don't *need* to. I have Emmett and Max to thank for that.

"But, *oh*," I make grabby hands towards Max, "my bag." He arches an eyebrow. I blush. "Please." This time, I barely stop myself from adding 'Daddy' to the end of my request.

How can I be so used to that after only a week?

Max smirks at me as though he's reading my thoughts, then unzips the backpack he brought in with him earlier. He reaches in and pulls out my soft white teddy bear. Ranger unfurls as he's pulled from the bag, doubling in size now that he has room. "Looking for this?"

My heart flutters the way it always does when I see Ranger. He was my first ever gift from my Daddies; a symbol of that very first night together. He's comforting and reminds me of how much they cared even then, when we weren't actually together and weren't really planning on repeating the experience.

Max holds him up but makes no move to bring him to me. I whine.

"Don't tease the boy, Max," Emmett huffs, sounding unimpressed. "You're not a cruel Dom, are you?"

I can't see Em, but I watch as Max chuckles and waggles Ranger at him. "You're such a softy," he accuses my other Daddy, and I wonder if anyone else thinks their flirting is hot as fuck, or if that's just me. "Josh needs to learn patience."

"Do you go this hard on him at work?" London asks Max, as though that explains this new dynamic we've got going. Considering they all know he looked after me when I was discharged from hospital, it's not a huge mental leap from there to the work connection.

Still, I snort. "I outrank him at work."

Max pulls Ranger further back. His eyebrow arch is insanely sexy, and I hear his silent threat that I had better start behaving if I don't want him to punish me later.

I affect an innocent expression. Butter wouldn't melt in my mouth. "I'll be good," I promise, reaching out again. "Please can I have my bear?"

Once more, the honorific is on the tip of my tongue. Who knew it would be this hard not to call Emmett and Max 'Daddy' for a few hours?

"If you're bratty, I'm taking Ranger back," Max tells me before he relents and steps into the living room to hand me my bear.

I hug Ranger tightly to my chest, while Matt looks up at Max with suspicion. "How'd you know the bear's name?"

"Duh," Asher says before Max can answer, "he took Josh home from the hospital 'n looked after him like a Daddy 'cos Joshie was Little in the hospital."

"Right," Max agrees easily, and he's not lying, but it still makes my stomach squirm with a sudden burst of guilt.

I don't think I like keeping them secret from my friends after all.

My Daddies wander off to join the others, leaving us Littles to our playtime. I manage to push my guilt down far enough to regress, but it sours my mood, making me a bit bratty.

I keep a tight hold of Ranger, denying Matt the chance to include him in our imaginative play. He's my bear. Mine. And the only thing reminding me that I have two Daddies who care about me, even if I've told them not to show it today.

"Let's play cars," Matty suggests, holding out a red sports car.

I scoff and reach for the yellow one, just to be difficult. "I don't like the red one anymore," I tell him.

My sweet best friend just shrugs. "I change favorites sometimes, too."

Some of my defenses come down and I try to shake off my mood. Play time with my friends is fun, after all, and I don't get to do it anywhere near as often as I'd like. Smiling, I zoom the car along the rug that's designed to look like a city, making it travel along the curving road. "Vroom vroom," the noise probably sounds more like a lawnmower than a car, but I don't care. "Let's race!"

Matt hunches over the other side of the rug, and we navigate our cars as far across the rug as we can reach. When I realize I'm losing, I make a screeching sound and have my car crash into one of the cartoon houses, going out in an imaginary blaze of glory.

Asher giggles from where he's flopped down to watch us play. "My turn next?"

I hand him the yellow car and reach for the red, shrugging at Matt when he looks between the car in my hand and my face. "Maybe the red is better after all."

And maybe I'm still feeling a bit out of sorts.

Chapter Seventeen – Emmett

Watching Josh play with the other Littles is a sweet kind of torture. He's adorable, even though he's not regressed anywhere near as deeply as he has with me and Max at home.

Home.

Huh.

My house has felt more like a home this past week than it ever has.

But it's only been a week.

Still, having Josh and Max there has made it warmer. More inviting. A space to do more than simply exist. The fact that I can already imagine my men being there permanently with me is a bit jarring. Have I ever gotten so attached so quickly?

But I can't help it.

Just like I can't help wanting to assert myself as Josh's Daddy like the other guys gathered here today can with their significant others.

"Hey! That's *my* bear!" Josh shouts and I look up from my

seat at the outdoor dining table just as Josh lunges at Matt in the living room. I have a direct view from my side of the table outside, through the sliding glass doors and across the internal kitchen/dining space of Charlie and Asher's home.

Max is on his feet, heading inside at the same time as London, and it strikes me that nobody blinks an eye at the fact that he's stepping in to discipline our boy. But if I did it, there would be questions.

I'm not the jealous type. Not usually. But right now? I can acknowledge that I feel a pang of something resembling the green-eyed monster. Sure, nobody thinks of Max as Josh's Daddy, but because of their work connection, and the fact that Max was Charlie's partner, it's not all that surprising that he would take up the mantle of temporary caregiver.

"He took Ranger!" Josh complains loudly in response to whatever admonishment Max has just given him.

I can't hear Max's reply from where I'm sitting, but I watch as he shakes his head and gestures calmly towards Matt, who is blinking wide-eyed and leaning towards London's legs for comfort.

It's not like Josh to behave irrationally, whether he's being bratty or not. And, of all the guys, I know he's closest with Matt. The burly, bearded Little doesn't have a cruel bone in his body, and is always sweet and soft-spoken. I'm itching to head over and mediate, because I can only assume that there was some sort of miscommunication between Josh and his friend.

"I wonder what happened there," Ted's voice interrupts my focus, and I turn to find my sometimes-colleague sliding into the seat at my side. He jerks his chin towards the living room. "Josh doesn't usually have outbursts like that. Or *any*, actually.

Especially not with Matt."

Ted's what you would call a silver fox. He's a handsome man, about my age, with streaks of gray at his temples and a devastating smile. He's a lawyer who specializes in contract law, and in recent years he has volunteered his services pro bono at The Center. We get along well, but right now I wish he would talk to someone else so I can keep an eye on my lovers.

That doesn't look like it's going to happen though.

Smothering a sigh, I shrug. "He did go through something traumatic only last week," I acknowledge. "This could be part of his brain's way of healing." Despite the fact that I've offered the words off the cuff, I hear the truth in them.

Josh has been coping well since the incident. Almost too well. I originally put that down to his personality and the fact that he's spent a lot of time regressing with me and Max...but what if he was just internalizing the trauma? Pushing it down until something random triggers him and he explodes?

Huh.

"Poor kid," Ted laments, directing his gaze over to where Max has hauled Josh to his feet and is directing him to the corner. Another pang of that not-quite-jealousy feeling goes through me. "But Max seems to have it in hand." There's a curious tone to Ted's voice. Then he nudges me. "Do you think our resident Dom is considering becoming a Daddy? Daddy Dom? Is that how that works?" I swivel my head back to face him as he shrugs. "I'll admit, I've mostly stayed in my own lane where kinks are concerned."

I'm too busy trying not to react to Ted's assumptions about the relationship developing between Max and Josh, that he blindsides me completely when he narrows his eyes and asks,

"Or do you and Max have something going on?"

"I…" *Shit. Fuck.* I can't lie. My cheeks burn and I'm thankful for my complexion not giving me away, despite the knowing glint in Ted's eye. "Ted," I sigh. "I'm going to need you to drop that line of questioning."

"I knew it!" He crows quietly.

Not quietly enough.

"Knew what?" Max asks, coming back to the seat he chose across from me and reaching for his beer.

Ted grins and gestures across the table, from Max to me and back again. "That you two have a thing going."

Max looks completely unruffled. "Oh. Right. Well," he takes a long drag from his bottle of beer, and I can't help the way my eyes zero in on the way his lips wrap around the lip of the bottle, or the way his Adam's apple works as he swallows, "it's very new."

"What's new?" Charlie asks as he places a tray of burger buns on the table. Ash is manning the grill, and I am starting to wish I was anywhere but here.

"Max and Emmett," Ted answers helpfully.

Charlie practically gives himself whiplash as he stares between me and Max. "Holy shit. No way. Since when?" Then he blinks and looks at me. "*He* was the date you were all spacey about?"

"Aww, you were spacey about me?" Max teases.

I point an accusatory finger at him. "Shut up." I look back at Charlie. "Kind of." I don't like leaving out a whole third of our relationship. It feels too much like we're sneaking around. I'm in my fifties. I am too old to be sneaking around.

"Kind of?" Charlie's eyebrows inch up his forehead.

"Hey, so, what was up with Josh?" I try to redirect the

conversation and also give Max a hint about my discomfort with this situation as a whole. Plus I'm genuinely concerned about our boy. "I see you've planted him in the corner."

Max nods, cool as a cucumber. He takes another long sip from his beer. "He should have asked Matt to give his bear back nicely. He didn't. He also refused to apologize. Instant corner time."

Charlie's eyes narrow and I can see him trying to put unspoken pieces together. "So," he asks slowly, "how, uh, how *do* a Dom and a Daddy connect?"

"You're making awfully big assumptions about my bedroom practices if you can't imagine that I'd enjoy being with a Dom, Charlie," I rebuke him mildly.

I'm not actually offended, because we're a very open group and I know his question wasn't intended to be insulting.

In fact, before I started trying new things with Max, I would have denied it could work, too. But now I'm curious about my desires to submit to him. I might have laughed at his attempt to praise me as he would a sub like Josh, but I loved being bossed around by him. And the thought of him punishing me with paddles or perhaps a flogger —when he's so much smaller than I am— makes my dick twitch with interest. We're going to have to explore that, but that's not at all what I need to be thinking about in this moment.

No, I need to distract Charlie before he realizes the true answer to that question. Because the issue isn't that Max and I aren't compatible, but I think we can both see that Josh brought us together.

Charlie holds up his hands in surrender. "Whoa, no, I wasn't...I didn't mean..." he looks to Ted beseechingly. "Help me."

Ted snorts.

I use the moment of distraction to look past Max and back into the living room, where Josh is nowhere to be found. I frown.

"How many minutes did you give him?" I ask Max, already pushing my seat back.

He checks his watch. "Five. It's been three."

"Well, he's not where you left him."

Charlie exhales. "My brother not following instructions? Shocking."

I want to tell him he's wrong. That Josh isn't the brat they all think he is. That he actually thrives on praise and cuddles. That his cheeky behavior is just for attention and is adorable rather than a nuisance.

I don't say any of that, though. I just rise to my feet and head into the house, waving Max off when he attempts to stand and follow me.

I head to the bottom of the stairs when a glance into the living room confirms his absence. "Josh?" I call, then cock my head, straining for his answer.

"I think he needed the bathroom," Zephyr tells me, coming to stand beside me.

He props his hand on his hip, emphasizing the tight cinch of his dress's waist. He's a dancer, long and lithe, and more Middle than Little. He and Ted make a stunning couple. "The one upstairs."

"Thanks, Zee," I nod.

He reaches for my arm, stalling me before I can head up. "Be gentle with him? I've never seen him regress like this. He's usually in a similar headspace to me, not *little* little, you know? And," he lowers his voice, despite nobody being around to hear us, "I know there's something going on between you, and I know Max is involved somehow, too. I won't say anything," he's quick to add. "I learned my lesson about meddling the hard way. But…don't get too mad with him, okay?"

"You're too perceptive," I grumble. "You and your Daddy both." I soften before he can say anything, appreciating that he's looking out for Josh when others seem happy to just write him off as being bratty. "But I promise not to be mad at him. He's gone through something traumatic and I think it's finally catching up with him."

Zephyr nods, smiling sadly. "He's needed a Daddy for a while, Emmett. I hope he's going to admit that and accept whatever support you and Max can give him." Then he pats my arm and wanders back into the living room, plopping down on the carpet between Tony and Katie and sinking back into playtime without even glancing back at me.

Ash, on the other hand, juts his chin at me and then towards the stairs. Matt has his back to me, thankfully. I don't need everyone getting into our business. Especially when Josh was so determined to keep our relationship to just ourselves for a while longer, though he completely underestimated how nosy our friends are.

I give Ash a nod and then head upstairs, turning left at the landing at the top before I knock on the closed door.

"Joshie," I start, "are you okay?"

At first I think he's going to ignore me, but then there's a weak "Not really" spoken in his Little voice.

My heart squeezes. "Can I come in?"

There's another pause before he answers, "Yeah."

I push the door open to find him sitting on the tiled floor with his back against the tub, his knees drawn to his chest.

"Oh, honey, what's wrong?" I ask, going to my knees so I can put my hand on top of his arm.

He sniffles, his brown eyes rimmed with red. "Daddy Maxxie got mad 'cause Matty took Ranger and—"

"Josh," I interrupt him calmly. "The real reason you're upset, please." We both know he wouldn't break down like this over a slight misunderstanding.

His lower lip wobbles. "I couldn't do the punishment. I was bad."

"I don't understand."

"I had to go potty, so I had to break the rules. I didn't want to break the rules. I wanted to be good."

"Oh, honey," I reach for him and pull him against me, squeezing him tight. "You were good. You're not diapered, so choosing the potty over time out was a good choice. Daddy Max isn't going to be mad, baby. I promise."

The fact that Josh has a huge chip on his shoulders about being in control of his bladder means Max and I are way more lenient on him with issues like this. Even though Josh has said he's okay with wetting humiliation play, it has to be on his terms and an agreed scene before it happens. Within his control. Having an accident outside of those terms is an instant red light.

"But I didn't stay in the corner for five minutes," he whines, pressing his face into the crook of my neck.

"You didn't leave the corner for playtime or to be bratty, though, did you?" I ask him. When he shrugs, I press further, "Do you think it would have been better if you'd had an accident and hadn't said anything?"

Finally, after a long moment of consideration, he shakes his head.

"Good boy," I tell him, and he sniffles. It doesn't surprise me. Even if he hadn't already been upset, Josh still gets emotional when he's praised. He hasn't received anywhere near enough positive affirmations during his previous Little experiences. Max and I are trying to change that.

"Now with that settled," I continue, rubbing his back to let him know I'm not about to chastise him, "want to tell me why you got so worked up over Matt picking Ranger up? I know you don't believe for a second that he was going to keep him from you. Matt's not like that."

My tone is soothing but firm. I'd like him to explain what happened, but I don't want him to think he's in trouble. He's already served his corner time and beaten himself up about not being able to complete it. And maybe that does make me a softy or a pushover, but I can't bring myself to be anything other than compassionate with my boy. He's not as tough and thick-skinned as he would like everyone to believe.

"I know," he eventually concedes, and his voice is small.

I'm still struggling to understand what changed in the hour or so since I arrived. He was all smiles and brazen humor when Max and I left him to play with the others.

I don't push him to talk, though. I wait patiently, content to hold him while he sorts out his thoughts.

It takes a few minutes, but he brings his fingers up to toy with the buttons of my shirt when he finally admits, "I felt guilty."

"About?"

"Making you and Max hide what we are to each other. What we *mean* to each other."

"Oh." I'll admit, I'm surprised by that. He seemed so sure that he wanted to keep our relationship his special secret for a while longer, just because it meant so much to him to explore it on his own while it was still so new. Kissing the top of his head, I murmur, "You should have come to us. Or just told everyone. Max and I are beyond proud that you're ours, you know."

He shakes his head, clinging even more tightly to me. "If this is gonna work, we all have to be on the same page. I'm not making those sorts of decisions without you."

I can't help smiling. It's just so typical of him to still think of others first.

My thoughts turn to the men downstairs. The group of Littles who have already astutely realized that there's something happening, but who are waiting for us to say anything. Then to the Daddies who have needled me and Max about our relationships, because they are meddling S.O.Bs, even though their intentions are good.

"Well, Ted's already worked out that there's something happening between me and Max, and Charlie was there when he asked us about it. I wasn't going to lie, but it didn't feel like the whole truth because you're integral to our relationship." I give him a squeeze as his breathing hitches. "You balance me and Max out, Josh. You get that, right?"

He snorts. "And you balance Max and me out. You calm us. Soften us. Support us." He finally pulls away from my neck. His smile is tremulous, but genuine. "And I would say that Max balances you and me out, too. Because you kind of suck at discipline outside of pre-agreed scenes, and I do like being bratty to get that attention sometimes. And he's hot when he gets all dominating."

My cock twitches at the memory of the other night and I nod, shifting at the spike of arousal. "That's an understatement."

After a beat, I redirect the conversation to where we started. "Anyway, Zephyr also cornered me to let me know that he's onto us, and I'm pretty sure Ash knows something's up, too."

Josh groans, but he's grinning now. "I guess I deserve their meddling," he says. "I've teased every single one of the guys when they met their partners...and I was the first to demand details, too." He waggles his eyebrows.

I chuckle and shake my head. "Well, then, they're being more respectful of us than you were of their relationships, aren't they?"

"Yeah..." He blows out a breath. "Can we tell them?"

I don't even have to think about my response. "Of course, honey. I'll text Max, but I know he's just as proud to be your Daddy as I am."

"What?" Charlie's voice comes from the open doorway behind me and Josh stiffens in my arms.

Giving Josh another reassuring squeeze, I turn my head calmly, not bothering to stand up. "Hi, Charlie."

He gapes at us, looking every bit a fish out of water. "You... and Josh...*and* Max?"

"Is that really so hard to imagine?" I ask in response.

"The two of you? No. But Max isn't a Daddy."

"He is now," Max interrupts, coming up behind Charlie.

We might as well invite the whole party upstairs and into this bathroom at this point.

Max takes one look at me and Josh before shouldering his way past his former partner, dropping to his knees next to us, reaching out for our boy. "Baby, what's wrong?"

Josh goes to him happily, clinging to him much the same way he was just clinging to me. "Our little spider monkey felt guilty for asking us to keep our relationship quiet," I tell Max, rubbing my hand over Josh's back.

Josh giggles. "Spider monkey?"

"Oh, I like that for a nickname," Max smirks at me. "He does like to cuddle, doesn't he?"

"Uh, hello?" Charlie cuts in, sounding bewildered. We all turn our attention back on him. He gestures vaguely over us. "When did this happen?"

He's not blowing up about it, which is a good sign. Charlie's a good man, but he can sometimes have tunnel vision and put his foot directly into his mouth, especially where people he cares about are concerned.

"It's new," Max answers him. "We kind of stumbled into it accidentally."

"But you're not…" Charlie starts, then hesitates. "I mean, the Age Play…"

"It works with Josh," Max says simply. "Emmett's got the experience that I don't, so I follow his lead for the diapers and stuff, but I find a lot of my Dom sensibilities work just as well as a Daddy when it comes to how we play together." He shrugs like it's no big deal. Maybe for him it really isn't.

God, he's just as sexy as our boy. His confidence drives me wild.

"I needed them," Josh speaks up, finally meeting his brother's gaze. It's like he draws on his inner brat, pulling up the ability to be brazen and firm. Or maybe he's fully back in his adult headspace, the strong, sharp detective instead of the sweet, needy Little. "I…I've been really lonely, Charlie. I needed a Daddy. Everyone thought I just wanted to do scenes or be a brat, but I needed more. Together, Max and Emmett give me everything I could have wished for."

It stings a tiny bit to think that I wouldn't have been enough for him on my own, but then I realize that what we said earlier was completely true: Max balances Josh and me out, too. On our own, we would have felt like something was missing, like something wasn't quite working properly. But with Max, everything feels right. Easy.

Perfect.

"Oh, Josh," Max kisses his cheek, "you're too sweet some-times, baby."

"Spider monkey," Josh corrects him with a cheeky smile. He closes his eyes and shifts his head away from Max's lips. "I won't answer to 'baby' or 'honey' anymore. I like the new nickname better."

"Well," Charlie observes with amusement, now leaning against the doorjamb with a more relaxed air about him. "It's good to see some things don't change. Good luck wrangling him. You're going to need it."

Eyes still closed, Josh gives his brother the finger.

Chapter Eighteen — Max

The whole group explodes into a cacophony of applause, cheers, and good-natured jeering once we're all back downstairs. I'm fairly certain I see Chance slide London a twenty-dollar bill, too. Josh turns pink and hides his face in Em's chest, while Ted observes the three of us and says, "Well, I understand the dynamic even better now."

"Yeah," Chance teases playfully, "Josh is such a handful he needs *two* Daddies to keep him in line."

Kade hits his bicep. "Maybe it's more like Josh just has such a big heart he needs two Daddies to share all his love with."

Matt nods in solidarity with his Little friend and snuggles into London's side. He shoots Josh a roguish grin. "Didn't you once say you wanted a harem?"

Emmett splutters and I can't help laughing. "I can totally imagine Josh saying something like that," I admit. "But Em and I are kind of possessive. He'll have to settle for a harem of two."

"Damn," Josh sighs dramatically, finally pulling back from Emmett's chest to look around at his friends. "Guess I'll have to rescind the offers I've made to those underwear models and porn stars..."

Emmett swats at Josh's ass and he yelps, but his grin is completely unrepentant.

Meanwhile, Zephyr leans into Ted's side and whispers, "Is it wrong that I want *all* the details? Like, hot damn. Look at the three of them."

I wasn't meant to hear that, obviously, but I'm standing too close to them to have missed it. I can't resist looking their way and winking.

Zephyr, the brazen fucker, winks back, not at all ashamed at having been overheard.

"Behave, tiny dancer," Ted shakes his head. Then, in a lower tone, he adds, "Josh is my best friend's younger brother. That's—"

"A classic trope for romance novels," Spencer muses from his other side. He's also completely unashamed with his eavesdropping.

"What's this about romance novels?" Tony, who writes them, pipes up.

Ted shudders dramatically and shakes his head. "Gross, Spence."

"Maybe between you and Josh, yeah," the curly-haired man agrees, "but for some, those forbidden, sneaking around vibes are hot."

Asher ushers us to take our seats at the two glass-topped outdoor tables which have been pressed together to become one extra-long one, stretching the entire length of their outdoor patio area. As a group, we barely fit, with extra chairs from the inside dining table having been brought out and squeezed in alongside the outdoor ones. But even though it's squishy, it's comfortable.

Josh sits in between me and Emmett. He is the most relaxed I have seen him in ages, save for the time we've spent holed up in Em's house as a threesome. A throuple? A menage? Whatever the label, outside of our private bubble, Josh has otherwise still been somewhat tense and guarded until now. I'm glad to see that he's finally giving himself permission to just be himself.

"So, a Daddy Dom, then?" Spencer asks me from across the table and down a couple of seats. He cocks his head and smiles warmly when I nod. "How are you finding the new element? I'm guessing the Dom stuff doesn't change."

I pretty much reiterate what I told Charlie. "The Age Play itself is new, sure, but it's fundamentally similar. All kink is based on the same principles, I guess. And being a Daddy goes well with being a Dom, I think."

"I can't believe none of us considered that Josh might need a Dom," he continues. "What with the bratting and all. We all knew he was submissive, but I guess we assumed he just liked teasing us."

"I didn't realize I needed a Dom, either," Josh directs his own response towards Spencer before I can politely suggest that Spencer minds his own business. I understand the curiosity, especially when these guys all consider themselves to be big brothers to my boy, but they should know better than anyone else not to pry into a person's kinks.

Josh keeps going. "But I don't really think it was a Dom I needed. I just needed Max. I have for a long time." He squeezes my thigh beneath the table. "And it turned out we both needed

Em and we didn't know it."

This boy is getting so many rewards when we get home. I know that's usually Em's territory, but a good Dom can reward their sub as well as mete out punishments. It's all about balance.

Oh, hey look: a sneaky metaphor!

It's not often I'm so deep and philosophical, but now that I've made that link, I can't let it go. Our relationship together is about that same balance, after all.

"Now, don't take this the wrong way," Charlie interrupts, and we turn our attention towards him. His expression is pinched with concern as he addresses me and Emmett. "You're both significantly older than Josh…"

"And, as he said earlier, he outranks me at work. These are just facts that don't actually impact our relationship." I shrug, not quite understanding the point he's trying to make. "Not to mention there's over a decade between you and Ash." I don't point out the age gaps between some of the other couples in the group, but the men in question are sitting up a little straighter, looking at Charlie with the same confusion I feel. "The only difference here is that there are two of us." I gesture between Emmett and myself.

Charlie holds his hands up in surrender. "I know, I know. I just…I…" he flounders.

"Get stupidly overprotective?" Josh offers with his usual cheeky smirk.

"Will it make you feel better to give us the 'if you hurt him, you die' speech?" Emmett asks calmly. "I understand how close your family is, Charlie. But Max and I care about Josh deeply. He was our friend first, after all."

"I can give you the speech," Chance says, rubbing his hands

together eagerly.

"To be fair," Matt nods at Chance, "I think we all could. But," he keeps going as the others start to speak up with their agreement, "like you said, you're not strangers. You probably care just as much about keeping Josh safe and happy as you do any one of us."

Maybe even more, I think, but I don't say it.

Abruptly, Ash starts to giggle. His attempts to stifle the sound only make him snort and laugh harder. "Sorry," he chuckles, flapping his hand through the air as all the attention around the table shifts to him, "I was just thinking about how Marie's gonna react."

Josh and Charlie let out nearly identical groans and cover their faces with their hands.

"Do I have to tell Mom?" Josh whines. "Can't we, I don't know, run away and live in the Caribbean under assumed names for the rest of our lives?"

"I do like tropical fruit," I offer, and Emmett reaches around behind Josh to cuff the back of my head lightly.

"Come on, your mother's not that bad, is she?" Emmett asks cajolingly.

The grimaces and grumbles around the table suggest otherwise. I laugh and shake my head. "She's intense," I answer on Josh's behalf. "Harmless, but not always the most PC or, uh, considerate of others' feelings?" I look towards Charlie apologetically. "Sorry, man."

He just sighs. "It's not like anything you just said was a lie."

"But she really does love her kids and want them all to be happy. Even if sometimes her idea of what should make them happy differs to what does," Ash says, patting his husband's back consolingly. He looks around the table and adds, "She's been pestering us to have kids. She's given up hope that Maze will and we're the next in line."

"Good luck with that," Spencer shudders.

"But, hey, telling Mom that you're in a polyamorous relationship might get her off our backs for a while," Charlie brightens as he looks at Josh. "Oh, *please* let me be there when you tell her. Please? I'll bring popcorn."

"Em's only a few years younger than your mom, isn't he?" Chance offers, his smirk telling me that he knows exactly what he's doing.

"Try a decade," Josh answers him, his eyes narrowed in warning. "And I'm more concerned that, once the shock wears off, she'll smother them to death rather than freak out about their age."

I laugh and can't help the dry words that come out of my mouth. "How terrifying. Your mother's going to want to love us to death. What a horrible person."

Setting his cutlery down on his plate, Josh nudges my bicep with his. "You won't be sounding so cocky when she's nagging you about every ridiculous thing under the sun."

"Or when she's sending you links to online articles about BDSM or 'keeping your love life fresh,'" Ash shudders. "Or, worse, calling to talk at me for forty-five minutes about her belief that being Little means I'll have a 'special bond' with our fictional kids."

Beside him, Charlie grimaces again. He abandons his own meal in preference of leaning over to rub his hand over his husband's back. "Sorry, little lamb. I've asked her to back off."

Ash shakes his head, his mop of curls flying about wildly with the motion. "It's fine, really. I love your mom, you know that."

"Yeah, but you'd love her more if she wasn't a raving lunatic," Josh acknowledges with empathy. "We feel the same." He gestures towards Charlie, encompassing him in the 'we' part of that confession.

Charlie nods, and then his expression turns serious again as he takes in his little brother. "I'm sorry I didn't force the issue about you being more than just a scene player, Josh. This was something you needed and I was just waiting for you to say something. That was wrong of me."

Under his breath, Emmett says something that sounds suspiciously like 'I told you so', but Josh and I are the only ones to notice. From the corner of my eye, I watch Josh nudge Em the same way he nudged me only a minute or so ago. Then he shakes his head and smiles back at Charlie. "I probably would have been a brat about it if you had pushed me."

Chance snorts, but Charlie just sighs. "Even so, as a caregiver, I should have known better."

"We all should have," Ted acknowledges.

"Yeah, and we've also seen what happens when people are pushed to talk about things they're not ready." Zephyr pipes up from beside his Daddy, playing devil's advocate. "It was lose/lose. This way, you kept the peace…and Josh found his Daddies."

"Well, there is that," Charlie agrees, and the residual tension from his apology seems to completely evaporate. But even if Josh brushed his brother's words off, I think he needed to hear them.

I scoop up some potato salad and let the conversation continue to flow on around me. To be honest, I hadn't given much thought as to how our relationship might be received once it became open knowledge. I knew that this group of

kink-friendly guys and girls wouldn't even bat an eye, but...
telling Josh's parents? Telling my mom? What about work? At
some point, Josh and I will have to disclose our relationship
to each other, but I'm uncomfortable leaving Emmett out of
the equation.

Polyamorous relationships still aren't exactly considered
socially acceptable. Outside of The Grove or The Center,
we're guaranteed to get a few questioning looks or scathing
comments when we go out together. We'll likely never be
able to legally commit to each other as a threesome. And
Josh *is* substantially younger than me or Max. What if,
unlike his brother and sister, he does want kids? Pretty sure
being a throuple would not go down well with any adoption
agencies...

My thoughts screech to a halt.

We have officially been together for a week. A single week.
Seven days. Can you tell me why my thoughts have already
leapt into 'how could we make having a family work?'? Can
you? Because I sure as hell don't know. I don't even know
if that's something either one of my men would want, but if
they did, I'd bend over backwards to make it happen.

And there I go again.

It's a far cry from the man I was even a week and a half ago,
I know that, too. The man who was so overwhelmed by guilt
for Charlie's accident, and for the way things had gone with
Josh that same night. That's not to say I don't still feel pangs
of it echoing inside me every so often. Even now, after talking
it out with Josh and being assured that I have nothing to feel
guilty for, I still can't help but feel that if I had done things
differently Charlie might still be a cop.

But then Josh might never have come home with me. Never

given me a taste of being his Daddy. Never set me on a course of pining to recapture those feelings. To explore the chemistry between us.

Not to mention the fact that, without that night spent looking after Josh, I never would have followed him to Emmett's the week before last. I never would have experienced any of what we've since shared together.

And, if not for The Little Community Center, Emmett might never have crossed our paths at all.

So, while I still have moments where I question my past actions, I'm slowly making peace with them. Silver linings and all that.

Not that any of this accounts for how deeply serious my feelings have gotten in such a short amount of time. I'm thinking about hypothetical futures that I have no business considering after only a week. Kids. Pets. White picket fences. These concepts should freak me out, not comfort me, right?

Instead, I find myself wanting to hurry things along. Suddenly, I want to tell Josh's family about our relationship. I want to introduce my mother to my partners: *plural*. I want to hold both Josh and Emmett's hands as I take them out on dates. Kiss them both in public. Plan a future together.

And none of that freaks me out.

I've gone from being a happy bi bachelor, content with casual hookups and scenes at The Grove, to wanting to cement a life with two partners within a week and a half. Am I the only one feeling this way? Is it normal to fall so hard and fast?

"Hey," Emmett's voice in my ear, deep and calming, makes me jump. I look up to find that he's switched seats with Josh at some point, and Josh is now deep in conversation with Kade on Emmett's other side. "Are you okay?"

Chapter Eighteen — Max

I feel a flutter in my belly that has nothing to do with the fact that I ate *way* too much over dinner, and I smile at my lover. "Yeah," I answer, leaning in to accept a quick kiss to my lips. "I am. Just…thinking."

His dark eyes are assessing, but he nods and nuzzles my cheek with his, and my heart thumps hard in my chest.

Whether it's normal or not, I've fallen hard for my men. It's too soon to put the words out there, and I would never pressure either of them to return the feelings bubbling up inside me, but I can only hope that they will eventually follow suit.

Chapter Nineteen – Josh

When the bullet grazed me, I never would have imagined that I'd resent returning to work. If you'd told me that I would have one of the best weeks of my life away from the precinct, I would have laughed at you. Of course, before shit went down, work was a distraction from my loneliness. I enjoyed the long hours because they gave me a purpose I was otherwise lacking.

Sure, I had my friends and family, but they've all got their own lives. My time spent with them was always enjoyable, but I was only ever a temporary entertainment for them. Even for Charlie, despite him being my brother and one of my closest friends.

Then I got shot and everything changed.

Unlike for Charlie, my shooting only seemed to change life in positive ways.

For one, my injury was minor. It was nowhere near career ending and I recovered within a couple of days.

For another, it forced me to face my loneliness and my

embarrassment over my other issues head on.

And finally —and most importantly— it led me to my men. My Daddies.

While I really don't recommend taking a bullet to the arm to resolve your life issues, this time it worked out for me.

Charlie always says I was born under a lucky star. Maybe he's right.

But now that I've gone back to work, I'm not as into it as I used to be. Now, I find myself checking my watch and wondering what Em or Max are up to. I'm watching the clock, counting down the hours until I can see one —or both— of them again. When we can go out on a low-key date, or have some Daddy/boy time at Em's place, or fuck like bunnies late into the night.

I've barely spent any time in my own apartment since we started dating. The last time I did, I slept like shit and I had to strip the sheets when I woke up because I forgot to diaper myself before I went to bed. I'd cried on the phone to Emmett about that. It wasn't my proudest moment, but he knew all the right things to say to calm me down and minimize my embarrassment, even though nobody would have known if I hadn't told him.

I know that as the honeymoon period of the new relationship fades, I'll get re-invested in my job again, but right now it's hard to imagine that happening. I don't want to be at work. I want to be at Em's house, a place I'm starting to think of as home, snuggled up on the couch between my two boyfriends.

Not even the case Dana and I are working at the moment can hold my attention for long, and that's saying something. We're closing in on a new street gang in the area, linked to our body in a barrel case, and also to the guy who decided pulling his gun on me was a good idea. It's the kind of case I dreamed about taking on when I was just starting at the academy, but right now it just feels like it's standing in between me and time with my Daddies.

It's only been two weeks since I came back to work, but every day feels like a lifetime. Plus, the fact that Max and I are on opposite shifts means I really only get to see him once a week. Twice if I'm lucky. We do catch each other for a few minutes as our shifts crossover, but with the hustle and bustle of the station around us, we can't exactly embrace or kiss the way I want to.

So, it's not exactly a surprise that I'm feeling moody now that the second week is coming to a close. Even though I've had time in my Little headspace, there's a nervous energy building beneath my skin. After that week spent deeply indulging my need for regression, the snippets I've had since have not been enough for me.

Unfortunately, the way I've dealt with this feeling in the past is to misbehave.

And, as it turns out, ingrained habits and coping mechanisms are difficult to change.

"Joshua," Daddy Em says in a firm tone that I have rarely heard directed my way, "I'm asking you once more to pick up your blocks so we can clean up for dinner."

I am sitting in the middle of the living room with blocks scattered around me like a hurricane has come through here. And, technically, it did in the form of Hurricane Josh. I'd built a tower and when I couldn't find the yellow triangular piece I'd planned to put at the top, I'd knocked the whole thing down with an epic *crash*. Now I'm refusing to pick the pieces up. Why? Because being petulant and combative feels good.

I jut my chin. "No."

Emmett hasn't really had to see me bratty before. I've been cheeky, but not purposefully defiant for him. He stares me down in a way that, if I didn't know him so well, would be intimidating given his size.

"I'm going to count down from five," he says, collected but unimpressed, "and if you still haven't made a move to clean up, you're going to be writing lines."

I roll my eyes. "Lines? Really?"

"And the next time we fuck, you're wearing a cage."

My cock twitches at that, even as I gasp, "You wouldn't."

"Question me again, and I'll make you sit still on my cock for fifteen minutes."

We all know I struggle with slow lovemaking. I'm all about instant gratification. Cock warming as a concept makes me squirm because I *need* to move. I *need* to get off. Fifteen minutes sounds torturous.

But, because I'm feeling brave in my brattiness, I just smirk at him. "Bring it, Daddy."

* * *

I. Regret. Everything.

When Max comes home three hours later, I'm pretty sure he's not expecting to find me sitting on Emmett's cock, wearing a metal cage around my own, desperate tears slowly leaking down my cheeks. But that's what he stumbles upon.

Over the sound of the TV playing, I hear the front door open and shut. I hear the metallic jangle of Max's keys landing in the bowl on the side table in the foyer. I hear his bag hit the floor and his voice as he calls out, "Honeys, I'm home!"

I hear his footsteps as he heads our way, and usually I would smile at the way he starts describing the random things that happened to him while he patrolled the city, but I'm feeling very sorry for myself right now.

Emmett followed through on his punishments, and every time I've squirmed on his lap, he's added an extra minute to my penance. I feel like I should be aching hard and leaking, but the cage around my cock prevents that. My balls feel heavy and desperate for release, and I also feel overwhelmingly guilty for pushing my sweet, pushover of a Daddy into taking this kind of action.

(Don't get me wrong: later, I'm going to look back and find this insanely hot.)

Max rounds the couch, still chattering about his day, and he comes to an abrupt halt when he finally registers us. I look away as his eyes find Em's. "What's going on here?"

I whimper as Emmett shifts to give Max a space to sit beside us. His huge cock nudges my gland and it's a feeling of almost painful bliss which rockets through me, but I've also been instructed not to speak.

Despite my teasing to the contrary, Emmett is actually damn good at doling out punishments when he has to.

So much for my pushover Daddy.

Maybe he's been taking lessons from Max.

"Joshua is learning that I don't make idle threats," Em says calmly, leaning over to give Max a kiss. I don't turn around to watch them like I normally would, but I hear the familiar soft, sweet sounds they make as their lips meet.

"Oh," Max says, sounding completely unsurprised. "Was our boy a bit bratty tonight?"

"He was," Emmett answers, smoothing a hand down my

back. My breathing hitches and I feel a pang of guilt for being a naughty boy. Em instructs, "Tell Daddy Max why you're being punished."

Pressing my lips tightly together, I shake my head. Even now, even as I'm being disciplined, I'm still pushing boundaries.

"Josh," Daddy Em says in warning. "I *can* sit here like this for hours."

I whimper a little at that. The ultimate submission of wearing a chastity cage while my ass warms his massive cock is arousing me in ways I can't articulate. The torture of not being able to orgasm is the harshest punishment I've ever been dealt. I don't think I can handle more than another few minutes of this. I certainly won't survive hours. My cock tries to plump up and, thanks to the cage, fails at the attempt. It's frustrating and even a bit painful.

Pouting, I finally do as I'm told, though I keep my sullen gaze directed towards the floor. "I smashed my block tower," I admit. The silence after my words is expectant, and I should have known Max would be waiting for the whole story. I sigh. "Then I wouldn't pick up the mess. And I wouldn't clean up for dinner." I swallow. "And I sassed Daddy Em…and when he told me to write lines, I wrote 'Daddy Em is a meanie' instead."

"Good boy," Emmett's voice is a low purr, his warm palm soothing on my skin. "Thank you for being honest, Joshie."

If I thought the punishment was arousing, the praise —even while I'm still suffering the consequences of my poor behavior— sends a wave of pure pleasure through me, warming me from the base of my belly and through my extremities. I tremble with it, and more tears leak from my eyes and slide down my cheeks. I make no effort to wipe them away.

Max moves around until he's directly in front of me and he squats, forcing me to look at him. "You're taking Daddy Em's punishment so well, monkey." He looks over my shoulder. "How long does he have left?"

"Five minutes," Emmett answers.

I close my eyes and try not to whine. I need him to move inside me. I need this cage off. I need to come.

"You're not going to get to come, Josh," Max tells me as though he's read my mind. "That's a reward. Bratty boys don't get rewards."

The whine I'd been holding back tears its way out of my throat before I can stop it. "Please," I beg, unable to stop myself. "Please, Daddies. I'll be good. I'll be a good boy."

"I know you'll be a good boy after this," Max agrees consolingly, "but that's not going to earn you an orgasm from your punishment."

I want to cry out that it's not fair, but I know better than to think that will end well for me.

"In fact," Max muses, "I think we'll keep you caged after your time warming Em's cock is up, hmm?"

I bite my tongue to prevent the complaint from slipping past my lips.

Max smirks like he knows what I'm thinking anyway. "That's it, good boy." He checks his watch, then looks back up at Emmett. "Do I get to suck you off when you're done teaching our boy his lesson?"

The cock inside me twitches. I fucking feel it. It's the most delicious torture I have ever felt.

How can I simultaneously love this and hate this so intensely?

I'm adding 'orgasm denial' to the list of punishments I never want to repeat.

Except it feels amazing to be punished like this.

Ugh.

"I was thinking we could jerk off for our boy. Make him watch while he's still caged," Emmett adds to the torture, speaking as casually as one might about what to order for dinner. "Unless you have a better idea?"

In front of me, Max's eyes take on a devilish gleam. He pushes to his feet and starts tugging off his clothes, tossing them onto the armchair in a haphazard —but contained— pile.

I distract myself from the full, uncomfortable feeling of Em's cock inside me by focusing on the flex of Max's perfectly toned ass as he bends over and tugs off his shoes, socks, and pants. When he turns back around, his cock is hard, the tip flushed a deep pink.

I lick my lips instinctively.

"What do you say, Em?" Max asks, "Is he allowed to put his pretty lips on my cock?"

I hold as still as I can, swallowing roughly as I wait for Daddy Em's verdict. He groans and his hips finally —fucking *finally*— move, rocking his cock down and then back up into my ass, stimulating my prostate all over again.

I want to wail against the sensation of desperately wanting to get hard but being unable to.

His raw demand drives me further over the edge of desperation. "Suck Daddy Max's cock, Josh. Suck him while I fuck you nice and slowly."

Max steps in front of me and I open wide as instructed. There's no hesitance in his action, no slow, romantic tease. He sinks his cock into my waiting mouth without preamble, making me gag with how far he pushes in, reaching the back of my throat before I'm ready. But it feels so good to suck him, messy as it is with the saliva and tears dripping down my face. He tastes salty and delicious, the scent of his skin musky and strong.

Max leans over me to kiss Emmett, and the sounds they make are so damn erotic. Little moans and growls that make me want to pull off Max's cock so I can look up and watch them.

But I don't do that. I don't want to risk not being allowed to come at all tonight. Instead I suck harder, adding my slurping to the porny soundtrack we are creating together.

Emmett continues to rock his hips in slow, deep movements. He doesn't have a lot of room to slip out, but he grinds on every thrust back up into me and I don't even realize that I'm crying out around Max's dick until he pulls out from my mouth and the sounds reach my own ears.

"Please," I start sobbing once I can speak uninhibited, "please take the cage off. Please. I'm sorry I was bratty. I'm sorry. I'm sorry."

The release of emotion is a relief all of its own. It's a head rush as the tension of my previous foul mood cracks and breaks. I'm barely aware of Max helping to lift me up while Emmett carefully slips out of me and disposes of the condom in a wad of tissues, or of the way they cuddle me between them while I ride out the wave of feelings. The boneless, relaxed feeling that follows as the tears and sobs subside is magical. My head feels all light and floaty. It's amazing.

It's so amazing that I even forget about the chastity cage and my desperate desire to get hard and come with my men.

"That's it, monkey," Emmett croons, "Let it all out. We've

got you."

"You haven't come yet," I realize, frowning and trying to look from one to the other. My eyelids feel heavy, even while my head feels so light.

"You're more important," Max insists softly.

That warmth from before bubbles up inside me again. I love how much they care about me, these Daddies of mine.

Pushing off the couch, I sink to my knees on the floor in front of them, in between both men. I reach for their cocks and take one in each hand, stroking in tandem.

"I want you both to come," I tell them. "I want you to paint me with it. Mark me as yours."

"Oh, fuck, Josh," Max moans, his cock slicking up with precum as I stroke, the pearly liquid dribbling down from the head and onto his shaft, aided by the movement of my hand.

"Then after you do that," I continue as though he didn't speak, "you can give me a bath, and dress me, and feed me dinner like I know you both want to."

Both my Daddies *love* giving aftercare, and once this high fades and the exhaustion of my emotional release hits me, I'm going to need it.

Emmett's cock is growing impossibly harder beneath my palm. He's rocking his hips into my fist, and I'm pretty sure he's okay with my plan.

"You're fucking perfect, Josh," Max says, taking the lead for both of them. As he pushes to his feet with Emmett doing the same at his side, his hand reaches out towards me. He cards his fingers through my hair and then tugs at the short strands while I twist my wrist and squeeze his leaking dick on every upstroke.

Em's hand lands on top of Max's, and they twine their fingers together, cupping the back of my head to hold me in place.

It's hot to watch both my men come undone at my hand on any given occasion, but tonight feels even more intense than usual. Maybe it's the cage I'm still wearing, the knowledge that they literally control my cock right now, or the lingering floaty, fuzzy feelings from being punished and used so beautifully. Maybe it's the fact that they're both watching me pleasure them, neither giving in to their usual urges to close their eyes or toss their heads back in bliss. Maybe it's the fact that they're watching me get them both off at once, and I'm still in a submissive position on the floor in front of them. Maybe it's the fact that I'm falling head over heels in love with them and I know it's written all over my face just as surely as their cum will be in a few minutes' time.

Maybe it's all of the above.

Emmett's breathing turns ragged first, his hips losing rhythm before the first spurts of his warm, creamy release land on my cheeks and forehead.

"Fuck," Max draws out the word, his pupils so dilated that his eyes almost look black, "that's the hottest thing I've ever seen."

Emmett's still going, emptying his balls over my face with a guttural groan.

"Come on, Daddy Maxxie," I urge, "come all over me. I need it. I need you to —oh, God, *yes*."

He lets out a shout as his orgasm hits, but he watches as every rope of his cum splashes over me. I feel like a Jackson Pollock painting: speckled and striped, chaotic and beautiful in their eyes. At least, that's what I interpret from the matching dazed but softly awed looks on their handsome faces.

"I think," Emmett says once he regains the ability to put words together, "you've earned the right to have the cage removed."

Max nods and pets my hair gently. I lean into the affectionate touch, allowing my eyes to flutter shut. "You're a good boy, Joshie. A very, very good boy."

Those are probably the most beautiful words he could have said.

Well, except for the three I'm too afraid to say myself, anyway.

It's too soon, I tell myself.

It doesn't stop me from thinking them anyway. As my Daddies scoop me up from the floor and lead me through the house for my promised aftercare, they're on repeat in my head.

I love you, I think as they bathe me.

I love you, I think as they diaper me and hand me my bear.

I love you, I think as they take turns feeding me my dinner.

"I love you," I murmur as I drift off, snuggled between them in bed.

I'm asleep before I can realize I said the words aloud...or before I can hear either of them say it back.

Chapter Twenty – Emmett

My heart thunders in my chest as Josh's words, murmured so sweetly as he succumbed to sleep, circle in my thoughts.

"I love you," he'd said.

It's like he put voice to the feelings I've been trying to hide for weeks now. I was so afraid that I would scare him off. That I would scare Max off.

I'm usually so analytical. So methodical. So *not* impulsive or easily swayed by emotion.

But being with Josh and Max has been a whirlwind of nothing but impulsive decisions and emotions…and it has been *so good.*

I haven't once regretted not weighing the pros and cons. I haven't felt the need to do risk assessments or flow charts about potential pitfalls or consequences to my actions. I haven't worried that being impetuous was going to bite me in the ass. I've trusted my gut for the first time in my life and, in doing so, I've somehow found everything I ever wanted out of life and then some.

When Josh was bratty earlier tonight, I was practically leaping for joy on the inside.

See, in the weeks since we've been together, my boy has been cheeky but never bratty. It was almost as if he'd held it back, hadn't completely trusted me and Max to stick by him through one of his turns.

Then tonight, he let his guard down. It wasn't an act: he was bratting because he needed the emotional outlet. And he finally felt comfortable enough to let go and let his Daddies help him through it.

I honestly thought I'd made the wrong call with the punishments I'd chosen. I'd gone with gut instinct, once again ignoring my analytical side, and he had been far more stubborn than I had anticipated. I'd thought that maybe I should have texted Max for his advice first because he's the experienced Dom, even if my psych degree bolstered my confidence in knowing what would get under Josh's skin the deepest. And then my beautiful, beautiful boy finally cracked.

I should have realized that he needed both me and Max before he felt unconsciously ready to let go.

Thankfully, we stumbled into that by accident. Watching our boy fully accept his punishment and release his guilt, pain, and frustration was heartbreaking and stunning to watch. He was so at peace afterwards that I know we did the right thing.

And then he was brave enough —or should that be unfiltered enough?— to be the first to say the words I've been wanting to shout for the past few weeks.

Catching Max's stunned, but equally love-struck expression in the dim lighting of my bedroom, I feel my heart squeeze all over again. Still, I find my voice and quietly say; "I love you both, too, you know."

Max has one arm tucked under the pillow beneath Josh's head, running parallel to my own so we can snuggle on our sides facing each other with our boy on his back between us. He reaches over the top of Josh with his free hand, finding mine and gripping it tightly.

"Me too," he confesses in a whisper that still seems to echo in the otherwise still night air. "I love you both, too. So much, Em." He pauses, then adds, "I think I have since that first night. Or at least I started falling then."

I can't contain my answering smile. "Yeah," I agree, "me too."

Max's eyes cut to Josh and he shakes his head ruefully. "I highly doubt he's going to remember saying it."

"Or he'll freak out," I offer as an alternative. "Either way, the genie's not going back in the bottle, and I can't wait to say it back to him."

"Mmm," Max's eyes are also closing now. "I can't wait to show him."

I drift off imagining all the ways we can reassure Josh that our feelings really are mutual and genuine.

* * *

I wake up alone in bed in the morning. Bright sunlight streams in from the window along the side of the room, warming the sheets and my skin. I roll over to grab my phone from the bedside table and feel my eyes widen at the late hour.

Nine o'clock?

Even though it's a weekend, I never sleep in. Seeing the number nine on my screen is more effective than a double shot of caffeine. I'm immediately alert and launching myself from the bed, heading into the bathroom to perform my morning ablutions before going off in search of my men.

I find them in the kitchen – Josh seated at the kitchen table with Ranger beside him, Max puttering around fixing breakfast. My stomach grumbles as the scent of bacon and eggs registers in my brain.

"Morning," Max greets me as I approach, tilting his head for a kiss.

I press my lips to his and wind my arm around his waist, looking over his shoulder into the pan of delicious breakfast goodness. "Good morning," I reply, my voice still gravelly with sleep. "This looks and smells amazing, babe. Can I help?" I'm usually the designated cook among the three of us, but Max has mastered the art of breakfast now.

"Make the coffee?" he suggests.

"On it." I wink at Josh who is tapping away at his phone screen at the table. "Good morning, monkey. Are you feeling better today?"

His cheeks pink up, but he nods. "I needed that yesterday," he says. "I know I should have warned you, or just asked for a scene…"

I shake my head as I place three mugs down on the counter. "We agreed we'd treat this as a lifestyle, not scene play. And, if I'm honest? I really enjoyed you being a brat for me, Josh. You put a lot of trust in us to take care of you and make it better, and that meant a lot."

Josh's cheeks turn a deeper pink and I let him ruminate on my words as I get the pot of coffee ready for pouring. By the time I'm sliding three steaming mugs onto the table, Max is bringing the plates of food over as well.

"Mmm," Josh moans around a mouthful of perfectly fluffy

scrambled eggs. "So good."

I have to agree. "I don't understand how you can completely butcher any other meal, but you can make a breakfast good enough to put any old-school diner to shame," I tease Max.

He shrugs and takes a bite of his buttered toast. "It's a talent, I guess."

"So, back to last night," I steer the conversation back to earlier, "you said something as you fell asleep. Do you remember?"

Josh pushes his fork through the remains of his eggs, not looking up at us. Still, he nods. "Yeah."

The single word sounds so uncertain. I can't have that.

"You fell asleep before we could reply," I keep my tone light and teasing. It's enough to stir his curiosity, at least, because he finally lifts his head to meet my gaze and then Max's.

"We love you, too, Josh," Max tells him simply. "And each other." He pauses, then meaningfully repeats, "I love you. Both of you."

Josh blinks. "Really?" his eyes shift to meet mine again, looking for confirmation. "It's not too soon? Or too much?"

"Really," I nod and reach for his hand, squeezing it as I try to impart all the warmth and genuine emotion that I can. "It turns out we've all been falling hard and fast. You were just the first to put words to it." Determined to chase away the lingering insecurity in his expression, I also repeat, "I love you both, Josh. You and Max."

Josh's handsome face breaks open into a devastatingly bright smile. "I love you both, too."

Hearing him make the declaration all soft and sleep addled was sweet, but it's even better to hear him say the words so confidently this morning. I lean in to kiss him, then he turns to repeat the action with Max on his other side, and then he pushes his chair back, scooting it around until he's positioned directly at the corner of the table, so we can all indulge in an uncoordinated, but no less enjoyable, three way kiss.

I lose myself in the moment. In the spicy scent of Max's cologne and the complimentary soft musk of Josh's. In the firm press of lips and the slide of tongues that taste of coffee and bacon and, in Josh's case, syrup. It's a little messy, but this is easily one of my favorite methods of expressing our feelings for each other.

We press our foreheads together and breathe as the kiss comes to an end, none of us seemingly willing to break the spell that has fallen over us. We're in a bubble of perfection where the outside world doesn't exist, and it is wonderful.

Naturally, one of us has to interrupt the moment eventually, and the honor goes to Josh, who bounces in his seat and asks, "So, does this mean I can introduce you to my parents now?"

* * *

Josh finds great enjoyment in telling the group chat about our agreement to meet his family as his partners. I watch as he types out a message at rapid fire speed, his thumbs flying over the screen of his phone. My phone pings and I see the GIF before I read the text.

It's a headstone that reads 'R.I.P' in big, bold letters.

Before I can say anything, either in person or in the chat, Chance pipes up.

Chance: Oh, dudes, please film Josh's mom's reaction. Please. I'm begging you.

Ted: Ignore him, @Max & @Emmett. The Walkers are lovely.

Charlie chooses that moment to send a GIF of a sailor saluting. He follows it up with *'It was nice knowing you both.'*

Beside me, Josh cackles.

Max rolls his eyes and swats at Josh's butt in warning. "Are you trying to earn another punishment, monkey?"

Josh shakes his head in denial, but his eyes are twinkling with an energy that spells trouble. He lifts his phone up and starts typing again.

When my phone pings again, it's with Josh's reaction.

Josh: I'll make sure I have popcorn! He's included a GIF of someone munching the aforementioned snack avidly.

Chance: I have no idea how your Daddies put up with you

Chance's words are accompanied by a playful emoji with its tongue sticking out.

Josh: They love me. They told me so. So there!

Max snorts. "Wait for it…" He says aloud.

Sure enough, a barrage of messages erupt in the chat, ranging from Ted's "I knew it!" to Ash and Zephyr's matching "Awww"s.

Josh's phone also rings, and he grins as he answers it. "Hey, Matty."

Max and I watch as he wanders out of the room, happily telling his best friend about our mutual declarations of love. It's cute, and I'm once again filled with warmth at his excitement and happiness over the development of our relationship.

"You realize we're not going to hear the end of this for days, right?" Max asks me in amusement.

I nod. "Yeah, but that means they accept us and our relationship, so I'm happy to suffer the teasing."

Max smirks. "You're *such* a softy."

"Not all of me is soft," I banter back, waggling my eyebrows suggestively.

"Oh, I know. And, I've gotta tell you, walking in on you punishing Josh the way you did last night was hot, Em. Using that big cock of yours so creatively…I'm going to be hard for weeks just thinking about it."

It only takes a couple of strides for me to close the space between us, backing him up against the kitchen counter with my hands on his narrow waist. "Well now, I might know a couple of guys who can help you out with that."

"Oh, I'm counting on it."

Chapter Twenty-One — Max

I'm not expecting to see quite so many cars when we pull up outside Josh's parents' house. Their double driveway is full, meaning we have to park on the street.

At least that will make for an easier getaway, I muse, wondering what we're actually walking into.

Because of our conflicting work schedules, it has taken a few weeks for Josh to actually organize this dinner. All joking aside, a part of me is nervous that his parents will take issue with some part of our relationship, be it our ages, the fact that there are two of us, or the fact that Josh calls us both Daddy. Any one of those factors would understandably concern most parents, even if they are cool with Ash and Charlie's dynamic.

I've met Marie and Grant before. On multiple occasions, actually. They are nice people, and they love their kids dearly. It's that last bit that causes me concern. What if they do take issue with me and Em professing to love their middle son? What if the three of us being together causes problems for Josh?

He's only now really getting back into the swing of things at work. He's only now fully embracing his Little side and his kink. He's only now learning not to be embarrassed when he wakes up needing to be changed. He's only now truly coming out of his shell and being himself instead of the person he thinks others expect him to be.

His parents' potential negative reaction could set all of that back.

For all that Josh pretends that his mother is an annoyance, I know he adores her. It will crush him if she freaks out about this new part of his life, one that makes him so happy. And it will crush me and Emmett if we have to step aside so as not to disrupt his family.

"Oh, look who's being the pessimist again," Emmett murmurs into my ear and I turn to glower at him. He rolls his eyes. "Do I need to lecture you like I did the night we met? Because I can."

"We'd met before then," I argue, because it's still easier to try to distract him than to face my issues.

Emmett rolls his beautiful dark eyes and bends his big body to bump his bicep against mine. "I didn't *really* meet you until that night at The Grove. Before that, you were just Charlie's hot cop friend."

I smirk. "Oh, so you *did* think I was hot before that night, then?"

"I had eyes, didn't I?" he sasses me right back. "And don't think I'm not aware of your tactics here. You're avoiding the question."

"Well, technically the question was if I wanted another lecture. I do not."

We've made our way out of the car and are walking up the

cobbled path that leads to the front door of the large, brick family home. I've only been here a couple of times before, but it has always struck me as welcoming.

The brick is a dark reddish brown, the accents all tan colored. From memory, the inside of the home is kind of dated, with blue carpets and yellow walls. There's a shabby-chic side table running the length of the wall in the entryway, and on it sits a large glass vase full of seashells. The coastal vibe is strong for a home in a land-locked city. Or, at least it was the last time I was here, which was over six years ago.

Josh is leading the way in front of us, oblivious to our conversation, not that we're trying to hide it. He's just excited to properly introduce us as his lovers —boyfriends?— to his family.

Emmett scoffs. "You were wearing that same 'I'm not good enough' brooding look you had on when we brought Josh home that first night. Are you really that afraid this is going to go badly?"

"No. Yes. I don't know." I sigh. "I just can't help thinking about all the issues they could have with us. From our ages, or the fact that there are two of us, or the fact that I'm a cop and I work with Josh…" I shake my head. "I've never wanted a partner's parents to like me this badly before, and I'm getting in my head about it."

Em's big palm lands on the small of my back, a gesture of solidarity and support. "And that's all this is," he says as we come to a stop behind our boy, who is pressing the doorbell with a big smile on his bearded face. "You want this so badly you're second-guessing yourself."

"Wait, what?" Josh turns around, frowning, but the door opens before we can summarize the conversation.

"Joshie!" His mother cries, as though they don't speak at least once a fortnight. She's short and round, with dark curly hair and Josh's brown eyes. She throws her arms around him and smooshes her face into his chest. "You're late."

Josh scoffs and checks his watch. "By, like, two minutes. Jesus, Mom."

"Five," she sniffs, affronted. "And you know anything later than five minutes early is late."

Before he can continue to argue with her, she peers around him and up at me and Emmett. She practically has to lean backwards to take him all in, which is kind of hilarious.

"And you must be Josh's friend, Emmett. I'm Marie." She waves off Emmett's proffered hand and launches towards him for a hug. "All of my babies' friends are welcome here. You're family now."

The top of her head barely reaches the bottom of Em's pectorals, and I have to press my lips together to prevent myself from laughing at the juxtaposition. Then she looks back at me, abandoning one embrace for another.

"It's been too long, Max," she declares, then just as suddenly as she grabbed me, pulls away and starts ushering us through the house. "When was the last time we saw you? The wedding?"

"Yeah, Ash and Charlie's wedding," I confirm. I'd spent a good portion of the reception trying to avoid her. She either wanted to dance or was determined to set me up with any other single guests she had come across, which was awkward as it was a very intimate gathering and I knew most of the attendees.

Looping her arm through mine, she says, "You'll have to fill me in on *everything*." She casts a furtive glance over her shoulder in Em's direction before arching her eyebrow at me. "Is there anyone *special* in your life?"

I can answer that question honestly, at least. "Yeah, there is."

"Oooh," she squeals and tugs my elbow tightly against her in her excitement. "You even *sound* besotted. Tell me all about them, the lucky guy or girl."

"Mom," Josh intervenes. "Leave Max alone right now. Is everyone here?"

That reminds me of the sheer number of cars in the driveway and lining the street. "Who is everyone?"

"Charlie and Asher, of course. Maisy and Ed. Theodore and his lovely young partner...though I do forget the darling's name. It's something a little left of center."

"Zephyr," Emmett and I supply in unison.

"Oh, yes, that's it. Zephyr." Marie nods, then continues, "Axel's here, naturally, and he's invited his girlfriend from college. Dani. She's quite shy." She cocks her head and squints her eyes. "And that should be everyone."

That's quite an audience, I muse, but I keep those thoughts to myself. Like Emmett said, my nerves are purely based on how badly I want this to go well.

We finally reach the large dining space which opens up via folding glass doors to the patio outside. With such a large number of people, Josh's parents have opened the doors and pushed the outdoor dining table together with the indoor dining table, creating one long shared table that crosses over both spaces.

Unsurprisingly, Marie has gone all out: the tables are set with white linen tablecloths and brightly colored linen napkins. Porcelain plates and gleaming silver cutlery. Wine glasses, and vases filled with bouquets of bright flowers I couldn't begin to tell you the names of. It's much fancier and more formal than any of the get-togethers Charlie has hosted.

All the people she listed are seated around the table, as is her husband, Grant. He's an older, slightly shorter version of Charlie and Josh. Charlie's words from a couple of weeks ago ring in my ears, reminding me that me and Emmett are closer in age to Grant than we are to Josh, but I remind myself that age is just a number. Josh loves us and we love him.

I just hope they see it the same way.

Everyone greets us warmly, with the guys from our social circle getting up to hug us and exchange kisses on the cheek. Ted gives my biceps a squeeze, and he murmurs, "They already love you, this won't change that," into my ear before he pulls back to clap Emmett on the back. Emmett and I find ourselves seated on either side of our boy, who quickly starts up a conversation with his younger brother across the table from him.

Axel looks nothing like Charlie or Josh. He's short and stout like their mother, with the same dark, curly hair and rounded face. He's in his early twenties, but I've known him since his mid-teens. It's hard not to think of him as a kid, even though he's well and truly an adult now. His girlfriend is sitting beside him, opposite Em, and she is the only person here I've not met before. She's cute. Shorter than Axel, with jet black hair cut into a bob framing her heart shaped face and eyes as dark as Emmett's. I smile across the table at her and she returns the gesture, though her smile seems tight and anxious. Marie did say she was shy, though, so it's likely she's feeling overwhelmed by the large gathering. I can't exactly blame her: for all of my usual confidence, my nerves are getting to me today, too.

The thing is, I'm not anxious about me or my feelings. I just really want this to go well for Josh. Have I mentioned that already? I think I have. Great. Now my internal monologue has turned circular. That's how anxious I am.

"…more about this mystery partner of yours?" I catch the tail end of Marie's question and I blink, wondering how I ended up lucky —or not so lucky— enough to be seated directly across from her.

"Mom, this is why our friends refused to come over when we were in high school." Charlie rescues me this time, arriving at my side with four bottles of beer, dangling by their necks between his fingers. He takes his seat and I belatedly realize I am surrounded by Walkers.

Ash is directly across from Charlie, sharing an empathetic glance with me while Marie's attention shifts. How he wound up seated next to his mother-in-law is anyone's guess. Charlie and Josh's dad is sitting on Maisy's other side, a couple of seats away from Emmett. Somewhat resentfully, however jovial the thought is, I wonder how he managed to finagle that.

Marie rolls her eyes but lets the question drop. "You're exaggerating. I was the cool mom."

Her children all groan or scoff in unison and I do my best to conceal my amusement by taking a big drag from my drink. This launches the family into what I suspect is a conversation they've had many times before. Charlie kicks off with the story of the time she gave him and his buddies boxes of condoms in his Junior year, and Maisy follows that up with tales of their mother's attempts to include herself in her friends' sleepovers.

"What about that Halloween she dressed as a character from *Cats* and insisted on singing *Memory* at every group of trick-or-treaters?" Josh puts his offering forth to the chortles of the rest of the group. "Word got out and we never had trick-or-treaters again."

By this stage, Marie has puttered back and forth from the kitchen, setting up a veritable buffet of roast meats, salads, vegetables and at least three different kinds of bread along a makeshift buffet counter. Ash and Ted have been helping, and Marie joins in the laughter at her own expense when she sits down to the tail end of the most recent story, which has carried on as we all lined up to fill our plates and then sat down again.

"...insists on calling me her baby whenever she visits me at college," Axel complains, but there's a fondness to his words, even while his girlfriend grimaces and tries to hide the expression when she catches me looking.

"You're my youngest and will always be my baby," Marie tells him with a shrug, completely unrepentant. "You'll understand when you have kids of your own."

I watch Ash wince, but Maisy speaks up before anyone else can. "I've told you before, Mom. You can't pressure us into having kids."

Marie sighs dramatically. "You would think the odds would be with me. I have four of you. Not one of you wants to continue the family line? To give me grandbabies to cherish? Really?"

Axel clears his throat. "Actually..."

"*Now*? You're doing this now?" Dani hisses from between her teeth. "Really?"

"Doing what now?" Marie leans forward over her plate of dinner, peering around her youngest son, suspicion creasing her forehead.

The rest of us sit up straighter, sensing what's coming

before Axel grasps at his girlfriend's hand and declares, "Dani's pregnant."

Bedlam erupts.

It's a cacophony of sound and movement. Marie's sobbing as she attempts to wrap her son and his decidedly green-tinged girlfriend in a hug, Charlie's insisting that he knew his youngest sibling would be the first to spring a surprise baby on the family, Maisy is crowing about being off the hook, and Josh...

Well, Josh is pushing his chair back and leaving the table.

By unspoken agreement, Emmett and I follow him through the house.

"You okay?" I ask our boy when we're far enough away from the commotion. We're in the formal lounge room: a space comprised of white walls and deep blue carpet. The coastal theme has followed through into this room, with a giant photographic print taking up the majority of the main wall above the white four-seater couch. I sidestep the white timber coffee table with its blue table runner and reach for Josh, whose shoulders are set with tension.

He shakes his head in answer to my question and folds willingly into my embrace. "I'm being stupid," he tells me, and I have to strain to make out the words with how muffled they are against my skin.

I meet Em's gaze over Josh's shoulder.

"You're not," Emmett tells him in that deep, soothing way of his. He's warm and empathetic, but with the air of his profession lingering in the delivery of his assurances. "Your feelings are always valid, Josh. You can't control them. You can only control the way you behave when you're feeling them." He places his palm on Josh's back. I can feel his solid, supportive presence without feeling the touch myself. "I'm proud of you for having the presence of mind to walk away, monkey."

Josh nods and presses his face in closer to the crook of my neck. "I wanted tonight to be *our* night, you know? *My* night."

"I know, baby," I reply with genuine understanding. "I know."

The more time I've spent with Josh, the more I've learned about his position in his family. He's the epitome of a middle child, and I'm pretty sure that has contributed to his need to be bratty whenever he's feeling overwhelmed and in need of affection or attention. He's also terribly self-sacrificing, prioritizing his siblings' feelings and needs over his own, not that they ever seem to realize that he's doing it.

Suddenly, I'm frustrated on his behalf. My poor boy who was so excited to tell his family that he's found love with two men who adore him and each other equally. "We can still tell them," I insist, but he shakes his head.

"Mom's not going to pay any attention to anything else tonight. And Axel will kill me if I try to steal his thunder."

"But you're the one who suggested this dinner in the first place," I argue indignantly. "He stole yours."

Josh shrugs. "I'm used to it. He's the baby. He's been stealing my thunder since the day he was born." The laugh he adds at the end of the sentiment is strained. It's almost like he's trying to convince himself that it's funny and not a painful truth.

After all, Josh used to be the baby. He had something like six or seven years of it before his younger brother came along.

"Well, you're *our* baby," I argue, squeezing him tightly. "And you'll always have our complete attention."

Josh is quiet for a few moments, absorbing the words before

he asks, "Is it okay if I'm bratty tonight? When we get home, I mean?"

Neither Em nor I need to think twice about our answer. "Of course, monkey."

Chapter Twenty-Two — Josh

"Hey, so I'm sorry I hijacked your dinner party," Axel says when he calls me a few days later. My butt is still sore from the paddling I earned myself when we got home that night. The temper tantrum I threw, combined with the punishment my Daddies dished out, was so cathartic that I almost forgot how annoyed I was with my little brother.

Almost.

"Yeah, well, it happens," I sigh, looking out of the window of my car and across the road at the target I'm currently staking out. Dana is on foot, and I have my earpiece in my other ear, ready for her signal should I need to leap into action.

Sadly, I don't think that's going to happen. The past three stakeouts on this case have also been a bust. We haven't made much headway on the street gang case we've been working on for months now, but Dana's convinced we're getting close to something. They wouldn't have shot at us otherwise. We just need to collate some actual evidence before we can dig in deep.

They're not exactly criminal masterminds, so something has to give.

Funny how the sentiment 'something's gotta give' applies to so many things in my life right now.

"Come on, bro," Axel pleads, grating on my nerves, "I didn't mean to take over. But the topic of conversation was *right there* and I needed to do it before I lost my nerve." He huffs impatiently when I don't reply. "Look, Dani's not happy with me right now, either. She didn't want to tell anyone because she's still not sure she wants to keep the baby, and—"

"And I'm at work right now, Axe," I cut him off, aware that I'm being a bit of an ass. "Maybe you should have listened to your girlfriend's wishes before you got all impulsive."

I stamp down on the guilt threatening to undermine my resolve. I've always prided myself on being there for my brothers and my sister. But I'm still irritated and frustrated that the one big piece of news I wanted to share with my family was thwarted and overshadowed by something I'll never be able to compete with.

Something I'll probably never have for myself, either.

Not that I've really given much thought to having kids, mind you. It's never really seemed to mesh with my lifestyle. Not with being a cop and keeping odd hours, not with being a Little, not with the utter lack of serious romantic relationships. That last one has changed, but the other factors remain true.

That said, plenty of cops have families and balanced home lives. And plenty of people in the kink community have kids. I know my arguments are feeble at best, but they're still enough to give me pause, and if talking to Ted has taught me anything, it's that parenthood is something I should be sure about before I commit to it. Having never slept with someone capable of conceiving, I have the luxury of being able to plan and decide. Axel, on the other hand, did not.

And there I go again, suddenly empathizing with my brother instead of holding on to my resentment. Can't I just wallow in my own woes like I want to? Just this once?

I wanted my family to know that I'm in love. Axe took that from me. Bad Axe. Bad.

But his news was kind of life altering and he's probably been freaking out and...

Damn it!

Scrubbing my hand over my face, wishing I could snuggle Ranger in my crib at Daddy Em's instead of being an adult right now, I sigh into the hurt silence. "I'm sorry. That was harsh."

"Yeah, but I hijacked whatever it was you were planning on telling Mom and Dad, so I guess I deserved that." After a beat, he asks, "Did, um, did you want to talk about it? I know you're tighter with Charlie, but..."

My lips tick upwards into a half smile, the realization that Axel has his own hang-ups about our sibling relationships slowly dawning. "Charlie and I have a bit more in common," I acknowledge, "but we're still tight too, Axe. Even if you have been stealing my thunder your whole life."

"Just because you're both gay doesn't mean we're all that different," he huffs back at me.

My family knows about Charlie's kink, considering how open he and Ash are about it, but I've never told them about mine. Now is not the time to open that can of worms. Especially not with my baby brother. "Yeah, well, I wanted to introduce Mom and Dad to my boyfriends—"

"Boyfriends? *Plural?*" He sounds bewildered. I scan the

building I'm watching while I wait for him to gather his thoughts. "Wait. Both of those old guys? Max and, uh…"

"Emmett," I supply, nodding. "And yeah. Both of them." I frown. "And they're not that old."

"Dude. They're both, what? Fifty? They're old. And, um, they know about each other, and they're okay with you dating them both at the same time?"

"We're all together equally. A threesome. A throuple. Poly. Whatever you want to call it."

There's another moment of stunned silence. "Holy shit. That's, uh, kinkier than I expected. So, yeah, maybe you have more in common with Charlie after all."

I roll my eyes at his babbling. If only he knew the truth to those words. "There's nothing *that* kinky about three people in love with each other."

"I just…I…I mean, you're all guys. Not that there's a problem with that! But I…ugh. I'm screwing this up. But you love each other, so…that's awesome."

I start to chuckle, but frown as I catch the tail-end of an alert over the radio. It sounds like an officer has been abducted off the streets. My stomach turns over. Regardless of who it is, my colleagues are my friends. We have each other's backs. To lose one in a situation like this is unthinkable.

"I've gotta go," I tell my brother. "Work emergency. I'm fine," I add, just in case he starts to worry about me. "But I've gotta go."

I hang up before he can reply.

I pick up the handset for the radio and announce that Dana and I will be on our way. Our stakeout has been a bust again anyway. She's already ahead of me, sliding into the passenger seat as I place the handset back on its hook.

"Josh," she reaches out her hand, gently touching my forearm and stalling my attempt to start the car. Something in her tone makes me sit up and take notice. "It's Max. The officer that got snatched. It's Max."

My heart is pounding and panic threatens to overwhelm me.

"Max?" I echo with disbelief. I shake my head. "No. Why would anyone abduct Max?"

Nobody knows about our romantic relationship yet. We were planning on disclosing it soon. But my partner is a damn good Detective, and I'm sure I've let things slip about how close I've gotten with my older brother's former partner.

She sighs and gives me a knowing look, tinged with empathy. "Because they know how important he is to you."

* * *

Because I haven't disclosed my relationship, and Dana is good enough not to say anything, our Captain has no reason to refuse my demand to run lead on recovering our officer. It's connected to our case, after all. The dumb shits that grabbed my Daddy off the street in broad daylight were known members of the gang we're investigating.

Captain Briggs isn't an idiot, though. He asked me a thousand questions about why Max might be a target, and the best I could offer him was that Max has been seen out in public with me because we're friends outside of work. It felt like a really thin excuse, but Briggs seemed to buy it.

Our station has been rounded up, and my entire attention is currently on Briggs as he debriefs us. Max and his partner were on a routine patrol. A bunch of the gang members

Dana and I have been investigating came out of nowhere, knocking Max and Vince out before they dragged Max away. He was shoved into a van which then sped away from the scene, according to the few witnesses who went to help Vince.

Captain Briggs is quick to assign teams to work on recovering our lost colleague as soon as possible. People are sent to get traffic cam footage, while others will double down on putting pressure on the gang members we currently have in custody in the hopes someone will break and give us information about the possible locations they might have taken my Daddy.

There's a determined air in the station as people take to phones, computers, and the street. It's just as serious as any other abduction, but I'd say we're taking this one more personally because it involves one of our own.

Once more, I am glad our relationship hasn't been disclosed because it means I can work the case. There's no way in hell Briggs would let me work it if he knew I was emotionally compromised. As it is, I had to work hard to convince him that my social relationship with Max, courtesy of Charlie, wouldn't impact my performance.

But, oh, I am definitely emotionally compromised.

It's even worse when I realize that I have to call Emmett. He's not listed as Max's emergency contact, and I'd rather he hears this from me than from Charlie when he inevitably finds out from one of the other guys.

I manage to sneak away from the organized chaos of our bullpen, dialing Em's number and bringing the phone to my ear with a heavy heart. I need his comfort desperately, but I can't ask that of him when I'm about to deliver devastating news. When I know that I at least have access to firsthand knowledge and he will probably feel useless and frustrated as he waits for updates.

When he answers with a low, sexy greeting full of suggestion, my heart breaks all over again.

"Daddy," I try to hold my voice steady, but I'm pretty sure it cracks, "they took Max."

* * *

"You kidnapped a fucking cop!" an angry voice is screaming.

I hide around a corner, peering around the exposed brick-work anxiously. My heart is pounding. I don't want to get caught. I'm on a rescue mission, after all.

I can't make out the conversation between the bad guys. I can only see their backs, and the pair of uniformed legs stretched out on the ground in front of them.

Max's legs.

These men have my Daddy and it's wrong. It's so wrong.

My thoughts go all wonky with my panic.

Some voice in the back of my head says I'm missing something vital right now, but I brush it aside. I don't know where Dana is, but I can't tear my eyes away from those legs. That's all I can see of Max. His legs. The two men blocking my view are still arguing between themselves.

I want my Daddy back.

I try to pull back, to reassess the situation, but I can't seem to force my body to cooperate. That's weird.

My instincts scream at me that I'm missing something big here.

To be honest, there's a lot that's wrong about this situation, but I can't pinpoint why I'm so confused.

I'm also starting to panic because why can't I get my body

to cooperate? Why can't I pull back, regroup, come up with a plan of action? Where's my partner? My backup? How did I get here in the first place?

I feel dizzy and, before I can even register that it's going to happen, I lurch forward, holding my service pistol in front of me, crying out "Let my Daddy go!" My hands are shaking.

This is very, very bad.

Why can't I stop myself?

The men turn to face me, still blocking my view of my Daddy, and it's so weird that I can see their faces but I can't register them.

"You're not getting your Daddy," one taunts me. His voice is mean.

My legs tremble. I shake my gun at him. "Gimme my Daddy!"

I don't understand what's going on. My Little side is taking over. I'm letting it.

I have never regressed on the job before. As mocking laughter fills my ears, seemingly echoing around the random room I've found myself in, I find I can't fight it any more than I could prevent myself from bursting in without a plan.

"D-daddy!" I call out, trying to peer around the strange men. I still can't really work out their features, even while they're right in front of me. I swear one of them looks a bit like the villain from the last action movie I watched, but that's stupid, right?

And why won't Max answer me?

"W-what have you done to him?" I demand, clinging to my Big headspace for as long as possible. Just until backup can arrive.

"Tell you what," movie villain guy says, "we'll swap. You're the one we wanted anyway."

"You'll let Daddy go?" I shouldn't trust their word, but Max wouldn't be in this mess if not for me. I'll do anything if he's going to be safe.

His feet on the ground don't even twitch.

Why can't I see him properly?

"Sure, kid," says the bad guy.

Then, as if in slow motion, he punches me.

In shock and fear, my bladder releases and I cry out, dropping to the ground. The world around me goes hazy, and I huddle into a ball, sobbing for Daddy.

"Jesus Christ, he's pissed himself," one of the bad guys says "I ain't touching him."

Flinching, I bring my knees up as far as I can and catch the smell of my accident. I gag a little, unable to stop the tears. I'm embarrassed at myself. Embarrassed and terrified. I've lost track of my Daddy, too, and I feel useless on top of it all. I wail.

"The fuck is wrong with him?" Angry Voice demands.

Some part of my brain is telling me this is all wrong, but I'm too regressed and too scared to listen to it.

The calmer guy doesn't sound as calm when he replies, but the words sound fuzzy now. I let their yelling wash over me while I try not to wail so loudly.

I want my Daddies. Max was *just there*! Where'd he go? Who are these people?

I yelp when I'm yanked to my feet and pushed roughly forward with the demand to "Walk!" shouted at me. My clothes are sticking to my skin, wet because I'm so pathetic that I peed as soon as I got scared, and I try to ignore how uncomfortable I feel. These men aren't my Daddies. They're not going to care if I tell them I'm hurting and feel yucky.

I walk into three walls as I'm navigated through whatever space we're in, even though time and space seems to be acting all funny, and then I can feel the difference in the air when I'm shoved into what I think is a tiled room. The floor feels different underfoot, even beneath my shoes, and the words the men are shouting are echoing in a way they weren't before.

Then I'm pushed roughly against a cold, tiled wall and, before I can say anything, I'm hit with a blast of cold water, which splatters my face and soaks my entire front, like a bucket was tossed over me. Another follows, and another, and another, until I start to scream.

"It's okay," a deep voice, roughened with exhaustion says as an arm wraps around me. "Shh, honey. It's okay."

I blink, feeling disoriented and confused as the cold tiles at my back and under my butt seem to vanish, replaced by softness.

"Josh, monkey, wake up. You're having a nightmare."

I blink harder now, frowning into the hazy darkness of Emmett's bedroom. A nightmare? But it felt *so* real. The pain, the yelling, the...*oh no*.

The wetness is real. It's cloyingly, disturbingly real.

I cringe and huddle in on myself, shame overwhelming me.

I barely remember being forced to go home from work last night, no closer to finding or rescuing Max. Briggs promised I would be the first to know if there was any update and told me I wouldn't be any good to anyone if I worked myself to complete exhaustion, so I eventually went willingly. Arguing with him would have seen me pulled from the case entirely.

When I got to Em's place, we just held each other. Words were too hard, but the silence was even harder. It was like a gaping reminder of what (*who*) we were missing. But neither one of us mentioned it. And, hey, at least we had each other, right? Unlike Max, who is alone, having God-only-knows what done to him, and…No. Nope. Not going there. It's not helpful.

I don't remember passing out in Daddy Em's arms, but I must have. And he must have brought me straight to bed, forgoing our usual nightly rituals. And now…now I've had the worst nightmare I've had in months, and I've practically flooded the bed, my clothes and probably Em's as well in my terror.

Why can't I just be normal? I think as I start to sob, yesterday's events and the nightmare finally catching up to me. Regardless of how much I hate that word, I've finally broken and admitted my deepest grievance with my situation to myself. I just want to be like mostly everyone else, at least where my bodily functions are concerned. *Why is this my body's way of dealing with stress? How can anyone take me seriously when I can't control my own God damn bladder?*

I know I'm turning vaguely hysterical, but I just can't help it. My chest heaves and aches, and my heart feels like it's going to explode, but I can't stop the spiral of thoughts. They only get darker.

Why couldn't I find Max? It's my fault he got snatched to begin with. He's going to hate me. Both my Daddies should hate me. This is all my fault.

"Josh, stop. Breathe for me. In and out. Come on." Emmett sounds calm and patient. Soothing. There's not a hint of disgust or reproach. "You're having a panic attack. I need you to focus on my voice. Try for me, Joshua."

The hint of authority is enough to appeal to my submissive

nature, and I force myself to take a deep, shaky breath, my sobs hitching.

"Good boy, now let it out slowly."

I comply.

"Good. Again."

This repeats for a while, but I've got no way of knowing how long. I'm trembling by the time Emmett deems me calm enough to stop, and my breathing hitches when he says, "Now, we need to get you cleaned up."

I cringe away from him, but he's not having any of it. His palm cups my jaw and tilts my head up to face him.

"Don't hide from me, Josh. Not now." I open my eyes at the plaintive request, unable to prevent myself from doing so. He sounds tired and pained, and I feel a pang of guilt for wallowing in my own grief and shame when he's also struggling with Max being gone. Em's dark eyes squint with appreciation and sadness when I meet them. "Not ever. Please."

"Sorry, Daddy," I apologize, my voice breaking. "I...I..."

There's so much I want to tell him. I want to apologize for the mess I've made of his bed —and our nightclothes— and for disturbing any shred of rest he might have been trying to get. I want to explain how responsible I feel for Max's current predicament, and how frustrated I am that I wasn't able to just sweep in and save him within a few hours. I want to tell him that I'm scared of what might be happening to our lover, that I firmly believe it should have been me in his place. I want to thank him for not hating me for throwing all our lives into this sort of upheaval. I want to tell him how grateful I am to have him here with me now, even though I know he's stressed out, too.

"I know," he says, still in that measured, soothing way. "You don't always have to be strong, Josh. Neither one of us do. Especially not now. And," he presses his thick index finger to my lips when I go to protest, "when we get Max back, we're going to tell him the same thing."

I have to stamp down on the wave of anxiety that hits me when I once again think about what Max might be going through. My nightmare was pretty tame, all things considered, and yet I had been terrified.

But Max is a Dom. He's a Daddy. If anyone can hold it together and stare these assholes down until we find him and make them pay, it's him.

I have to tell myself that to avoid thinking of how helpless I'd felt in my nightmare. A Daddy wouldn't regress like I had. A Daddy would bide his time to dole out punishments. And, okay, I know that's not quite how it works, but my Little side accepts that reassurance and, with my pants wet and clinging to me, and the ammonia scent of my accident lingering in the bedding and on our clothes, regressing seems inevitable right now.

It's yet another thing that's not fair to throw onto Emmett. I shouldn't just expect him to comfort me and be Daddy while I slip away from the helplessness of this situation, but I *need* to be Little for a bit. I can't afford to accidentally regress when I go back to work, and nothing else seems to help me de-stress quite like being Little. I've gotten used to relying on it these past couple of months.

"It's okay," Emmett tells me, kissing the top of my head as I blurt all of those thoughts aloud. "I'm not a cop, Josh. I can't do anything to help find Max. But if I can help you get into the right headspace to find our man, I will do it any way I can."

Tears of gratitude well in my eyes and slide down my cheeks. "I love you," I tell him, and it hits me how glad I am that we exchanged these words weeks ago. That Max knows how much we love him, too. That when we say it again, it's not going to be seen as a knee-jerk reaction to trauma. "I love you," I repeat, softer still.

"And I love you."

That's all I need to hear. I close my eyes and let Emmett guide my breathing again, until I'm comfortable enough to slip into my Little headspace. When I'm finally there, I'm sad that Daddy Maxxie is gone, but the fear and terror of it is no longer overwhelming. I'm reassured when Daddy Em promises Maxxie will be back soon.

"I'm wet 'n yucky, Daddy," I tell him, scrunching my nose against the discomfort I can no longer deal with.

"I know, monkey. Let's get cleaned up."

Daddy pushes out of bed, bundling the sheets and blankets and sodden mattress protector into a heap, adding our clothes to the pile. Then he takes me into the bathroom and runs a bath in his huge tub. It's not quite big enough to fit three people, but big enough for the two of us.

In the warm water, we don't play with toys like we usually do. We don't tease each other with grown-up touches, either. We just cuddle, drawing silent support in the still night air, and it's everything I need in the moment.

Well, almost everything.

I still need Daddy Maxxie, but that's a problem for Big Josh to deal with.

Tomorrow.

Chapter Twenty-Three — Max

Kidnapped. I've been kidnapped.

This is easily the most surreal thing I have ever thought. Definitely the most surreal experience I've ever had.

I mean, honestly, in what world does a random, bottom-of-the-totem-pole Officer like me get nabbed off the street in broad daylight by half-witted thugs who have gotten all of their criminal inspiration from TV?

That's the only thing keeping my head firmly on my shoulders at the moment, the knowledge that these goons are morons. They're dangerous for that same fact, but they're less likely to kill me than seasoned mafiosos or members of a properly established street gang.

After trying their hands at interrogating me, however clumsily, and realizing that I don't actually know anything about Josh's case, they fought among themselves about what other uses I could serve for them and then left me locked in this tiny, concrete room which I can only assume used to be a storage closet.

My head is throbbing from where I took the blow that knocked me out, and I'm exhausted and dehydrated, but I'm otherwise unharmed. Even while they interrogated me, the worst they did was slap me around a bit. Considering my experience as a Dom, a few poorly wielded smacks to the face didn't really bother me.

The exhaustion and dehydration, though? That's beginning to be a problem.

I have no idea how long I've been held captive. I don't know how long I was unconscious for, either. I can't see outside from my dark little cell, and none of my captors have worn wristwatches. I'm determined not to pass out again if I can help it, though. Not even for much-needed sleep. Doing so might mean missing a chance to escape, or gathering intel from the idiots who keep pausing to argue outside my cell door.

I try not to think about how worried Josh and Emmett must be. If either of them had been snatched off the street, I would be beside myself. I'd also do everything in my power to find and rescue either one of them.

I know Josh is probably doing the same right now.

My boy is strong like that. He's a fucking amazing Detective, and he's never once let his Little side slip at work. But, then again, he's never had a Daddy get kidnapped out from under his nose, either.

Thank God he has Em to lean on. Our big, calm rock. With his psych training, there's nobody better to look after Josh at a time like this. To make sure he eats and rests and doesn't run himself ragged in his fight to find me. If anyone can outstubborn and keep my monkey in line, it's my other lover.

Fuck, I miss them.

It doesn't matter if I've been held against my will for a few hours or a few days at this point, I miss them both terribly.

I strain my ears and listen for other clues or tidbits of information that might help take these fuckers down. When I'm rescued —and that is definitely *when* and not *if*— I plan on making sure the whole lot of them go away to prison for a long, long time.

Sadly, there's nothing. No movement from outside my makeshift cell's door, and no sounds of life from beyond the thick, cold wall at my back. I wouldn't be surprised if this building, like The Grove, is soundproofed. It feels industrial, from its bare concrete floors to the plain plasterboard walls, so I can only imagine that I'm being held somewhere in the city's industrial area.

Well, that is unless I was unconscious for hours while they transported me to another city altogether.

The thought makes my stomach roil. If that's the case, it'll be harder for Josh to find me. Other cities' police would need to be involved, and even though a fellow cop's life is at stake, the chances of them working the case with the same intensity that my boy will is slim to none. And, worse still, if state lines are crossed, the whole issue gets even messier.

No. No, I have to assume that I was only out for a couple of hours maximum. Just enough time to be transported across the city and carried into my crappy little cell, left here until I woke up with a pounding headache, disoriented by the darkness around me. Even now, the only light filtering in is through the minuscule cracks of space around the outline of the doorframe. It's also the only space that lets the sound in.

My back aches from sitting on the cold hard ground for so long, but the room isn't long enough for me to lie down, and when I stand up I feel somewhat claustrophobic. I'm tempted to close my eyes and give in to the urge to let sleep overtake me, but I remind myself that I can't. I need to stay vigilant.

Nobody comes back to the room for what feels like hours.

I grit my teeth when my bladder starts to protest.

There's no way I'm going to piss on the floor in my cell. The lack of ventilation in here will make that unbearable.

So, despite wanting to stay unobtrusive in the hopes they'll forget me and let their guards down, I push to my feet and pound on the door.

"I need the bathroom!" I holler. "Unless you want me to piss everywhere! Trust me, I'll aim under the freaking door if I have to!"

I feel ridiculous making that kind of threat, and a vaguely hysterical smile tugs at my lips because I can so see Little Josh bratting it up in a similar way. Naturally, that thought shifts me into longing and frustration again.

I miss my monkey and my co-Daddy so fucking much. They must be worried sick. What kind of Dom allows his submissives to worry over him like this? What kind of Dom—

No.

No, I need to stop that line of thinking right now. I was taken by force by a group of men. I was outnumbered and knocked out. Nobody could have fought their way out of those odds. Not in reality.

I drag my focus back into the here and now. And, in the here and now, I'm desperate to pee. That's my first priority. I'll focus on dealing with the bigger picture after this issue is resolved.

Slamming my fists into the timber of the door again, I repeat my demand and my threat. I'm mid-way through repeating it again when the door swings outward suddenly, causing me to stumble forward.

I squint against the brightness of the light, having spent too long in nearly pitch blackness.

"Come on," a gruff voice huffs, grabbing my bicep and hauling me forward. My legs are wobbly, probably from the dehydration, lack of food, and from being sat on my ass for God only knows how long.

He drags me into a grimy men's room and I scrunch up my nose at the smell of it. Still, my cell would have eventually reeked this way if I hadn't demanded to be let out to empty my bladder. My captor shoves me hard towards the ancient, moldy and rusted urinal trough, then stands beside me with his gun drawn as I deliberately take my time unzipping my fly.

The second I let go, though, the evidence of how desperate I really was is impossible to contain. I can barely keep the sigh of absolute relief at bay, but my refusal to let these assholes see just how affected I've been by their capture is strong enough to prevent it.

I've barely got my dick tucked back into my underwear before I'm being manhandled back out of the bathroom and down the short hallway which leads to my cell.

The walls are bare, and there aren't any windows. The light is all from the fluorescent bulbs above us. The flooring is all rough, scuffed cement.

No clues to my location there, then. I haven't even seen my captor's face yet, either. My eyes took too long to adjust to the light, then I was too distracted by relieving myself to look in the mirror. And now he's behind me again, pushing me forward at a rough, fast pace.

Rookie fucking error.

We reach the only door swung wide open and I am shoved hard into the depths of the former storage closet, stumbling as I hit the far wall, only just managing to stop my forward propelled motion with my hands against the plaster at the last possible second. I turn to snap at my guard, but I barely catch a glimpse of dark hair before the door slams shut and the lock clicks.

Being plunged back into darkness sucks, but the pounding in my head has subsided, and my back and ass feel better for having gotten to walk around even just that small amount.

After this, though, I think I'm going to have to add sensory deprivation to my list of hard limits when I'm playing with a sub —with Josh or with Emmett— because there's no way I could willingly put someone else through this kind of experience. Not even if I thought they'd enjoy it.

Thinking about all the sexy fun things I *will* do with my men once I'm free turns out to be just a good a way as any to pass the time while I wait for an opportunity to break out again, though, so that's what I settle in to do.

God, I miss them.

Chapter Twenty-Four – Josh

G lancing angrily at the clock, I bite my lip and type rapidly at my keyboard. I'm searching through property records, trying to find a clue as to where my Daddy is being hidden.

It's been over twenty-four hours now. Unlike in the movies, we can't just go barreling down doors until we find the right location. We can't pick people up off the streets for questioning without due cause. We can't use threats of physical violence.

Investigating is time consuming. And every minute that ticks by is another one in which I haven't found my Daddy.

My nightmare still lurks in the recesses of my mind. There's nothing scarier than feeling helpless and impotent. Max had been within my grasp and I hadn't been able to help him.

It was just a dream, I remind myself, feeling the burn of humiliation simmering under my skin.

Some part of me is afraid that, when we do find him, I'll do pretty much exactly what I did in my dream: lose control of myself. Regress. Cry. Wet myself in fear.

It's not just my reputation on the line if that happens. It's Max's life.

Dana's hand stills my bouncing knee, startling me enough to look up at her. She looks as exhausted as I feel, and I'm grateful to have a partner who cares as much as she does.

"We'll find him, Josh," she assures me in her steely, no-nonsense tone. I'm glad that she's not being uncharacteristically sympathetic, even though her eyes are filled with a maternal sort of warmth. "It's only been—"

"It's been over twenty-four hours!" I snap. "At this point, rescue might become recovery. You know the statistics as well as I do."

Her lips form a thin line. "The whole precinct is working this case," she reminds me. "We work with good cops, Josh. We. Will. Find. Him."

I don't snark that it's the matter of whether we'll find him alive or dead that's getting to me. That sort of attitude isn't fair on her, and thinking about the worst-case scenario won't help me to get my head into the right place to do my job properly.

One of the other Detectives caught a break yesterday when one of the potential gang members he was questioning slipped up and mentioned 'holding the cop' somewhere. That meant Max was most likely inside a building somewhere and not at the bottom of a lake.

It was one of the only pieces of information we had to go on.

Now we're all scouring property records and leases for people linked to the gang, and to their families and known associates. It's slow work, nothing like the techno wizzes on certain TV shows would lead you to believe, and I'm getting anxious.

So far, we've short-listed five potential properties and dismissed another three.

"What about sub-leases?" I demand when another hour of searching yields no further results. "Or under the table agreements? How are we going to track those?"

Dana frowns, staring at her monitor. She holds up her index finger to silence me, then types rapidly for a moment. I sit up straighter. I know that look.

I finally allow hope to blossom when she turns to me with a shark-like grin. Her eyes glint. "I think I've got it."

* * *

Rescue missions aren't exactly what Hollywood makes them out to be. We don't usually go in guns blazing, shooting first and asking questions later. We have plans and backup plans, and we try to minimize loss of life or collateral damage. But, damn it all, for once I wish I could just draw my service pistol and burst through the doors, taking down every single one of the guys who took my Daddy away. I've never shot anyone before, never even fired my weapon, but as our cavalcade of vehicles set up, surrounding the warehouse exit points, I find my trigger finger getting itchy.

The building in front of me is nondescript. It's like every other warehouse in the area, no different even to the outer façade of The Grove. There's no signage, nor is there any hustle and bustle of workers. It's just a big, gray building with a reinforced roller door and a single security-barred entry door.

There's also no sound coming from inside.

It's not imposing or looming.

It's just a warehouse.

But my Daddy is being held hostage inside and that makes the whole thing seem ominous anyway.

Our various teams get into position, all of us wearing bulletproof vests and radios, our guns drawn and held securely, their muzzles facing the ground, directed away from each other and ourselves.

My heart is pounding so hard I swear my colleagues can hear it.

Because Dana and I took lead on the investigation, we're going in first with a collection of other officers and detectives. As much as I trust all of these people implicitly, I'm glad that I'll be getting the first chance to sweep the building. If I inadvertently got Max into this mess, I'll damn well be the one to get him out of it. And even if it's not my fault, he's my Daddy and my lover. We take care of each other. Always.

As soon as we get confirmation that we can enter the premises, I practically race towards the front door. The door itself is protected by a security gate. The metal bars, covered in a chipped, peeling layer of white paint, are padlocked from the inside, but there's enough room between each bars for us to cut the damn thing off.

As expected, the big, bulky lock is no match for the epic set of bolt cutters we came prepared with, and it gives way and clatters to the ground in a series of satisfying thumps against the door on its way down.

"Well, I guess we just announced our presence," Dana says wryly.

I shrug. "As if they aren't watching through the security

camera anyway." I point up at the device mounted above the door and wave at it with a shit-eating grin.

Adrenaline and the prospect of bringing my Daddy home *might* be channeling my inner brat.

Just a *tiny* bit.

Dana just shakes her head. "Max has his hands full with you, doesn't he?"

I don't bother answering beyond grinning a bit wider. Just the mention of Max's name is enough to refocus my efforts in getting to him. I kick the flimsy timber door in, relishing in the way the plywood cracks and splinters before giving way. I'm expecting to be met with their brute force or at least half a dozen weapons pointed at the doorway...but when we push through into what was once an office space, it's empty.

I scowl.

Like I said, these things aren't often very much like TV.

Two teams trickle in through the doorway behind us, and I know we have two others manning the exit points at the rear of the building. Nobody's going to get past us if they're trying to make a sneaky getaway.

We split up into pairs, our weapons raised, sweeping the small catacomb of dated offices and storage rooms in our search for our missing colleague and his captors. There's a large open warehouse space to the left of these smaller rooms, and two pairs of cops head that way. Their shouts and the muted sounds of footsteps running on concrete, accompanied by crashes, tell me that they've found someone in the building.

I'm torn between sticking with the job I'm supposed to be doing and taking off in the direction of the noise. It's only logic which keeps me going with my actual task. The likelihood of Max being kept in a securable, internal room is much higher than the possibility that he's chained to a radiator or something out on the warehouse floor. He's less likely to escape or cause trouble if he's contained, especially if it's in a room without windows, and with only one potential exit to guard. The smaller the better, if only to make it more difficult for him to take a run up and use physical momentum against these guys.

Of course, these guys aren't the sharpest tools in the metaphoric shed, so maybe they have been keeping him out in the warehouse. It's not as though the building is crawling with people to keep an eye on their hostage, after all.

When we complete our sweep of the ground floor offices and come up empty handed, my stomach sinks. Was our intel wrong? We were so certain that this would be the right building. The lease is linked to two members of the gang. It's on the outskirts of the industrial area, bordering onto the undeveloped land at the edges of the city. It's the perfect location for them to hide stolen merchandise, to tear down stolen vehicles, to even stash their drugs. These people aren't smart enough or fiscally sound enough to have more than one den of debauchery, and if Max isn't here, I have no idea where to look.

"Ground floor clear," Dana says into her radio, then jerks her chin in the direction of the rickety looking stairs at the end of the narrow, grungy hallway. "Proceeding to level two."

Like The Grove, this building has a second level. I highly doubt this building will compare. But, if it's where I'll finally find my Daddy, it'll be ten times better than The Grove ever could be.

For some odd reason, the second floor is where all the bad guys have been hiding. They greet us in force at the top of the stairwell, shooting down at our team as we reach the landing which turns left before we're directed up again.

"Fall back!" Dana yells as bullets rain down towards us, whizzing past, tearing through the plasterboard wall behind the landing.

Okay, so maybe these things *are* sometimes just like Hollywood makes them out to be. Especially when our perps have modeled their gang's presence on whatever they've seen on TV or the movies.

Morons.

There's not a lot of precision in their shooting, and they go nuts with it, emptying their clips when we're not even visible. It works in our favor, so I silently thank Hollywood for its inaccurate portrayal of unlimited ammo. Our team surges up the stairs as soon as the hail of bullets peters out into ineffectual clicks that echo down the staircase.

We throw ourselves bodily into the wall of predominantly young people when we reach the second floor, attempting to get as many of them cuffed and immobilized in a short time as possible. They're a scrappy bunch, most of them not looking any older than twenty-five, and some part of me feels a pang of empathy for them. Especially the youngest ones, who don't even look like they're old enough to drink.

From the case we've been running, I know that they've all lived fairly rough lives. Many of them have been in and out of juvie since before puberty, and being in a gang is the closest thing to family they've known. But even though I feel for them, their backgrounds don't excuse their criminal behaviors, and escalating from petty things to serious attacks on members of the public —to kidnapping and shooting at cops— is even worse. Most of these kids will probably wind up doing a lot of time in prison, considering how serious these newer offenses are.

Once this lot are contained, we break off into teams again, sweeping and clearing out the rooms up here. The flooring is scuffed linoleum, a tiny step up from the bare concrete of downstairs. The walls are still bare plasterboard, though, and the fixtures are minimalist and dated. I suppose street gangs don't care about the modernization of their office spaces.

Ahead of me, one of the Officers with us reaches a locked door between two of the larger offices. I imagine it's a storage space of some kind, and my heart jumps as I watch Robbins rattle the knob. He calls something out, then stands back and kicks the door in, holstering his weapon before striding inside the room, calling out "Found him!" before he disappears.

I don't even need to think about it. Even though I should be sticking with Dana, I break into a run.

Chapter Twenty-Five - Max

More time passes. I can't tell you how long. My eyes are gritty and heavy, but I've continued to fight sleep. When my door bursts open, the sudden sound and light has me flinching backwards. Two men enter my little cell, each taking a side and hefting my up by my biceps. My legs are numb as I try to walk between them, but they don't seem to have an issue dragging me along the narrow hallway.

I wonder if they're going to attempt another ham-fisted interrogation, or something more sinister, but they just haul me up the stairwell at the end of the hallway, leading me to a second floor with the same dinged up, bare walls, but a floor covered in mottled old linoleum. I guess the upstairs space was intended for the higher echelon of whatever company previously occupied this place.

Thug One and Thug Two ignore my demands for answers about what they want from me and where we're going, leading me to yet another door sandwiched between two others, opening it and shoving me inside.

Another storage closet with no light.

Great.

The lock clicks and there's a heavy thud on the other side of the door, like someone has reclined against it.

At least my new cell has upgraded flooring. Small wins, right?

I sigh heavily and settle back against the far wall, glaring at the pinpricks of light filtering around the shape of the door. I'm so tired, and I feel so useless, but I need to hold out for as long as I can.

I manage to stay awake, straining my ears at every tiny sound until the first signs of commotion filter through the building to my cell.

I get to my feet, sighing with relief as I hear what I assume is my colleagues getting closer, the sounds of fighting and gunfire not as off-putting as they should be, because I know that they'll have come in force and I will be getting out of here.

Well, unless my captors try to use me as a human shield or a bargaining chip, but I have faith in the cops I work with. Plus, this is too small a space for them to maneuver around me that easily. And I'll be waiting just in case the people who open the door are not on my side.

Sure enough, I hear someone nearby call "Clear!" before the doorknob rattles. The sound of timber cracking as the door is presumably kicked in follows soon after, and then I hear the same voice say "Found him!" just as I squint against the pervasive brightness from the hallway spilling into my cell, framing a broad shouldered figure.

My knees buckle as the relief starts to sweep over me. However long without food, water, or sleep will do that to a man, I guess.

"Max, man, we've got you," my rescuer says as he catches me while I stumble forward, more unsteady on my feet than I expected I would be. I recognize his voice. Sam Robbins. One of the other Officers on my usual rotation. "Are you okay? Are you hurt?"

I nod. "Head hurts," I manage to answer, still squinting. "Ugh. Too bright."

"Sorry," Sam says just as the sound of more feet racing towards us reaches my ears. "Let's get you out of here. Can you walk?"

I nod, fighting the pins and needles in my legs and, with the strong hands assisting me, totter unsteadily out into the hallway.

"Da—*Max!*" Josh's voice is full of relief as he races down the hallway, ignoring the uniformed officer who found me as he rushes over.

My knees go weak at just the sound of his voice, and my eyes widen even though the desire to squint against the unbearable brightness is still so strong. He came for me. My sweet boy came for me.

I'd known he would. Or, rather, I knew he would try. But after God only knows how long spent missing him and Emmett and yearning for them both, just hearing his voice and seeing his handsome, bearded face has tears prickling at the backs of my eyes.

I don't care who sees them, either.

"Mon..." I start and then practically bite my tongue as I stop myself from saying the wrong thing. "*Josh.*" My voice breaks as the relief of seeing him finally overwhelms me, and I can't help the hitching sob that escapes my throat when he wraps his muscular arms around me, taking my full weight off the other Officer.

I'm not ashamed of my emotions. Our usual roles in kink and in the bedroom don't negate human responses to trauma, or loss, or grief. A good Dom can show weakness. Can cry. Can admit that they need help. And a good boy can be the strong one. The hero. The person shouldering his or her Daddy's weight —literal and metaphorical— as they collapse with relief and joy.

"I've got you, Da...*babe*," he says, holding me close, running his hands through the hair on the back of my head. The new pet name sounds strange coming from him and not Emmett, but I understand why he can't use his usual loving title for me. It doesn't mean that I don't miss my usual title, but I kind of like 'babe', too.

Hissing, I wince at his touch, though. He stops immediately.

"Pistol whipped," I explain, and I feel him cringe.

"Sorry. I'll be careful."

"Captain's going to read you the riot act, Walker," Sam says as he steps back up to my other side, seemingly determined to help escort me from the building even though it's clear Josh has got this. "You should have declared your personal relationship before you volunteered to—"

Josh cuts him off. "If I'd done that, Briggs wouldn't have let me come. And there was no way I was going to pace the length of the station while you were all out here saving my man, Robbins. I'd rather ask forgiveness than permission."

"Fucking cowboy," Robbins snarks, but there's no heat to it. "Guess you're riding in the bus with him?"

Josh's bearded cheek rubs the side of my head as he nods. "Damn straight. Briggs can tear me a new one tomorrow."

I lean heavily on Josh as we leave the building, despite my lack of injuries. I'm exhausted, my head aches, and I don't want to let go of my boy for one second if I can help it.

It's all I can do not to snap when the paramedics separate us so I can lie back on the stretcher in the back of the ambulance. They don't even blink when I reach for Josh's hand and refuse to let it go, even when we start moving in the direction of the hospital.

"Emmett?" I crane my head to ask Josh, the sound muffled beneath the oxygen mask I've been fitted with for some reason. I finally notice how wrung out he looks, dark circles and stress lines carved into his handsome face. He offers me a small but genuine smile and squeezes my hand.

"I've texted him. He'll meet us there."

And despite feeling bad for putting my lovers through this kind of stress, I'm glad to hear that Em will be at the hospital, too. I need to see him just as badly as I needed to see Josh, and I won't rest until I do.

Chapter Twenty-Six — Emmett

I watch Max sleep, the steady *beep-beep-beep* of his heart monitor reassuring me that he's okay. Uninjured, beside the concussion he sustained, just recovering from sleep deprivation and dehydration. The doctors think he'll probably sleep for twelve hours at least. His body needs the rest. All I want to do is wrap him up in my arms, carry him home, and pamper the ever-loving crap out of my stubborn Dom.

The past few days have been a blur. A roller-coaster of emotions, most of which were not pleasant. From the second Josh called to tell me that Max had been grabbed by some street gang, to the agonizing wait for any updates, to the news that they were pretty sure they'd located him and would be storming in guns blazing, I could barely catch my breath.

It doesn't matter that the whole ordeal was thankfully over within forty-eight hours, those hours felt like a lifetime.

Obviously, I wasn't alone in my stress or fear. Charlie and Ash have been right there with me the whole time, while Josh's family and the rest of our social circle also spent the time on tenterhooks, but when Josh joined the rescue mission or whatever the hell they were calling it, I was more than aware that *both* the men I loved were in danger. I was also aware that I was completely useless, while Josh was able to throw himself directly into the rescue itself. But that was his job. Mine will be to help Max heal. To help them both heal.

I have never been more relieved than when I received Josh's short text telling me that they'd gotten Max out safe and that nobody was badly injured. I understood that he couldn't call me, but it didn't make the wait to see them any easier to bear. All I wanted was to hold my men in my arms and never let either one out of my sight again.

From the moment Josh and I were allowed into Max's room, we set up camp here, only leaving to allow cops in to take statements. Josh even flashed his badge and used his most dominating tone when the nurses tried to kick us out after visiting hours, which was kind of hot considering his generally submissive nature. We slept fitfully in these awful, uncomfortable chairs, waking up at any sound of discomfort or random bleat of the machines monitoring Max's heart and oxygen levels.

I wouldn't have been anywhere else.

"Hmmm," Max's familiar hum as he approaches wakefulness draws my complete attention and I focus on him as his eyes open in slits. He turns his head on his thin hospital pillow, taking in his surroundings before looking back over at me, blinking almost lazily. "Em?" he asks on a yawn.

"Hey, babe," I greet him softly. I wonder how much he remembers about yesterday, when we tearfully embraced before he lost the battle against his overwhelming exhaustion. To say his and Josh's colleagues are confused is an understatement, but we don't owe anyone an explanation about what we mean to each other. "How are you feeling?" I'm already at his side, pressing the button to raise the back of his hospital bed. It responds with an electric *whir*, and I carefully help him rearrange himself on the mattress.

"Stiff, and not in a good way," he says, then looks around again, his brow furrowing.

"I sent him to get coffee," I inform him before he can ask. "He was starting to go a little stir-crazy." As it was, Josh had whined about wearing a diaper in a public place, but we'd both agreed we were camping out in Max's hospital room, and Josh's nightmares have only gotten worse with this new traumatic event having played out. I scrub my open palm over my face, feeling the stubble prickling my skin. "I think we're in for a few days of bratty Josh once we get home."

"Home, huh?" Max grins lazily up at me. "I'm assuming you don't mean our respective abodes."

I snort. "As if either of you prefer your places to mine."

My place is the biggest. It has the nursery set up, and we've been working to install a flogging bench in the master bedroom, too, as well as a cabinet for Max to store his assortment of paddles, cock cages, shibari ropes and other Dom paraphernalia. I'm certain that Josh and I are going to enjoy experimenting with each and every one, even if the flogging bench is more for his punishments than my submission.

At any rate, we're kidding ourselves if we pretend that Josh and Max haven't been spending every available moment at my place anyway.

Max's expression turns soft. "Are you asking us to move in officially, Em?"

I think about how empty and lonely my house feels when either —or, worse, *both*— of my lovers are staying in their own apartments and I nod, making sure to keep my gaze pinned to his. "I am."

He smirks. "I can't believe it took me getting kidnapped for you to finally ask."

A groan barrels through my chest and out of my mouth. "It's too soon for jokes about it. I was worried, Max."

Max's face drops and he has the grace to appear apologetic. "I know. I'm sorry."

I reach for his hand and squeeze it. "You're back. You're safe. You're not hurt. That's all that matters."

He nods, causing a lock of his greasy blonde hair to flop forward. He makes no effort to brush it back. A tear slides down his cheek. "All I could think about was how much I missed you and Josh. How worried you must be. How useless I felt."

"You kept yourself out of trouble and alive," I insist, wondering if this new self-flagellation will cause his previous feelings of guilt over Charlie's shooting to flare back up. It wouldn't surprise me, but I'd rather try and get ahead of that and prevent it from happening. "You did the smart thing, Max. You did the right thing. You did what Josh and I needed you to do for us."

It's not emotionally manipulative to remind him of that last fact. It's not.

I try not to think about how badly things could have gone if the assholes who snatched him had been more competent and more experienced. Or if Max had tried to fight his way out. The gang, from what Josh has told me, is a new one on the scene, trying to make a name for themselves without proper understanding of the realities of being actual bad guys. Mostly teens and men in their early to mid-twenties, previously involved in petty crimes, whose only understanding of underworld crime is informed by Hollywood blockbusters and TV shows. That was why they were so sloppy. Why they were so easy to catch. Why they weren't prepared to actually kill a cop, even on their second attempt.

Even so, what they've done is enough to guarantee them long prison sentences.

It's also enough to guarantee that all three of us —Josh, Max, and I— will probably need some sort of trauma counseling. I mean, Max was kidnapped for fuck's sake. A cop. When does that honestly happen in reality? I'm convinced the gang was inspired by scenes from *Law & Order* or *Criminal Minds*, because real mafiosos would not be stupid enough to attempt such a thing in broad daylight. It would almost be laughable to think of if it hadn't actually happened, and to someone I love at that.

I close my eyes, unable to prevent flashing back to answering my phone the other day, grinning at Josh's name on my screen.

"Hey monkey," I'd said, prepared for some lunch-hour flirting with one of my lovers.

"*Daddy*," even in that one word, I could hear Josh's pain and terror. His resignation and his desperate need for comfort. Whatever was going on, I knew it was bad.

I knew it was a worst-case scenario when Charlie burst into my office at the same time, his phone held to his ear, his face pale.

"They took Max," Josh told me, and I'd been glad to have already been sitting, because my knees would have surely given way otherwise. "Snatched him right off the street."

I'd felt sick, and I could tell Josh was barely keeping it together. "Wha...how?"

Charlie's blue eyes were boring into me from where he sat heavily in one of the chairs on the other side of my desk, but I couldn't focus on him. My head felt fuzzy, and my heart was in my throat as Josh gave me all the information he knew, which didn't seem like much. Not in the grand scheme of things.

Some thugs had nabbed my lover and I couldn't do anything about it, and my other man was going to put his own life on the line to try and find him...

Max clearing his throat brings me out of my spiraling thoughts. It turns out that he's doing what he usually does, deftly changing the subject before I can continue to lecture him. "Could you call the nurse? I need the bathroom."

My stubborn, stubborn Dom.

He's lucky I love him.

* * *

"I tried to stop them." These are the words Charlie says when I answer his call two days after Max comes home.

My boss, being the understanding, compassionate man that he is, has given me carte blanche to stay home with my men for as long as I need to. It probably doesn't hurt that my lovers happen to be his younger brother and his former partner; men he cares about quite deeply. So, with that in mind, I'm not quite sure what he's talking about.

I blink. "Uh...?"

His sigh is heavy. I can envision him scrubbing his hand over his face. "Mom and Dad will probably be on your doorstep in half an hour. Maybe less."

"Why my doorstep?"

"Uh, because Josh has pretty much moved in with you?" Charlie's answer is delivered slowly, like I have the processing capacity of a toddler or an orange-tinted politician.

I suppose he has a point. But: "Why wouldn't they call him?"

"Because my bratty little brother has been dodging their calls."

Shoulders slumping, my head tilts back until I'm staring at the ceiling, and I close my eyes for a brief moment. As anticipated, Josh *has* been quite bratty these last few days. He's also spent a lot of time in his Little headspace. That has proven to be good for Max, who has been working through his frustration at his professional impotence (his words, not mine) by taking charge of all of Josh's discipline.

I've been providing aftercare to both of them. That has worked for me, because my need to pamper and protect my lovers has only increased tenfold since Max was abducted.

"Now's not a good time," I tell Charlie, even though I know my protests will be futile. I've met his mother: once she gets something in her head, there's no swaying her.

But Josh is currently sprawled on his back on the living room rug, thrashing his legs and refusing to get up to be bathed and changed. Max has already promised him fifteen smacks to his ass, but he's going to find himself wearing the cock cage again if he keeps this tantrum up.

"I wanna play with Ranger!" my boy howls petulantly, as if illustrating my point for Charlie. "I don't want a bath!"

On the other end of the line, my boss sighs. "How long has that been going on?"

I just shrug, and the nonchalance comes out in my answer.

"Maybe ten minutes? Max has got it under control."

"Under control enough that he'll be ready to face Mom in twenty minutes?" Charlie sounds skeptical.

I don't blame him.

"You're a big, dumb, meanie!" Josh declares loudly.

I stifle a chuckle and call over my shoulder, "You're bigger than Max, monkey!"

"Don't encourage him!" Max yells back at me, but I can hear the smile in his voice.

"Yeah…" Charlie drawls, "I'm going to let you go. Warn Josh about Mom. That might help." He hangs up before I can dissuade him of that particular notion. For some reason, Josh has been reluctant to talk to his family since he rescued Max. He's been avoiding their calls, only sending the odd text to assure them that he's alive and that he's fine.

The 'fine' part is debatable.

I'm not entirely sure why he's avoiding them. They were just as worried about Max as if it had been Josh that had been held hostage. Then, when they found out that Josh would be leading the team to recover their lost Officer, they'd been worried about both men. They loved them. Even Max has spoken to Marie since he woke up in hospital, but Josh has been sidestepping every opportunity.

Slipping my phone back into my hip pocket, I wander back into the living room, finding the scene almost identical to the way I'd left it when I walked out to take Charlie's call. Josh is pouting, flat on his back on the rug, a mess of toys strewn around him. Max is leaning against the nearest wall, his arms folded, his expression neutral.

Josh's eyes widen and seem to get brighter when he sees me. "Daddy Em! Tell Daddy Maxxie he's a poopy head!"

"Not a chance," I reply, striding across the space and tucking my hands under his armpits. "This has gone on long enough. That was your brother on the phone. Your parents are on their way—"

"What? No!" The childish petulance shifts into something closer to panic. "No! I don't wanna see them."

We do not have enough time for me to patiently wheedle his reasoning from him. "Unfortunately, you're not getting a choice." I grunt as I pull him upright. First into a seated position, and then, after I've adjusted my stance so I don't put my back out as I lift, to his feet. "So, bath time. Now."

He sulks his way into the bathroom, then complains when Max and I tell him he needs to shower instead of soak in a bath.

"You could have had a bath if you'd listened earlier," Max reminds him as he helps tug Josh's paint-splattered soft blue t-shirt over his head. He helps Josh out of his play shorts and training pants next. "Completely dry. Good job, monkey."

Josh shrugs, but I can see the way he's trying not to preen under the praise. With his nighttime accidents increasing in frequency, his regression and daytime play has focused on his control more than usual.

I can understand why. It's an issue that plays on his mind constantly, something that stresses him out and embarrasses him. Confronting it in his Little headspace is a safe way to regain confidence and control, and the role-play satisfies all of us.

"I'm going to leave you guys to it," I tell my lovers, confident that the worst of Josh's tantrum has passed. Once his family are gone, we'll talk about what's bothering him, and we'll discuss why he's been so determined to avoid his family, too.

"I'll get a pot of coffee going and see what kind of snacks I can put out for our unexpected guests."

Josh groans, allowing Max to usher him under the warm shower spray. As Charlie predicted, he's rousing from Little space, sounding Big, if resigned and defeated as he says, "I'm sorry about them."

I shake my head. "They're your family. This is your home now. They're always welcome. Now, get cleaned up."

I don't leave any room for argument as I leave my men to it.

Just as I'm placing a tray of cookies and fruit on the dining table, the doorbell rings. Hoping Josh and Max are almost done, I head to the front door and, taking a moment to brace myself, swing it open.

Marie doesn't even give me a chance to say hello. She launches herself over the threshold and wraps her arms around my waist, her head barely reaching the center of my chest.

"Hello," I direct down at the mop of curls, amusement coloring my tone.

"Oh, *Emmett*," she says emphatically, "why didn't you and Josh say anything?"

I look towards Grant with an eyebrow raised in question. Josh's dad shrugs.

Marie keeps going. "About your relationship, I mean." She finally pulls back, steadying herself with her hands on my forearms. Her brown eyes are beseeching. "You didn't worry that we wouldn't approve because of the age difference, did you? Because it isn't an issue for us. We just want our kids to be happy. And with Josh moving in so soon, he must be happy."

"I am, Mom," Josh says, coming out of the hallway that leads to the bedrooms. He's dressed in his standard adult casual outfit – jeans that complement his fantastic ass and strong legs, and a worn gray t-shirt which clings to his biceps and pecs. "But Axe made his announcement before we could."

Marie's eyes widen as Max follows Josh out of the hallway. She looks between Josh, me, and Max with confusion.

"Come have a coffee," I urge, gesturing for us to leave the foyer of my home. "We'll answer whatever questions you have…within reason, obviously."

Josh sits between me and Max at the table, his parents taking seats across from us. With amusement, I wonder if anyone else feels like this is akin to a job interview, or an interrogation.

Like a good host, I pour coffees and gesture to the platter of sweet treats, but only Josh reaches for the cookies.

He shoots smug glances at both me and Max, as if daring us to tell him he can't have the treats or discipline him.

I squeeze his thigh under the table. "Behave," I warn, my tone light.

Before he can say whatever taunting, naughty thing is on the tip of his tongue (if the glimmer in his eye is anything to go by), his mother cautiously asks, "What's going on here?"

Once again proving that his Little side and submissive nature don't necessarily mean he shies away from potential conflict, Josh steels his jaw and meets his mother's stare head on. "We're in a relationship. Together. Max, Em, and me." He sighs. "We wanted to tell you at dinner last week, but after Axe dropped his bomb, I figured it wasn't as important." The defeat in his voice kills me. "Then everything this week happened and…" Josh trails off, his voice thick. He shakes his head. "We should've just told you anyway. *I* should have."

"Oh, monkey," Max wraps an arm around our boy and

squeezes him as understanding dawns over us both.

Josh keeps talking, taking advantage of his mother's un-characteristic stunned silence. "I almost lost Max. *We* almost lost Max. I know you worried about him, but you couldn't have understood what I was going through. What we were going through. And that's because I was too annoyed with Axe stealing my thunder. I made our relationship all about me, and I shouldn't have." Tears slide down his cheeks as he looks pointedly into Max's eyes and then turns to look into mine. "We're equals in this. Telling Mom and Dad shouldn't have been about making an announcement or whatever. It should have just been about telling them how happy we are together."

This is part of what's been eating him up inside. This guilt about not telling his family when we had the chance. This assumption that, in wanting to make a special announcement because he was excited and happy about us, he was somehow being selfish.

My sweet, ridiculous boy.

Lowering my forehead to his, I stare right back into his dark brown eyes and tell him, "I never felt like you were making it about you, baby. You wanted a moment that was all yours to tell the other people you love how happy you are. That's not wrong or selfish."

He sniffles. "But when Max got abducted, I felt...I felt..."

"Like it was too late?" Max offers gently. Josh nods.

Ignoring our audience, Max and I share a long glance over Josh's head. There's no way to change what happened, and Josh's feelings are valid and understandable. But it's in the past, and we need to work through it. I'm still trying to find the right words when Marie speaks up.

"It's not too late," she tells her son, and when I look over, her expression is chagrined. "I'm sorry I got wrapped up in your brother's news, but I'm listening now. And we worried for Max terribly when we heard what happened. Even without knowing about this," her hand swoops through the air in an arc across the three of us, "we worried terribly about how you felt. We knew you were close friends, that much was obvious from dinner."

There's nothing over the top about her mannerisms right now. Marie Walker is speaking softly, and the out of character behavior gives her words more weight. "I'm sorry you felt you couldn't tell us when you wanted to. I can only imagine what the past few days have been like for you. For all of you."

Max and I wait for Josh to react. These are his parents, after all. This is what he's been struggling with.

He takes a shuddering breath and then exhales. "Max balances me and Em out," he starts, repeating words I said to him weeks ago, bringing a smile to my lips as he continues, his tone shifting as he starts to shed some of the guilt he's been carrying, "and Em balances me and Max out."

"And you balance us out," Max finishes for him, giving him an affectionate shake and then a kiss to the top of his head. "Our perfect brat."

Marie claps her hands together and squeals, the moment of gravity having passed.

"Go on, then," she urges, finally wrapping her palms around her coffee mug and taking a delicate sip, "tell me everything. How did this relationship come about?"

Max and I sit back with matching grins while Josh launches into a slightly modified story about our humble beginnings, and I can't help but think that things are once again exactly as they should be.

* * *

"Daddy," Josh whines, squirming on the couch. The sound of a slap rings out, and Josh whimpers immediately.

I look over from the armchair, my eyebrow arched. "That's another two minutes."

From behind Josh, Max sighs. "You'd make a good Dom, babe," he tells me. "You've come a long way from the pushover you were when we first got together."

That's not entirely true, and we all know it, but I'm enjoying myself right now.

Both of my sexy lovers are naked. Currently, Max is warming his cock inside Josh's perfect ass, our boy denied motion or friction. We haven't given him a cage as part of his punishment for his earlier temper tantrums, but it was a close thing. It was only empathy for Josh's misplaced guilt that prevented us from bringing out the implement of torture. (I think my softness is starting to rub off on Max.)

They're lying on their sides on the couch while we try to watch a movie together. I'm achingly hard in my jeans, just the sight of Josh's punishment turning me on beyond measure.

"Daddy," Josh mewls again, but keeps himself still. "Please, Daddy. I'm sorry. Please."

Before we started this part of his punishment, Max had spanked him as promised. The curve of his perfect ass is still blush pink from what little I can see of it, given our angle. His cock is hard and leaking. It practically pulses with the desperation I imagine he's feeling.

"Joshua, this is your final warning," I tell him firmly. "You're going to let Daddy Maxxie soak for another," I pause to check my watch and do some quick calculations, "six minutes. And then you're going to let me diaper you, and after that you'll watch your Daddies make love — without touching yourself."

Josh whines.

Max smooths a pale hand down Josh's golden-tanned flank. "You're taking this punishment so well, monkey. Maybe next time you'll think before you misbehave, hmm?"

Max and I have already agreed between ourselves that, if Josh can last long enough to watch Max fuck me for a couple of minutes, we'll relent and rescind the orgasm denial part of his punishment. That's more for our benefit than his, but he doesn't need to know it.

"This is what happens when you call your Daddies names," I add, as though he really needs the reminder.

He bites his lip, swallowing roughly as he nods. Such a stubborn boy. I love it.

I love him.

I love them both.

They make such a gorgeous picture like this. I spend the next six minutes drinking it in, Max's pale skin and lean form against Josh's tanned muscles. Max's blonde hair against Josh's dark locks. The smattering of freckles across Max's body, the unblemished expanse of our boy's. Max's white as snow ass, tensed as his equally pale hip is pressed up flush against Josh's rounded globes. Their legs entwined, fine hairs more noticeable on Josh's than Max's. They're like a work of art.

Having been in Max's position, my cock buried deep in our boy's warm, lubricated channel, I can imagine what Max is feeling. I admire his restraint, the lax expression on his face, his dedication to seeing this punishment through to the end instead of giving in to the temptation of rocking into Josh's ass, feeling our boy squeeze around him.

When I check my watch again, I'm reluctant to call time on the vision in front of me. I commit it to memory and then tell Josh he's been a good boy for getting through that part of his punishment, delighting in the full body shudder that wracks him as Max carefully pulls out.

Max kisses the back of Josh's neck before I climb out of my seat and offer my men my hands, assisting Josh and then Max up off the couch, one after the other.

I kiss them both deeply, and it turns into a sloppy three-way kiss that has my already hard cock leaking in my briefs. I'm the only one of us fully clothed, and it's time to remedy that.

"You get our boy diapered, babe. I'll get rid of this," Max says as we get to the doorway of Josh's nursery. He holds up the condom he'd removed after he slid out of Josh, and I nod.

"Meet you back in the bedroom for round two." I can't resist pinching his ass before ushering Josh into the nursery.

"I really am so proud of you, Josh," I tell him, lifting him up onto the change table: a move I know he loves. It makes him feel small, resettling him in his Little headspace. "I'm proud of you for being so open with your family. And I'm proud of you for accepting your punishment and making it through."

He raises his thumb to his mouth, sliding it between his teeth. It's an action he tends to only bring out when he's feeling very Little and vulnerable. With today's events and his punishment, it's not a surprise to see it. "Punishment's not over," he reminds me, only a tiny hint of sulkiness in his tone as he raises his hips and lets me slide a diaper under his ass. His cock arches up towards his belly, the crown an angry red, the head glistening and damp.

I smother my answering smirk. "Keep being a good boy, monkey. Good boys get rewarded."

He squints at me as I complete the diapering process, covering his erection and strapping down the tabs on his hips, but he doesn't say any more. Instead, he just makes grabby hands at me once he's sitting back up, and I chuckle as I lift him from the table and carry him from the nursery and into the bedroom. He snags Ranger from the middle of the bed as I deposit him on the mattress, cuddling his bear close.

Max is already in bed, slowly stroking his cock.

"Strip, Em," he demands, his voice low and sultry.

I do as he commands, making a show of the slow removal of my t-shirt, tugged up and over my head. I tease with my jeans, popping the button and lowering the fly at what feels like one pair of tiny zipper teeth at a time. I hook my fingers into my waistbands and tug them down. My cock practically springs free, betraying just how desperate to get off I am.

I crawl onto the bed, over the top of Max, trailing kisses over his skin. Next to us, Josh groans, thrusting his hips upwards. But he keeps his hands clamped around his bear.

"Good boy," I commend him. His fingers twitch in Ranger's fur.

I make it to Max's lips and capture them with mine. Our cocks connect, hot, hard, and leaking. We make matching moaning sounds into each other's mouths.

"Fuck, this feels so good," Max arches his back, grinding his length against mine.

All I can do is nod, dipping my head as thrills of pleasure course through me.

We move against each other just like this, our precum providing just enough lube to aid the slide of shaft against shaft.

I turn my head when Josh's needy whine rents the air.

"I've changed my mind," I tell him, feeling cruel to deny him when emotions have run so high today. "You can touch yourself, baby. Or join in. Or...or...oh, *fuck*," I lose track of my thoughts as Max's lubed hand wraps around our cocks, adding new sensations to the mix. I close my eyes against the intense bliss. "Whatever you want, baby. Punishment's over."

"Thank you, Daddy," Josh practically sobs.

I reach over and cup the back of his head, tugging him down for a messy, desperate kiss.

"Can I still just watch?" Josh pants when he pulls back. "Like...like the first time?"

I swear I almost come remembering that first night we spent together sexually. It's significant that Josh wants to revisit that experience, and it feels important to me, as well. Like we're acknowledging how special it was that we got together.

Honestly, I know I'm usually more eloquent, but I'm distracted by Max rolling his hips and squeezing his fist, and most coherent thoughts disappear altogether.

"Whatever you want," I repeat, then groan as Max rocks his hips, fucking into his fist.

The sensations of doing this, just frotting against each other, are exquisite. The slide of sweat-slicked skin on sweat-slicked skin. Our pants and moans. Our heavy breathing and murmured encouragements. Sweet words followed by filthy demands to move faster, fuck harder, squeeze tighter. Even filthier words, admiration of each other's bodies, the way we taste to each other, how much precum we're producing. The sensation of the mattress bouncing at a faster rhythm than Max and I are producing.

"Oh, Jesus, Em, look at him..." Max mutters, sounding strained, and I turn my head to take in our other lover.

Josh has rolled over into his front and he's rolling his hips, frantically fucking the mattress as he watches me and Max rubbing off against each other.

No, not the mattress. Ranger.

He's fucking his bear, just like he did that first night. I can only just see a fluffy white leg jutting out from underneath the front of Josh's diaper, bouncing in time with his thrusts.

And, just as it was that first time, the action is the perfect blend of kinky, sweet, and hot as fuck.

Until Josh, I'd never imagined I'd be aroused by the action of a boy stimulating himself with his stuffie, but now I'm mesmerized. I wonder about the friction he's feeling, dampened by the constrictive scrap of plastic and cotton between his cock and his toy. I imagine the soft give of the plush bear, the way it molds and yields for him. The way the soft tufts of fur must be tickling Josh's exposed belly and upper thighs.

"*Fuck*," I breathe as I watch him, unable to tear my gaze away, still rocking my length against Max's.

Max's attention is equally rapt on our boy because he pants, "Told you. He's perfect. He's perfect and he's ours."

"D-Daddies," Josh stammers when his eyes lock on ours, the strips of skin above his beard line reddening at our appraisal, "I'm coming. I'm coming. Oh, fuck, I can't...*ohhhh*." His hips jerk, his skin flushes all over, and he all but howls as his orgasm hits him. It's one of the most gorgeous things I've ever seen, and my balls tighten in response. Especially when he flops down, his nose crinkling as he puts a hand to his covered crotch and complains, "Now I'm all messy."

My cock jerks and dribbles out another stream of precum

as the pleasurable tension inside me coils tighter. But those words push Max over the edge first.

"Oh, shit," Max's curse is the only warning I get before his cock pulses against mine and he spurts jets of his hot, sticky cum between our bodies and over my cock. His hands scrabble at my slippery back, settling on my ass, gripping tight. His fingers dig into the soft flesh he finds there almost painfully. Certainly hard enough to bruise. But he grinds against me until he's wrung every last drop of his release out.

The sight and feel of him is the last straw for my own resolve and I toss my head back and let out a roar of absolute bliss as I come harder than I've ever come in my life. I come for *days*, painting Max in the evidence of my orgasm, the creamy jets of my cum mixing with his. I'm lightheaded by the time my balls have emptied, but I have the presence of mind to roll sideways —the opposite side to where Josh is sprawled out— so I don't crush my dominant lover.

"Holy fuck," Josh groans, reaching out to run a finger through the mess on Max's belly. He swirls it, combining our essences, before scooping a dollop into his finger and sucking on it.

My deflating dick twitches pathetically at the display. At my age, especially after how hard I just came, I'm surprised it had even that much movement left in it.

"We're *so* doing that again," he says, sounding about as wiped out as I feel.

Max makes a strangled sound of agreement. I nod.

"Seriously, though," Josh says as a comfortable silence descends and I contemplate how necessary clean up is, "thank you. Not just for this," he waves his hand over the disorder, and I assume he means the sex, "but for everything. For being

271

my Daddies. For taking care of me, and punishing me, and…" he cuts himself off, sniffling as his voice breaks. "Happy tears," he promises as Max and I start to sit up with matching looks of concern on our faces. He swallows. "I didn't know how badly I needed you both until I had you. I feel like I've won the lottery or something."

"The Daddy lottery?" Max snorts, half-heartedly tickling at Josh's ribs.

"Yeah," Josh agrees, grinning now. "The Daddy lottery. I…I never thought I'd find someone who could manage me, you know? For one-offs, sure, but for a relationship…I thought I was too much work. And, on some level, I guess I was."

I go to protest, but he holds up a hand, preventing me from saying anything.

"I *am* too much work for one Daddy. But I've got you two. And you're everything I ever wanted and more. So…jackpot."

My own throat is tight, thinking over how lonely I was until that night I took a chance and let them both into my home. How I'd felt like I hadn't yet found the right Little for me. And, it turns out, it wasn't just a Little I needed. I needed a stubborn, self-deprecating Dom as well, I just hadn't realized it until he'd wormed his way under my skin.

I nod, a smile of my own tugging at my lips. "Jackpot indeed," I agree.

Max laughs, wrapping an arm around me and the other around Josh. He tugs us into him, heedless of the cum cooling on his skin and of the cleanup we desperately need. "Jackpot indeed," he repeats, and I can't help but think he's on the same page as me and Josh. He needed us, too, even if he hadn't known it.

We've still got a long way to go to recover properly from

Max's ordeal, but right now, all we need is a shower and a good night's sleep. And then maybe a repeat of tonight's performance in the morning.

Jackpot indeed.

Epilogue — Josh

I am an absolute wreck right now…but it's in the best possible way.

In the year since Max's abduction, life has changed beyond anything I could have imagined. Obviously, Max and I moved into Em's place officially. All three of us underwent some intense therapy sessions, individually and as a throuple, and Max and I stayed on at work, despite both considering leaving at one point or another.

So, on the surface, life looks pretty much the same as it always did, only I live with two men who I love, and my family and friends are all cool with it.

Except I have changed. Pretty significantly, I think.

I'm totally happy to admit that I'm not a scene Little. I'm one hundred percent a lifestyle Little. I'm open with my social circle about my emotional needs. I tell my family when I'm feeling those usual 'middle child syndrome' things, too.

I've started to face my nighttime issues in my Big headspace, as well. It's hard not regressing when I wake up wet, even if I am still sleeping in a diaper every night. It's hard discussing my continued embarrassment and resentment about it with my Daddies and with my therapist.

But I'm coming to terms with the idea that there's no quick fix for it. Hell, I might never fully stop wetting the bed, even if it's only happening every second or third night now. And that's okay. It doesn't make me any less of a man, any less of a cop, any less of a lover. It doesn't make me weird or abnormal. It's just a condition like any other. There are days where I still hate it, but most days I've accepted that it's just a part of my life.

And I've taken a big step in letting go of my tight control when I'm in my Little headspace, which my Daddies reward me for. Case in point, I've just been thoroughly fucked on my change table, with a clean, dry diaper open under my ass and my favorite spider monkey t-shirt scrunched up under my pecs.

Pretty sure Daddy Em only intended to give me a hand job, but then Daddy Maxxie got all moan-y and the lube came out from under the change table…and, yeah. Having Daddy Em sliding into me with his huge cock while Daddy Maxxie encouraged me to suck his dick was heaven. I didn't even tease Daddy Maxxie for needing a step-stool to be at the right height for the change table because I was too distracted by how naughty and perfect the whole experience was.

So, yeah, I'm an absolute wreck right now. My own cum is splattered up my belly, flecks of it having landed on my bunched up shirt and even on the underside of my chin. I can feel Daddy Em's release trickling out of my ass, dribbling onto the previously clean diaper beneath me. We all got tested and had the 'we're exclusive and have no plans for that to change' talk six months ago, and I don't think there's a better feeling than having one —or both— of my Daddies filling me up so much that I can't hold it all in. I squirm with pleasure, clenching and unclenching, enjoying the squishy wetness.

"You're all messy," Daddy Max says, sounding as blissed out as I feel. He runs his hand through my hair, smiling down at me adoringly. That expression still fills me with warm, fuzzy feelings. "How about a bath?"

I grin and nuzzle into his touch. "Yes please, Daddy."

Em gives me a quick wipe with a wet wipe he warms between his big palms first, then he carries me into the bathroom. I don't think I'll ever get used to that feeling, either. Finding a Daddy bigger than me, strong enough to carry me, wasn't ever something I dared dream might happen. But here he is, my giant Daddy, and I thrill in how Little he can make me feel.

Daddy Em sets me down beside the tub, which Daddy Maxxie has started to fill. Sometimes one of them will climb in with me, but I always feel a bit guilty that all three of us can't fit. Today, neither of them makes a move to get undressed, so it looks like the bath is mine and mine alone. Daddy Em gets my bath crayons and Daddy Maxxie grabs the loofah.

In this moment, I'm struck again by just how perfect my life is right now. I get to regress whenever I need, whenever I want, and I'm the furthest I could possibly be from alone. I don't have to be bratty to get attention, though I still enjoy being cheeky sometimes (my Daddies come up with some of the best punishments ever!) and when I'm stressed, I feel safe lashing out with true misbehavior, knowing that my Daddies will make it all better. They don't get annoyed or angry with me. They don't expect things of me. They just love me for me.

"What are we drawing today, monkey?" Daddy Em asks once I'm submerged in the warm water, the blue bath crayon already in his hand. I reach over the edge of the tub, sloshing water onto the floor as I grab for the yellow one.

"A monster!" I enthuse. "A big, furry monster. With tentacles. And claws. And polka dots."

Daddy Maxxie snorts and grabs the purple crayon. "It definitely sounds monstrous," he agrees. "Does this monster eat little boys?"

I giggle as I start to draw on the inside wall of the tub. My bright yellow crayon stands out against the white porcelain. "No, silly. It eats hamsters."

"Eww," Daddy Maxxie scrunches up his nose. "Poor little hamsters."

"Nah," I assure him, "they're evil hamsters from Planet Hamron."

"Oh, I see," he rolls with it, helping me flesh out my drawing.

We scribble and scrawl over the porcelain together, making up a story about the hero monsters and the evil hamsters. The monsters win, obviously. They eat all the hamsters and enact a coup on Planet Hamron, taking over and creating a utopia for other monsters from the whole galaxy.

I love that my Daddies enjoy playing with me this way, too. That they don't mind if I want to spend entire days in Little space. That I'm able to be silly more than I am sexy.

I'm sure there will be more problems for us to face in the future, but as far as I'm concerned, we've weathered the worst-case scenarios and come out on top.

Together.

* * *

This is going to sound weird, but the best part about life now? It's feeling like I finally belong in my social circle. Having spent years watching the people I love find their forever Littles and forever Daddies, I never thought I'd be one of them. I never thought I'd fit in properly.

They never made me feel like I wasn't one of them. Any one of the Daddies would have stepped in as a placeholder caregiver if I had asked, and the other Littles have always let me play with them without making me feel like a loner. But now I'm one hundred percent one of them. I have Daddies to look after me, too. To bring me juice, or take me to the potty, or sit and join in on any of our games. And it feels damn good. I feel good attending get-togethers knowing that we're all stupidly happy in love and with the way our lives have turned out.

Today is going to be just one more example of that.

See, Charlie's throwing Asher a 'last birthday of your twenties' party. My brother is an awesome husband to his Little, and an even better Daddy, but I have outdone even him with Ash's birthday present, if I do say so myself. I told my Daddies that I had the perfect thing in mind, and that I was picking it up on my way to the party, seeing as I had to work this morning, so I'm going to surprise even them.

As I pull up to Ash and Charlie's house, I grab the box from the passenger seat and let myself in through the front door. Charlie's once magazine ready home, decorated in tasteful grays and whites, currently looks like a circus threw up in it. There are streamers and balloons everywhere in a rainbow of colors. Loud, happy music is playing from the vicinity of the living room, and I can hear the squeals and laughter of my Little friends coming from further inside the house — maybe even from the backyard.

I follow the sounds, grinning as I take in the absolute chaos of the scene in front of me.

It's a kid's party on crack. Charlie's even gone as far as to create a ball pit in his small backyard, using an oversized inflatable pool and God only knows how many thousand plastic balls. Right now, Kade is issuing a war cry and throwing himself into it on top of a shell-shocked Katie. The plastic sound of the balls making way on impact, hitting each other and scattering out of the sides of the pool is covered only by my friends' raucous laughter.

On the outdoor table and the inside dining table, there are plates upon plates of party food. Sugar as far as the eye can see. Cakes, candy, chocolates…I want to dive into all of that, but it will undo the hard hours I've put in at the gym, or the jogs I still go on with some of the guys in our group. Besides, I still have Ash's gift in my hands, and I'm not giving it to anyone but him. I can't wait to see his face when he opens it.

"Joshie!" Matt calls out from off to my left, and I turn to catch him and London coming out of the downstairs bathroom together, Matt's play shorts kind of askew. London hurries after his boy, trying to adjust the elastic waistband of Matty's shorts while Matt practically bounces over to me.

His enthusiasm is infectious, and the rest of the party has me happily settling into my Little headspace. I'm already dressed for the part, having swung by home and dressed myself before I headed over. I would have preferred my Daddies to dress me, but that would have meant showing them Ash's surprise and I didn't want to do that.

With my hands full, I lean in to Matt's open-armed embrace. "Hey Matty, having fun?"

"Yup. But I drank too much juice so I had to go potty." He beams at me from beneath his messy beard. "Daddy helped."

"Daddies are the best," I agree, once again loving that I can speak from experience now. Real experience, not just playing in a club. Not that there's anything wrong with just playing in a club: it's just not what I wanted. Not really.

"Have you said hello to your Daddies yet?" London prompts me, smirking knowingly.

I shrug, but I can feel my own cheeky smile tugging at my lips. "I said hello this morning?"

Matt's Daddy sighs, but it's an affectionate sound. "You should go find them. They've been looking forward to showing you some of the games Charlie's set up for the party."

"I sawed the ball pit," I tell him excitedly, sinking even deeper into my headspace. The box in my hands suddenly feels heavier as I do, and that reminds me that I am on a mission. Birthday present delivery first, play later! "Where's Ash? I gotsta give him his present." I hold the box up a little for emphasis.

"Last I saw, he was outside," London answers, already leading the way. "Yep. There. On the slide." He points beyond the ball pit that got my attention, to the adult-sized inflatable slide that takes up the rest of Charlie's backyard.

I blink, not quite understanding how I could have been so distracted that I didn't see it to start with. "Whoa."

Tony slides down with a whoop of joy, scrambling to his feet at the bottom and racing back towards the bouncy climbing platforms on the slide's side, loudly declaring his intentions to go again. Ash slides down with a cheer of his own, but Matt calls out to him before he can follow after Tony with the same enthusiasm.

"Joshie has a present for you!"

Ash claps his hands and races towards us, collecting Charlie —who had been standing only a few feet from the bottom of the slide, watching like a hawk alongside Spence— on the way.

"Hi Joshie! Thanks for comin' to my party!" Ash says, and if I was big, I'd say the words were rehearsed, especially because he turns his curl-covered head towards Charlie. "See? I'm a good boy."

"You sure are, little lamb," Charlie agrees and ruffles Ash's mop of hair.

"Joshie gotted me a present!" Ash tells him. "Can I open it?"

I watch my big brother's eyes drift over the box in my hands. The outward facing side is nondescript, plain brown cardboard, and I've been smart enough to keep the air holes facing my body. Charlie's eyes narrow at me. "What did you do, Josh?" He looks over my shoulder, and that's when I realize that my Daddies are approaching from the snack table.

I need to do this fast.

"I got Ash a present," I reply and thrust the box towards its recipient, taking care with it as I do. He can't see the air holes, but Matt and London do, with Matty gasping and London making a sound that's a half-laugh, half-groan. "Open it," I urge, just as Daddy Em's big, beefy hand lands on my shoulder.

"Oh, God," Max says, coming up on my other side. "Joshua. Tell me you didn't."

But it's too late. Ash has his present now. They can't take it from him. That would make him very sad. And Charlie will never make Ash sad if he can help it.

Ash sits himself on the ground and places the box in front of him, opening the folded over flaps. The rest of our group has all gathered around to see what's happening. Ash stares down at the mottled ball of fluff for half a second, and it peers back at him with wide, yellow eyes before it lets out a tiny '*mew*'.

Awww.

"*Kitty!*" my brother-in-law exclaims happily, then looks back up at me with wet eyes. He's beaming. "You got me a kitty!"

Told you it was the best present ever.

Daddy Em's hand tightens on my shoulder. "We need to have a talk, monkey," he says in that tone of voice that says I've done something very, very naughty.

"Daddy!" Ash reaches into the box and pulls the tiny cat out, cradling it with care against his chest. Then in a fluid motion, without need for his hands, he pushes back up to his feet and turns to Charlie. "Joshie got me a kitty! See!"

"I do see," Charlie's tone is similar to the time he caught me using his favorite leather jacket as an art smock. He glares at me over the top of Ash's head. I smile back innocently. Somewhere behind Charlie, Chance guffaws. I can hear Spence chuckling, too. Even Cherie is trying to hide a smile behind her hand.

Max's hand suddenly mirror's Em's, clamping down on my other shoulder.

"Inside," Max demands. "*Now.*"

I'm well aware that I'm in a lot of trouble for this stunt. My butt is already anticipating the spanking. It'll be all reddened up in only a few minutes.

But, as I glance around our group, at the amusement on some of my friends' faces, and the complete joy on Ash's. I know it's worth it. My reputation as a brat is totally worth it.

For these guys? *Anything* is worth it.

And that's the way it's always going to be.

THE END

Thank you so much for reading *Josh's Jackpot.* I genuinely hope you enjoyed it, because (as always) it was super enjoyable to write. With this being the final book in the series, I wanted to go out with a bang and I know I squished a LOT of fun stuff in here.

Anyway, I'd love it if you could leave a review on your retailer of purchase or on Goodreads.

Reviews not only tell the algorithms that our books deserve attention, but honest feedback also encourages and inspires me to keep writing. Even a star rating helps, and I greatly appreciate you making time to do so.

Speaking of my writing, I don't have a sneak peek for you with this one, but the 'Also By The Author' section has links to all of my other books currently available (at time of publishing).

And, if you'd like a free ebook copy of *Charlie's Contentment* (a 10,000 word zero-angst, low-plot, high-fluff novella which functions as an extended epilogue for *Asher's Answer,* but can also be read as a super sweet stand-alone) subscribe to my newsletter here:

https://annasparrows.com/newsletter-subscription/

For updates, release dates, competitions and more, follow me on Facebook. The link is in the 'About The Author' page.

About the Author

I've been writing* for as long as I can remember. I started with silly short stories as a kid, moved on to fanfiction in my teens (and still write it now), and am also a published MF romance author under a second pen name.

I have been an avid reader of MM romance my whole life. (Ask me about my beginnings with *Buffy* fanfic, haha.) I wrote a sweet and kinky MM romance novel in 2022 and the reader response changed my life. From there, I knew I had found my niche.

And thus Anna Sparrows was born.

*All of my writing is 100% my own. No part of it is generated by Artificial Intelligence (AI) software of any kind. Yes, that means that it's sometimes flawed, but I'm okay with that.

You can connect with me on:

◐ https://annasparrows.com

▊ https://www.facebook.com/AnnaSparrowsAuthor

✐ https://www.instagram.com/annasparrows

Subscribe to my newsletter:

✉ https://annasparrows.com/newsletter-subscription

Also by Anna Sparrows

I write ridiculously sweet & steamy MM romance with guaranteed HEAs…and sometimes with a side of kink.

The Littles & Lace Series
The Littles & Lace series is an MM Age Play series, following a group of like minded friends in the BDSM community. You'll find ABDL, light Pet Play, Femme Play and more here.

Book 1: Asher's Answer

Book 2: Matteo's Mettle

Book 3: Ted's Temerity

Book 4: Spencer's Satisfaction

Book 5: Chance's Choice

Book 6: Josh's Jackpot (MMM)

The Dads & Adages Series
Venture to Australia's stunning Gold Coast, where a group of single dads are going to learn a few life lessons on their way to their HEAs.

Book 1: Where There's A Will

Book 2: You Don't Know Jack

Book 3: A Match Made In Evan (release TBA)

Shifters Sanctuary Series
In a world where alphas are thought to be extinct, a number of 'human' men are about to have their worlds rocked.

Book 1: His Alpha Unlocked

Book 2: His Prodigal Alpha (release TBA)